A Circle of Stones

By Donald P Marple

ISBN- 10: 0692743111

ISBN- 13: 9780692743119

This book is dedicated to all who search for the courage to do what's right, to those who try and fail and get back up again.

Table of Contents

ACKNOWLEDGEMENTS

I just want to say a gigantic THANK YOU to everyone who supported me through this process and to the writers who inspired me.

Chapter 1
The Great Outdoors

Everyone was distracted by the commotion down the street. Their attention was turned away from a little boy left alone in his front yard. With the sound of sirens growing closer in the distance, the crowds of neighbors were all engrossed in the unfolding drama. But one face in the gathering watched the boy out of the corner of his eye and lingered back as everyone else moved forward. The plan was to abduct the child that night, but he saw that the opportunity was now. The dark hearted man had been watching the child for months. He had purposely strolled by his house on a regular base to let the child get use to seeing him. He smiled and waved just like any good neighbor would. He was just a two bit thief, but if he could pull this off, he had been promised more. There were those in power that wanted this five year old boy and the reasons why didn't matter to the man. They had given him everything he needed to get the job done, even purchased a house on the same street as the boy's family.

The child was tossing a small smooth stone into the air and then catching it again. The boy liked to play catch. When his father came home after work they always played a little catch in the front yard together. So when the man tossed the exact same Seattle Seahawks Nerf football into the back yard of the boy's house, the little tike took the bait. The predators hands were covered with a set of transparent gloves that protected him from a drug which, he was told, was potent enough to knock the boy unconscious immediately. The child innocently picked up the toy football and was smiling as he turned to retrieve it. He was a darling little guy dressed in blue jeans, Nike shoes and a Seattle Seahawks t-shirt. For a moment, the predator was anxious. The boy should be out cold by now, not even able to stand. When the child started walking the ball back to him he became very alarmed. Then suddenly, the boy veered off course and fell in the grass behind his house, out of his mother's line of sight. She remained distracted by the emergency down the street, just like everyone else. The boy struggled to get up but finally gave way to the invading neuromuscular agents. The little boy's world was about to change forever. The monster had him now.

Five years later.

The scenic drive to the trailhead gave Eric Savage time to consider the adventure before him. The blacktop road dipped and curved with the rhythm of the land, climbing out of the western lowlands of the Puget Sound and up into the old growth forests of the Cascade Mountains. It was still dark when he left his home in Seattle early that morning, but now the sunrise in the east revealed some breathtaking views. As he drove, he looked out over the vast wilderness. As far as the eye could see were tall snow capped mountains, fast moving rivers, and deep cedar forests. This was going to be the journey of a life time. Eric Savage had always been a hiker and a lover of all things outdoors; Camping, fishing, hunting, exploring, kayaking, or just walking a trail in the early morning to see the way the first golden light touched the tops of the highest trees. There was a kinship he felt with the earth.

The question he asked himself on the edge of this adventure was simple. Was he ready? His backpack was full of only what was necessary. It was a balance between survival needs and the weight he could carry. He enjoyed being alone for short periods of time but how would he handle weeks? He would miss Amy, his wife, but this had been a dream of his for the longest time and she had urged him to go.

"I have two busy weeks at work coming anyway. You have three weeks off before you start your new job. Go!! Or you'll just be bored out of your mind and drive me crazy," she had told him with a wink and a smile.

Eric pulled into the parking area and made one last equipment check. He took out his map and ran his finger from where he now stood to his goal about seventy five miles away. This was it! He felt excitement mixed with a little healthy fear of the unknown. He freely admitted to himself that he was no survivalist. But he had prepared as best he knew how and he would survive somehow. Eric ran his fingers through his dark brown hair. His smiling eyes were as blue as the sky on a summer day. His body was fit from years of trips to the gym and weekly jogs. The trail ahead called to him and before he knew it he was hiking into the forest. The air smelled sweet and the sun was shining with a few white puffy clouds floating about. The lofty evergreens stood at attention on every hillside, higher and higher, leading through the mountain passes. It was a good start.

After covering a respectable distance for the day Eric found a good place to camp for the night. The August summer weather of the Pacific Northwest was perfect and the energy of the first day had taken him far. The trail converged with the river after about seven miles. He decided to do some fishing in order to save his packed supplies for later. After setting up camp, which wasn't much more than his small tent and a circle of stones for his fire, he walked to the river's edge and cast his line into the moving waters. Hopefully, a few hungry trout lived here and he would catch three or four, but after a few hours, he settled for one good sized Rainbow Trout. He wasn't out to impress anyone, he was out to enjoy. He had no problem starting a fire with good kindling and wax matches packed. There were plenty of dry fallen branches lying around. He cleaned his fish, placed his fillets in his one fry pan and over the fire they went, seasoned just the way he liked. Eric enjoyed the glow of his campfire, the sound of fish frying in a skillet and the smell of cedar. Night fell slowly, as the light of the sun changed colors and scaled the surrounding mountains.

A man has time to think out here, Eric thought as the stillness of the set in. His one regret was that his father Noland was not there with him.. Their plan was always to do this together. But Eric and his father did not always see eye to eye and at the moment their relationship was broken. Eric had not seen or talked with his father in twelve months. His dad was a retired Navy Seal and had his own way of doing things. He had groomed Eric for the U.S. Military, trained him how to fight in hand-to-hand combat and coached him as a marksman from a young age. Never-the -less, after Eric did his four years, he passed on the opportunities to follow in his dad's footsteps. He had seen, first hand, what the stress of being a member of the U.S. Militaries' Special Operation Forces could do to a family and wanted something better for Amy. Eric was a gifted computer programmer, code writer, and had just landed a job at a large internet security firm. He had taken a different road than his father. But he was still his father's son and shared his dad's passion for the outdoors. Being on the trail reminded Eric of his father's better qualities.

As Eric got comfortable in his tent, ready to call it a day, he lounge back listening to the sounds of the forest. He knew there were deer nearby, having seen tracks by the river. He also knew these mountains were home to some larger predators. Black bear were common, than there was the occasional story of a mountain lion or grizzly bear. But this far south, he considered a grizzly to be a distant threat. Smiling to himself he imagined the whole forest around him, wild and free. He was free too. He was on an adventure. Tomorrow he would travel deeper into the unknown.

Not more than a hundred yards away two eyes focused on Eric's dying fire. He was afraid of the man but he was also hungry. That night he would sneak into the man's camp and search for food. He waited until the fire was completely out and while the moon was still low in the night. Walking as quietly as possible he stepped across the opening that was between the tree line and the circle of stones. He looked about straining his eyes for anything, but there was nothing. The man had taken his pack in the tent with him for the night. There were no scraps left in the pan next to the fire and whatever had been cooked in it was long gone. Yet the smell of something good lingered causing his stomach to grumble with disappointment. Despite his efforts to walk softly he accidently stepped on a twig and snapped it in two. It sounded so loud in the quiet night air that he froze in place, afraid the man would awaken. But after some time with no movement from the tent he slipped quietly back into the forest unaware of the muddy prints he was leaving behind. What was he going to do? Without food he would starve?

The next day Eric was up with the sun and decided on making some breakfast. He had some dried eggs and bacon that only required hot water to bring to life. All at once he saw the muddy tracks! His eyes grew wide and his heart pounded a little harder. Someone had been in his camp last night. But after closer examination he was puzzled. The tracks were small, like those of a child. They were certainly not left by him. He looked about the forest.

"Hello?" he called out. "Hello, is somebody out there?" There was no answer.

He compared the size of the track to his own. It was no more than half the size of his shoe. What was a child doing out in the forest miles from the trailhead? He followed the tracks till they were lost to the forest. They were headed deeper into the woods, parallel to the trail.

"This is odd," Eric said to himself.

He tried to remember if he had heard about any lost children on the news before he had left home, nothing came to mind. Should he hike back out and get help? But what if the kid was with others and had just wandered off. He decided he would just call it in. He had brought along a cell phone for emergencies. He held his phone high but couldn't get a signal.

No reception out here this low. He thought in disappointment.

This meant that he would have to hike to some high ridge or small mountain top and try again. This was not a part of his plans for the day and would throw him off schedule. Yet the thought of some lost child out here alone was enough to overcome his feeling of inconvenience. Eric packed up his little camp, and took the trail heading in the same general direction as the small prints had gone.

Hidden in the dense underbrush the little boy watched as the man passed him on the trail below. He felt both drawn to the man and fearful of him at the same time. This man was his only known source of help, but he feared the man would be angry and cruel with him. The men that he had known were always angry. He had finally found the courage to run away from them. He would rather die out there in the woods alone than return to where he had been. Still, he was hungry and needed to eat something soon.

While the boy spied from his hiding place, the walking man suddenly stopped on the trail and put down his pack. The boy crouched closer to the ground, worried that he had been spotted? The man retrieved a zip-lock bag from his pack and walked off the path just a bit to a bush and started picking juicy blackberries. He ate some and put the rest into his clear plastic zip-lock bag. When the little boy realized the man had found berries, he waited in hunger for his chance.

Eric decided not to hike far that second day in order to give the child the chance of finding him again. He took one detour off the trail to a high point and called in his discovery of the tracks to the local police. No one had heard of any missing children in the area. No reports had come in. They suggested that perhaps the tracks were already there when he set up camp and he just noticed them the next morning? Eric wasn't buying it.

After making his way back down to the trail he searched for a second camp site and scouted for any sign of tracks ahead of time. He made camp the same as before except this time, before going to sleep for the night, he placed a chocolate energy bar in the frying pan next to a new circle of stones. If someone wanted it, they would have to cross an open area that he insured would leave clear imprints. If the prints were the same as before, he would know the child was following him and probably hungry. He weighed the idea of trying to catch the child in the act. But if he frightened him or her away, they may never return. For now he was just going to take it slow and see what happened.

The boy reached out his hand and took his first bite. The bitter sweet flavor filled his mouth. He ate another and then another. They were the best tasting blackberries he had ever had in his whole life. He would stay next to this bush till the last berry was eaten. He did not need that man. He was not stupid. He would live off the berries. Now that he knew what to look for, he could find more bushes filled with blackberries.

The boy whispered it to himself, "I am not stupid."

The next morning Eric was a little excited to check on the power bar. He unzipped his tent and looked to where he had left it in the fry pan. But there it sat, undisturbed and covered with beads of morning dew. He was disappointed. Now what? Should he try looking around? Should he just continue on his adventure and let the police handle it? He had already taken the time to call it in. Had he done his duty? Wasn't this his vacation, his once in a lifetime shot at scratching something off his bucket list? But he knew the police would not come looking for a lost child with no missing persons report filed, the only evidence being some muddy tracks reported by a hiker. He also knew he could never live with himself if weeks later while reading the paper the story of a child found dead in this wilderness stared him in the face.

Eric decided he would change his tactics. He needed to make a scene. He needed to get the child's attention. He needed a big fire. He needed to make some noise. That kid needed to smell his food. That night he built a large bon fire and cooked a rainbow trout seasoned with bacon bits. He talked loudly into the forest about his fish and bacon. The fire lit up the tall trees all around. If the child was near he would certainly see it.

Indeed, the boy was drawn in by the smell of Eric's food. There was the glow of a campfire over the next rise. The berries had helped but he was still hungry. Eric saw movement in the woods. This was going to work. Kids are so curious. The noise moved closer now. The child was coming in, attracted by the hope of a meal. Eric called out in the direction of the movement. "This fish is sooo good! ummm, I guess I just made too much. I sure wish I had someone......"

A large black bear with two cubs in tow stood up. Eric's eyes became the size of dinner plates. What an idiot he was. And now he was going to die. He remembered his fire and picked up one of the burning sticks from its outer unburned end. The bear closed the distance between them. Eric backed away slowly holding his torch out in front as a deterrent. He looked at the tasty bacon flavored trout and realized, the bear wasn't going away. He put the bon fire between himself and the beast and then he slowly backed into the forest leaving everything behind. A black bear with her cubs was not to be messed with. The bear now owned his camp and there was nothing he could do about it.

Eric was angry. Not at the bear. She was just doing what mother bears do, finding food for her cubs. Not even at the lost child. Eric was angry at himself. How long had he planned this trip? When would he ever have the time to do this again? How could he be so dumb? He had forgotten where he was and the respect that nature demands. He knew better than that. He watched from a safe distance and hiding spot as the bear and cubs shredded his tent, tore into his backpack and ate his fish.

Dear God, please let there be something left. Eric pleaded in his thoughts.

The bear was in no hurry and after a long while Eric reclined back in his hiding place and went to sleep. It was not a good sleep. Not a deep sleep, just a restless slumber. He awoke several times but could not discern in the dying firelight of his camp if it was safe to return. He would wait until daylight.

No more mistakes. He thought to himself.

The next morning Eric stood at the edge of his camp and surveyed the damage. Everything was spread out like a bomb had gone off. The bear had done a job with her claws and teeth. Every ready to eat meal was ruined; some were gone, completely missing. Even his toothpaste was chewed up. His hunting knife was still good. He could still make due with a broken fishing pole. Hack, a stick and a line would catch fish with hook and bait. His tent was torn badly but could be duck taped up enough to work, sort-of. Was he going back? Off-course he had to go back! Didn't he? He needed to resupply. But another part of Eric Savage welcomed this challenge. He had suffered a loss for sure, but who doesn't?

He started making three piles of his remaining

equipment. The first pile was garbage, the second was fixable things or things that could still be useful, and the third was undamaged. Where was his canteen? Where were his matches? His smaller Swiss army knife was also missing! Somewhere during this process he noticed the half print of a child's shoe. Eric could not believe it. But there it was, same prints and size as before. So the kid must have come in after the bears when he was asleep and helped himself to Eric's belongings. Eric didn't know what to think or feel about this. He just shook his head and walked away for a moment. He had been attacked by a bear and then robbed by a kid just for good measure. But after a minute he started to laugh to himself. He had wanted an adventure. This was going to be quite a story to tell.

The little boy started to carve his name into the side of the red Swiss Army Knife with the edge of a sharp rock but stopped short. They called him, Tiny Tim. But the name angered him. The title was slapped on him because he was so small for his age. At twelve years old everybody said he was tiny, Tiny Tim. They also called him stupid and other names. The question on his mind at the moment was his other name, the one he couldn't remember. He could remember being told over and over that his name was Tim. He could also remember receiving an especially cruel beating with a leather belt for saying a different name when asked by a new comer. Now the boy tried to recall that name, anything but Tiny Tim. He strained to dredge it up as if it were sunken treasure. *B..... Be........Benj........*

Then he heard it, like someone called to him, "*Benjamin.*" His other name was Benjamin.

It was the name no one wanted him to remember.

Benjamin, he liked the sound of that name. Tiny Tim scratched his other name as best he could into the red Swiss Army Knife. He had always wanted a knife of his own. He took off the cap of the canteen and drank the cool clean water. He felt for the box of matches in his pocket and smiled. He also had three dehydrated meals. He would have taken more from the man but he was afraid the bears would come back or the man would return to find him there. He was more afraid of the man than the bears. He had never been beaten by a bear but his body was scarred by the leather belt the man named Harvey had used on him. Tiny Tim could not remember a time in his life when he had ever been as free as he was right then. All his life, he had been forced to work, work, work, from early morning till late at night, to clean up messes left by the men or to take food to the sobbing girls in the cages. Yes, he was hungry now, but he was used to being hungry anyway. He would never go back to that place. He held the small knife up in his hands with all the determination his little soul could muster. He would never go back; he was going to learn to survive in the woods. And if they came looking for him, he would kill them.

The "honorable" Judge Fredrick Hurst lived in a large brick mansion surrounded by one hundred and forty five acres of wooded and pastured property. It was obvious that his wealth went beyond his judge's salary. It was rumored that he owned some oil interests but no one really knew or had the courage to question him.

His office was a paradox of dark claustrophobic meets oversized enormous. Deep stained mahogany wooden book shelves lines the walls. Trophies of deer, elk, mountain goat, and bear stared at you as you entered. They seemed to whisper a warning. You are entering the layer of a deadly hunter. It was evident that he was also a collector of artifacts and old manuscripts. They were displayed proudly, but more like captured prisoners then honored guests, each incased in glass or some other cell, present against their will. The men that stood in the shadows were sinister and threatening. In the back center of the room was a colossal ornate desk behind which sat the commanding figure of Judge Hurst.

The blow was sudden and the man named Harvey went down. The pain shot through his body like electricity. There was no escape, he would get no sympathy, the others laughed at his plight. They surrounded him like the vultures they were. He had made a mistake. He had let the boy escape. Tiny Tim was Harvey's responsibility. He had put them all in danger. The boots came at him from all sides. He would die a painful death. But just as suddenly as the attack started, it stopped. Judge Fredrick Hurst had simply raised a finger. He normally would not speak directly to Harvey. There was a chain of command and Harvey was low on that chain. Never-the –less, the boy was important. He had been with them a long time. He had been to many of their locations and most concerning; he had seen the judge's face several times.

The slave trade was both a growing business and a dangerous business in America. For a long time people just refused to believe it existed. Slavery was something of the past, a subject their children studied in history. Americans didn't want to believe something so hideous was growing in their cozy suburbs. But now, task forces were being formed. Media attention was growing. Girls had been rescued and were speaking out. Still, most of America didn't care. Not really. Not enough to do anything. He would get the boy back.

Judge Fredrick Hurst looked at Harvey's beaten body. Harvey was a monster, a huge beast of a man with animal instincts and no moral code. But he was the kind of monster the judge knew how to control and use. It was Harvey who had kidnapped the boy five years ago, on the judge's orders, right out of his backyard. It was an act of revenge on an old enemy. Harvey knew the boy and the boy feared Harvey. He would send the monster after the boy.

After Harvey was given his orders and thrown out, the judge handed a sealed envelope to a trusted runner. The envelope was to be delivered to their contact in Mexico. A plan needed to be set in motion, a rouse that would keep an adversary off the real trail of Tiny Tim's escape. Twenty four hours later it was being opened across the border. The order was clear and from the American Judge. *Find a ten year old Caucasian male that looked like the boy in these pictures. There is a birth mark on the lower back that would need to be added. Have it done by a professional. Hold the child at the Mexico City complex.* Clues would then be discretely dropped. It wouldn't take much. The man the judge needed to distract moved like a shark to blood and was twice as deadly.

Eric stopped along the trail at a natural overlook taking in the beauty of the mountains before him. From his vantage point, the forest of individual trees stood as one, blanketing the lower river valleys and reaching up the slopes of the surrounding mountainsides. The movement of the unseen wind became visible in the waves of their branches. It was mesmerizing to watch the rolling patterns form, curving and exciting the living vegetation. There was something magnificent about it all and Eric felt his own soul inspired and moved with the sight of it. He had traveled the world and seen a lot of places. But there was something special about the Cascade Mountains of Washington and Oregon. The view was breath-taking. The air was crisp, clean and full of the smell of cedar forests. He was not going back. He would face this challenge like he had faced so many other challenges in his life. He would adjust. He would adapt. He would even enjoy the contest. The boy had taken some of his supplies and the bears had destroyed others. But he had duck taped up his back-pack and his tent. He would still be able to fish and collect berries. Starting a fire with his back-up magnesium block would bring back some good memories. He was a fan of watching those survival shows and with his military training he would be just fine.

The boy was a mystery to Eric. He was assuming it was a boy child but could not be sure. It made no logical sense for a child to be out in the woods this deep. But Eric had a feeling he would find the boy tonight. If he knew anything about boys, he knew the desire to have a camp fire would be too tempting, and the boy had his matches.

Tiny Tim was enjoying the view of the Cascade Mountains even more than Eric. He had never seen anything like it before in his life. He loved the tall evergreens. He had rarely been allowed to play, not out-side anyway, just video games. This new world was full of wonder to him. It was something completely fresh and different. Now he climbed and played and battled imaginary enemies. The sticks became swords, and rocks he threw became hand grenades. The lofty green trees were everywhere. He climbed one and then another and another.

Even so, at times he would get scared and feel like someone was watching him. All the new sights played with his imagination. In the distance he saw a dark stump of a unique shape. In his mind, it looked like a dark evil man wide in the shoulders. Its shadows formed the face of Tiny Tim's nightmares. It was Harvey, coming to chain him again, like a forgotten dog. At first, Tiny Tim ran away, but looking back realized he was running from nothing. The voice of Harvey mocked him in his mind.

Afraid of your own shadow boy? It taunted him.

That made Tiny Tim angry and turned him around. If that stump wanted to fight he would fight, first with rocks from a distance, and then as he grew bolder, with the red Swiss Army knife, he battled the monster stump.

Yet the voice in his head spoke again. *You can run Tiny Tim but remember, I'll always find you in the end.* Harvey always did find him. In the factory when he hid, Harvey would always, always find him.

"Not this time!" the boy said as he attacked the stump.

"Not this time!"

The boy was wild, stabbing the old cedar stump again and again and again. He started to cry. He was never allowed to cry around Harvey. Harvey would back-hand him across the room if he was caught crying. Tiny Tim looked around at the trees almost expecting to be reprimanded. But no one was there to disapprove. He could cry if he wanted to. Tiny Tim decided that the knife wasn't doing enough damage to old stump Harvey. That's when he remembered the matches.

Eric came upon the burning stump an hour later. The ground around the stump had caught on fire and Eric had to rush around stumping it out before it got out of control. What had this child been thinking? He could have started a forest fire. There was something strange about this whole scene. Eric Savage stepped back and looked at the stump and the area around it. Rocks were everywhere; the burnt remains of sticks were protruding out of the stump. The child's shoe prints circled the stump in every direction digging into the dirt, trampling down the underbrush. Eric could feel the intensity of the boy's feelings or was he just reading into things a little too much. Maybe the boy was insane? A wild boy who lived in the woods? Now he was concerned. He would have to track this child down and find him before he burned the forest down. Eric felt the responsibility fall on him. Those were his matches. He had been careless enough to let them fall into the boy's hands. He saw the child's tracks heading north toward Mt. Rainier but also going farther off trail. He had to catch him soon.

The monster named Harvey was still feeling the pain of his brush with death, which only fueled his desire for revenge. He could not focus that desire at the judge or the others for now, but he would kill the boy. He had been told to only recapture the child but he would not control himself enough for that. He already had a lead. Some hiker had called the police about seeing the tracks of a child out in the woods some ways from the road where Tiny Tim had escaped. Harvey easily found the map to the trail on some outdoor trails web-site. He was packing for his trip. Harvey was not unaware of outdoor life. Although he preferred the city, he knew how to live and hunt in the woods if necessary. He only needed to get within a certain range of Tiny Tim and the hand held tracking device would pick up on the small capsule implanted just under the skin on his back. The others had mocked him for not having it with him the day Tiny Tim had fled.

Eric had to climb to the highest point in the area before he could get a signal. His cell phone had been in his side pocket when the bears came to visit. He had enough common sense to call his wife before heading off trail hunting for this child. He told her the whole story from the beginning, from the first prints to the burning stump. His wife was a good woman and Eric loved her, as his favorite author would have said. "She's a woman to ride the river with." No one talked that way anymore, but Eric enjoyed the old western novels.

Amy Savage took in the information as best she could. "So you think it's a boy?" "How old would you say he is?" "What did the police say?" "Are you OK?" She asked a few more questions about where he was and gave him a time frame to call her back. Eric gave her his current GPS location. That was it. Now she knew. It would worry her. Eric knew that. But it was the right thing to do.

Amy walked out the front door of their craftsmen style home onto their little front porch, down the stone walkway that Eric had painstakingly laid and through their white gate to get the mail. Her mind was on Eric and this mystery child. It had been five years since the disappearance of their son.

She refused to think of that. There was just too much pain to go there without good reason. But the idea boiled under the surface of her soul.

At the mailbox she looked up and saw a man three houses down packing his SUV. She had never liked the look of that man. He was a big man, wide in the shoulders but narrow between the eyes. It looked like he was going camping. Their gazes locked for just a moment but he looked away suddenly. Alarms were going off in Amy's stomach. The police and the private investigators had interviewed everyone on the street after their son's disappearance. So why did he look so guilty?

She thought about calling the police. The investigators down at the station knew her family by name. Most felt that the Savage family had gone too far in their search for Benjamin. Eric and his father Noland had ended up on the wrong side of the law by following leads where ever they went, including into some very dangerous situations. Papa Noland Savage was a retired Navy Seal. He was not about to give up on his only grandson. But about a year ago, Eric and Noland ended up incarcerated in South America and faced years of red tape before they would get a fair hearing. Amy had to bribe their way out. After that, Eric and his dad had a falling out. Eric could see that he was losing Amy in his search for Benjamin. He had to be home more. Amy needed him. Noland felt Eric was giving up. They had some hard words and parted ways.

Eric followed the boy's tracks, lost them and then found them again. Lucky for him the boy wasn't really trying to hide his trail. As a matter of fact, the child liked to kick rocks, break low branches, and draw circles in the dirt. Eric could hear him before he could see him. Just over the next rise, probably down by a small creek that fed the river. Eric moved slowly now. He wanted to see the boy. Up till now he had been a ghost boy who only left tracks. He wanted to put some flesh and blood on all this mystery. He made his way quietly as possible down the slope toward the creek. Suddenly, the head of a big buck came up with a start. The deer and Eric were both startled. With a bolt, the deer took off into the forest, making a commotion as he went.

Eric had lost his element of surprise but the boy had to be close. Eric called out into the trees, "You almost caught the forest on fire." No answer. "If you are going to start a fire put it out before you leave or you'll burn down all the trees." Nothing. "Make a circle of stones to keep the fire contained, OK!" He was talking to himself. Maybe this was going to be harder than he thought.

That night Tiny Tim gathered rocks into a circle, just like the man had told him, to make his first ever campfire. He used his stolen matches and had a fire going in no time. He liked the trees and did not want to burn the forest down. If this man liked the forest too, maybe he was a good man. Tiny Tim thought about that. He could not really remember any good men. Harvey had told him his mom and dad had thrown him away in the garbage. That wasn't nice. Then he remembered the "Courage" stone. Tiny Tim reached into his pocket and pulled it out. The "Courage" stone had been his for as long as he could remember. It was a smooth stone like those he found by the river. The word courage was deeply engraved into the stone on one side. Tiny Tim gazed at the word as the light of his campfire brought it to life in his hand. One time Harvey had taken it from him and tossed it out the window. "You're so stupid you've got rocks for brains," Harvey had snarled. Tiny Tim found the stone again later.

Tiny Tim couldn't read or write very well but over the years had picked up on a few things. Sometimes the girls in the cages would talk to him and he would ask them questions while bringing them their food. That is how he learned to read and write a little. One lady saw him looking at the stone and told him it was the word courage. She asked if she could hold it and Tiny Tim gave it to her. She let the rock rest in her hand and stared at the word. Without taking her eyes off the stone she told him, "No one in this hell hole would give you this. So you must have had it on you when they abducted you. Maybe your mom or dad gave you this? Hold on to it kid!" She gave it back to him and turned away.

Tiny Tim could not remember his mom and dad. He remembered crying for them one night and Harvey giving him a bad beating for it. After that the memory would not come to him. Tim remembered a garden with stones in it, like the one he had. There were other stones with other words on them like, love, joy, and family. Was that his mom's garden? Maybe Harvey had lied to him about his parents throwing him into the garbage? Maybe Harvey had lied about a lot of things?

Eric found the boys' camp the next morning. There was a circle of stones just like he had asked and the fire had been put out before the boy left. Eric couldn't help but be pleased with the child. He *had* been listening. Maybe he was still close by. Eric slowly turned and searched the forest with his eyes. The morning sunlight caught the gleam of metal reflecting off of Eric's canteen now strapped over the boy's shoulder. Eric pretended not to notice. He had another idea. "If you would leave three unused matches for me by your fire tomorrow morning, I'll trade you for a little fishing line and a hook. If you can learn to fish for your food you wouldn't have to steal anymore."

Tiny Tim liked the idea of catching a fish. He had never caught a fish in his life that he could remember.

Suddenly a voice in his head mocked him, it was Harvey's words. *Don't try it, stupid!*

What if I can't catch one and look stupid in front of the man? Tim thought to himself.

Tiny Tim put his hands over his ears and closed his eyes. *No!* He forced the negative thoughts away. If he was going to survive in the forest for the rest of his life he would need more food. He needed to learn to fish.

The next morning he counted out three matches and left them next to his circle of stones. When he came back to his camp later that day there was a willow branch with fishing line and a hook. There was also a zip lock baggy with some bright little balls of orange power bait and a chocolate power bar.

Eric watched the boy from a distance as he consumed the power bar and pondered his next move. Hopefully, he was winning the boys trust. Maybe it was time to try and make a face to face trade? The only way he could help this child was to get him to voluntarily walk out of these woods with him. The boy did not seem injured in any way. He did seem a little thin and dirty. But Eric had only seen him from a distance in the shadows.

He followed the boy to the river and hid upstream. He watched him fish for a time and realized, by the looks of it, the boy had never been fishing before. Eric decided to go and retrieve his own fishing gear. He would just start fishing a little ways away from the boy and let himself be seen. Hopefully, he could initiate some conversation without scaring the child away.

Eric followed a game trail back to where he had stashed his things. After retrieving what he needed he started back. Glancing to one side of the trail something caught his eye. Carved low on the trunk of a Douglas fir tree was the name Bengeman, Benjamin spelled wrong? Eric went to the tree and kneeled down to get a good look. It was fresh. It had to have been the boy. Was his name Benjamin? Eric almost would not let the thought take form. His name was Benjamin! Benjamin? It had been so long ago. Five years of so much pain for Amy and him. Dare he think this boy could be their Benjamin? Five years? This boy looked about the right age.

Eric dropped his fishing gear and ran through the whispering woods. As he ran, he prayed. Please still be there! God, please help me. As he ran, he tried to call Amy. No service. He was in a dream. Was this really happening? Why had he not acted sooner? The river was just ahead now. He could hear the rush of the water. Trees blocked his view. The willow branch lay half in the water. The canteen still hung from a tree branch. Where was the boy?

Eric looked in every direction. "Benjamin!!" He called out. He was not there. Eric forced himself to calm down. He looked for tracks. There were other foot prints everywhere, large man sized footprints. There had been a struggle. The boy tried to fight back. There was blood on the ground. Eric found his red Swiss Army knife. There was blood on the blade and scratched on the side was the name Bengeman. There was no doubt in his mind now. Somehow, someway, this lost boy was his missing son and this time he was not going to fail him.

Chapter 2
Dreams and Nightmares

The painful dream came to Amy as it had so many times before. It always started with the same scene in her mind. She was playing with little Benjamin in the front of their home on a bright sunny day. He was only five years old. He was her beautiful little boy. He looked like his daddy with his sky blue eyes and laughing smile. That made her happy. He was dressed in a Seattle Seahawks football shirt and blue jeans. Eric grew up in Washington and was a diehard Seahawk's fan. Little Benjamin already watched football games with his dad. He had recently started talking loudly to the players in the game like they could hear him, just like his father. They had a happy life.

It was years before this scene, at Grandma Savage's house where Benjamin laid hold of his first engraved stone. Papa Noland had given one to his wife as a gift. It was a white stone with the words, forever loved, engraved in beautiful script. Somehow the little guy got a hold of it. Benjamin had just started walking and putting everything into his mouth. Thankfully, it was too large for his mouth but he was slobbering all over it when Amy took it away from him. She read to him the words on the stone and it made him laugh. Amy liked the idea of words in stone. Some words should be that solid, that strong, they should last forever. She purchased a few on her own and Eric noticed, buying her one as a gift that read, unforgettable. Friends and family caught on and that's why the flowerbeds, walkways, and corner posts, in front and behind the Savage home were filled with

27

engraved stones. Love, Hope, Faith, Family, Laughter, Courage, and a host of others, over the years, found their way into the collection. One stone was engraved with the statement, *Nothing is written in stone*! Eric brought that one home for himself. Now that Benjamin was five, he played with the smaller stones and Amy would have to check his pockets before putting his play clothes in the wash.

Their front yard had a four foot fence with a gated entry. They did not live on a busy street but with a very active five year old a fence was a good thing. It was the 4th of July and Eric was out picking up some fireworks for that evening. Some teenage boys down the street were detonating some very questionable sized explosives that were rattling the windows through-out the neighborhood. Where were their parents? Amy worked as an ER doctor and knew all too well what fireworks could do.

"BoooMM!!" The deafening sound of reverberation hit and painful cries for help followed. Amy ran into the house for her enhanced first aid kit and back out again quickly. She told Benjamin to stay in the yard as she closed the gate and ran down the street to where a group of teens were gawking in shock at the bloody shredded stump of flesh hanging from their friend's wrist. Amy immediately went to work to stop the bleeding.

"What's your name?" she asked calmly, while swiftly grabbing something for use as a tourniquet.

"......Steven , em"

"Hi Steven, my name is Doctor Savage. How old are you Steven?"

"....Auuu...Fourteen."

Amy pulled the tourniquet tight.

"What's your last name?"

"Mills,.. I can't feel my arm."

That's a good thing! Amy thought to herself.

"I think I cut up my hand."

No kid, you blew up your hand. She was already assessing the possibilities for reconstructive surgery.

Parents came running from the houses around. She could hear the calls being made to 911. It would take the EMT's 11min to reach them. She turned to an adult bystander. "I'm a doctor. I need a bag of clean ice. We have to find his hand and fingers. They need to be put on ice immediately!" She ordered. Some people helped, others backed away, grossed out.

The kid questioned, "Find my hand??" he passed out.

When the EMT'S arrived, she knew them by name. She gave them some instructions along with the salvaged parts of the boys hand on ice. She wanted to go with them but she couldn't leave Benjamin alone. Parents thanked her as they rushed to follow the ambulance. She had done what she could and headed home.

Benjamin was not in the front yard. He must have gone inside. Not like him to miss all the action. "Benjamin" she called out. She went through the house and into the backyard. No Benjamin. She called louder now. She checked the sides of the house. She went back through the house and checked again.

"Benjamin, if you are hiding in here the game is over. Come out right now or you'll be in big trouble!" She waited in hope. *Please be hiding.*

No Benjamin. She ran back out on the street. A few people were still lingering about talking about the injured boy's hand. She recognized some of them, but others were strangers. She did not see her Benjamin.

"Excuse me did you see a little boy. He was wearing a Seattle Sea Hawks shirt." No one had seen anything. Amy looked again at the empty yard and fear started to fill her heart.

"Benjamin!" she called out in every direction. He always came when she called and was not one for wondering off too far.

It was at that moment that Eric pulled around the corner unto their street. Amy ran to him and stopped him in the road. As she said the panicked words it hit her hard. "I can't find Benjamin!"

Amy woke up in a panic, jumping out of bed, she called out his name. She was half asleep. There it was again. All the old feelings came back, guilt, anger, fear, regret; it was all there like the day it happened.

She told herself to calm down, it was only the thousandth time she'd had that dream. She did not need to fall apart again. She wished Eric were home.

Harvey would have finished Tiny Tim on the spot if not for the hiker he had heard coming through the woods. He wanted no witnesses. He would take the boy deep into the woods on his ATV and dump his body where no one would ever find it. Surprisingly, the boy had fought back and drawn blood. *Every dog has his day*, Harvey thought to himself as he looked at the fresh cut on his forearm. The boy would pay for that before he died. He had knocked Tiny Tim senseless with a blow to the head and carried him off. His ride was right where he had left it. *No reason to work hard if you don't have to*, he thought to himself. The sign at the trail head said no four wheelers allowed. So no one would have one out here but him. Harvey liked having every advantage he could get over others.

Eric was panicked. He could not loose Benjamin again. He had to find him. Following the big man's trail, he guessed from the depth of the track that Benjamin was being carried. Eric was moving as fast as possible without losing their sign and prayed that he would overtake them soon. Ahead, he heard the sound of an engine starting and ran immediately in that direction. Jumping over a fallen tree on the run and into a small grassy clearing Eric saw the back side of a large man riding away on a four wheeler. The boy, his boy, Benjamin, was tied to the back rack like a dead deer. Eric ran for all he was worth. Harvey did not hear him coming over the noise of the engine. Rushing in from behind, he had a chance to catch them. Eric leaped for the back rack of the vehicle, catching the bar next to his son; he started to pull himself up. Harvey finally noticed and gunned the engine. The wheels kicked rocks into Eric's lower body but he held on with one hand. But then Harvey took a sharp left and sent Eric rolling.

Coming to a stop, Harvey swiftly pulled out his gun and took aim at Eric. Eric had not been expecting such an immediate and aggressive response and froze like a deer in the headlights. Nothing but providence saved him there. The shot was too high and kicked up dirt two feet passed Eric's head. Instincts kicked in and Eric rolled over a bank and into a natural ditch but not before a second shot just missed his shoulder. Eric Savage hurried on all fours into the safety of the trees. Harvey took off in pursuit, struggling to fire his 9mm on the move. The lead slammed into the trees around Eric as he ran an evasive pattern through the forest.

Harvey couldn't get a clear shot with all the trees in the way and uneven ground, but he would not give up the chase now. This man had seen him with the boy. Eric ran into the thickest stand of trees he could find trying to make his path difficult to follow. But the sound behind him never diminished. It was only a matter of time. His heart was pumping fast and great beads of sweat were running down his face. This was now a race for his life and the odds were with the guy on the ATV with the gun.

He had to change the game. On the run, he picked up the largest, sturdiest looking branch he could find and froze up against the back side of a wide tree. If he could time this just right, he had a chance. Waiting for the sound of pursuit to get right on top of him, Eric put all of his strength into grand slam home run swing aimed right at Harvey's head. The blow landed true, cracking the branch in two over Harvey's forehead and sending him flying unconscious to the ground. The four wheeler rolled to a stop by itself with Benjamin still roped to the back.

Eric went to his son and untied his hands and feet. He gently lifted his body from the back rack of the four wheeler and sat on the forest floor holding the boy. Eric checked his breathing and his pulse. He was alive. There was a nasty burse forming on his right temple. He needed Amy to look at that. He couldn't help but just look at the boy. The family resemblance was there, this boy was a Savage. Without a doubt this was his Benjamin Savage, his son. Where had he been all these years? What had he been through? Who was this man?

Suddenly, a sound came from the direction of the fallen Man.

Harvey struggled to his feet like a grizzly bear waking in the winter. He shook off the blow and fixed his eyes on Eric.

Eric carefully placed Benjamin aside and stood to face the man.

"Who are you?" There was a rage building up in Eric Savages blood like he had never known before in his life. "What are you doing with my son?"

"Your son?" Harvey was rubbing his forehead but his thick skull had saved him from any real harm. "You're the boy's father? Now that is funny. I think I'll tell you! I think you really need to know, being his father and all."

Harvey abruptly picked up the gun that had fallen just feet from where he was and pointed it at Eric. It was then that Harvey realized he couldn't focus his eyes very well. Eric he could see, but the gun in his own hand was a blur. He tried not to show it.

"You were stupid to let me get this in my hands again," Harvey boasted. "But I'll answer your questions, just because you asked so nicely," he said sarcastically. "I'll tell you just before you and your son die."

Eric did not back down but rather took a step closer. Harvey took aim with the gun but still couldn't see the sights. It didn't concern him because at this distance, he couldn't miss.

"Eric Savage." Harvey grinned and shook his head realizing who stood before him. "You don't celebrate the 4th of July anymore do you?" Harvey taunted him. "I can understand why, the feeling of guilt must really come up on those anniversaries. You have missed out on some memories with that boy over there haven't you? But I haven't." Eric saw his face turn dark and evil. "He doesn't even talk about you anymore…"

Eric had been slowly closing the distance between them as Harvey spoke. With gun in hand Harvey was confident and wanted to brag. But Eric had been counting shots as he ran and now seeing the gun up close knew what Harvey couldn't see.

"Click"

Harvey was out of bullets.

The white hot fury building up in Eric Savage exploded with a blinding attack of right and left punches to Harvey's face. Harvey tried to use the empty gun to shield himself but Eric responded with a front kick to his stomach. Harvey was a big man and this was not his first rodeo. He lunged low at Eric and took him down with his superior weight, intent on changing the fight into a wrestling match where he would have the advantage. But Eric kneed him in the chin as they fell together and used the moment to roll out from under him and back to his feet.

Eric remembered his father teaching him how to fight a bigger man. It all came rushing back, the hours of training, the need to use the man's weight against him.

As Harvey was getting up he scooped up a hand full of dirt and flung it into Eric's face and eyes. It was a child's trick but nothing was too low for him. Eric was momentarily blind. Harvey seized the moment with a powerful right cross to the head and Eric almost lost consciousness. But then Harvey telegraphed a kick with his boots and Eric sidestepped. He pushed his foot higher into the air. Harvey slipped and landed hard on his back. Harvey rolled fast thinking Eric would kick him while he was down but Eric didn't need desperate measures. Harvey did not admire what he thought was weakness and cursed Eric with contempt. Eric ignored him and attacked again. Harvey fought back but could not match the intensity coming out of Eric Savage, but he was a bear of a man and counted on Eric growing weak first.

Eric remembered the day his father Noland made him cut down a huge tree on their property. The tree seemed so thick, so hard, and so strong. With every swing of the axe his muscles burned. Every time he wanted to quit his father would encourage him to never give up.

"Don't let it beat you son, you can do this!" Noland would say.

Eric reminded himself of who finally won that battle as he and Harvey circled each other looking for weaknesses. One would attack and land a few blows and then the other would do the same. Harvey wanted to get his powerful hands on him but Eric was too fast and turned his attempts to get in close against him to land deadly strikes to his core.

Eric found the combination of moves that best kept Harvey off balance and started chopping. His muscles burned and his fists were bloody and num, but Eric just kept chopping. The big man felt his strength failing him. Eric saw his moment and threw his weight into a straight power punch into Harvey's face. Harvey fell back and landed on his rear end. He did not get up. Only then did Eric stop and look over to where he had laid Benjamin, but the boy was gone.

Eric glanced around to find him but he was nowhere to be seen. He searched for some sign of which direction he might have gone and found a faint trail. Harvey seeing his chance to escape jumped on the ATV. He started the engine and speed away like a whipped dog with his tail between his legs. Eric Savage let him go and instead followed the trail left by Benjamin leading in the opposite direction.

Back in Seattle, Amy couldn't shake the feeling that something wasn't right. Eric had not checked in with her when he was scheduled too. The day before when she saw that man down the street, he gave her a look that made her skin crawl and he was packing like he was headed into the woods. Then there was this mystery child Eric was following. The dream of that dreaded day had returned after such a long absence. Was something trying to warn her? She decided to call Noland, Eric's Dad.

He was probably out there somewhere still searching for Benjamin. After grandma Savage passed away and he and Eric stopped talking it was all he ever did. She would have to leave a message that he probably wouldn't get for weeks.

The phone rang. She waited.

"Please leave your message after the beep."

"Hey dad, this is Amy. Eric went hiking in the Cascades. I think he may be in trouble. He called me because he was going off-trail to investigate something and was supposed to call me again but I haven't heard from him." She phased, should she say more? "There is more, he was tracking a child lost in the woods. He thinks it's a boy. I just have the feeling something is wrong. I'm going to get Gary Holland to take me in after Eric to try to find him. I'll keep a cell phone with me but reception will probably be sketchy. I know this sounds crazy but everything in my gut says this all has

35

something to do with Benjamin. Love you. Bye."

Gary Holland was a long time friend of the family. Noland and Gary had enlisted together when they were both eighteen. Noland became a Navy Seal and Gary a hotshot pilot. He loved Amy and Eric like they were his own kids. He called a friend who worked for the forest service and got a chopper pilot who would drop them off as close as possible to Eric's last known location. It may all be for nothing. He may be fine. The police would do nothing because there was no real evidence that anything was wrong at this point. The Savage family had cried wolf one too many times in the eyes of Police Chef Hobbs and without something solid they would get little help.

Judge Fredrick Hurst received the news that Harvey had returned empty handed with irritated dissatisfaction. The judge had him brought in. Harvey stood there like a kid in the principal's office. His face was swollen and bruised from his fight with Eric Savage.

The judge was mocking, "What happened to you Harvey? Did Tiny Tim beat your face in with a stick?"

Harvey heard the snickering around the room. He knew better than to answer in anger but it seethed inside his heart. Instead, he thought of the best lie he could think of to save himself. "Tiny Tim had help to escape from me. He didn't do it alone. They must have planned this. Out there in the woods, he was with his family. The whole Savage Clan got the drop on me. You know Noland Savage. The Navy Seal! I didn't stand a chance."

No one laughed at the name of Noland Savage.

Judge Fredrick Hurst sat back in his English leather chair and took a drink of his scotch. Could he believe this man? Could he afford not to believe him? Noland Savage was supposed to be in Mexico. He had carefully planted information and false leads that would throw him off the real trail. But the man was damn hard to keep track of. If Noland ever found out that he was involved with the kidnapping and slave labor of his grandson there would be no legal formalities to hide behind. Noland was cut from stone. He would be judge, jury, and executioner.

Harvey saw the effect the name Noland Savage had on the judge. He would keep that ace up his sleeve just in case.

Judge Hurst put his drink down and stared intently at Harvey before he spoke. "Describe Noland Savage. What did he look like?"

Harvey knew he was walking on thin ice. "Eric Savage is the one I saw face to face. He was the one I fought with."

That actually added up to Hurst. If he had fought Noland, he'd be dead.

"Eric is tall with brown hair, blue eyes, generally well fit guy who knows how to throw a hard right. Noland stood by Tiny Tim; I didn't get a good look at him."

"Why would Noland let you leave?"

"Tiny Tim distracted him, got scared because he saw me and ran off. Noland went after him. I saw my chance and got the hell out of there."

"Who got you with the knife?" the judge asked seeing the fresh cut on his forearm.

"Eric Savage," was all Harvey said but was disgusted with the thought that Tiny Tim had gotten the better of him.

The judge's men made some calls and unfortunately Harvey's story checked out. Eric Savage was known to be in the Cascade Mountains hiking. No one knew the location of Noland. But Amy Savage and a good family friend were dropped by chopper somewhere near the Mt. Rainier National Forest just hours ago.

Judge Hurst didn't like all the unanswered questions this situation brought to his mind. Why take the child into the forest? Why not go right to the police? He smiled at the thought of that. If they had gone to the police the boy would be dead by now. Did they know that? Unlikely! How much did they know? Even if they had watched the factory for months or had a spy on the inside, there would be no connection to himself or Chief Hobbs. A plan was forming in the judge's mind. They had seen Harvey and fought with him. If Harvey returned and was killed by the police, the Savage family would be grateful. They would come out of the woods. He did not like the odds of finding and defeating Noland Savage in the deep woods. Judge Hurst picked up the secure phone. He would need Chief Hobbs help on this one.

Tiny Tim ran through the woods in fear. Harvey was after him. Harvey would beat him. Harvey had killed the nice man who gave him the fishing pole. Nothing ever worked out for Tiny Tim. He was stupid to think he could get away. He was stupid to think he could catch a fish. Stupid! Stupid! STUPID!! The cliff came up suddenly, without time for him to stop. He went over the edge and dropped like a stone into the waters below. Tiny Tim did not know how to swim.

Eric Savage dove off the cliff seconds later and fished the boy out of the depths of the river. He brought him to the shore and pumped the water from his lungs. The boy came around, coughed up some more and took a wheezing breath, but then he pulled away from Eric in fear.

"It's ok, you're safe, It's going to be alright," Eric pleaded.

The boy was panicked. He tried to run away but the cliff and the river boxed him in on all sides. He had nowhere to run.

"Are you hurt?" Eric asked him, hoping to calm him down.

"Harvey's after me!" Tiny Tim explained.

"Who is Harvey?"

"Harvey's my dad," Tiny Tim said it out of habit, ashamed.

Eric Savage looked at his boy. Fear was all over him. What had they done to his bright, energetic, confident child? Someone was going to pay when he caught up to them. But that could wait.

"What's your name?"

Benjamin hesitated, "Tim."

"How old are you?"

"Twelve, I'm small for my age." He dropped his head. "They call me Tiny Tim."

Eric Savage looked at his son with all the love in his heart.

"You are not small for your age, because you are not twelve, you are only ten. And your name is not Tiny Tim. Your name is Benjamin Noland Savage."

Miles away in the city of Seattle, Officer Daniel Lane opened a chest filled with keepsakes from his late father. It had been a long time since he last went through the old photos. He was fourteen years old when his father died in the line of duty. That was just seven years ago. His dad had been his hero, his whole life. His death had devastated him and his mother. Despite his mother's fears, after just one year of college he dropped out and decided to follow in his father's footsteps and become a police officer. It was what he had always dreamed of becoming, but for some reason now that he was finally a City of Seattle Police Officer, he was restless. There were those still around on the force that remembered his dad and respected that Daniel would want to be an officer, but than there were those who seemed to avoid him. They watched him from a distance and looked on him with some secret distain. Daniel was fresh out of the academy and expected some razing, but this was different. Even his own Chief of Police, William Hobbs, kept Daniel at a professional distance while welcoming other new officers. He was not invited out after work to hang out with the guys. Conversations seemed to stop when he walked into the room. Maybe he needed to give it more time or maybe there was something about his father that no one was telling him.

As he went through his father things, not really knowing what he was looking for, he got sucked into the pictures of him and his dad. When he looked into his dad's eyes he felt guilty for thinking that maybe his father had done something wrong and that *he* was now paying for it. He put the pictures back and was about to close the lid when he saw a stray photo in the corner of the crest, one that he had never noticed before, it was of his dad and Chief Hobbs. He wasn't aware that they had ever known each other. Hobbs never brought it up and now, Daniel wondered why.

Amy Savage allowed Gary Holland to lead the way to the GPS location Eric had last given her. Gary was a good man to take her out into the forest on a wild goose chase. Eric would be surprised to see them, to say the least. She would never live this one down. Maybe she had over reacted. They arrived at the exact location where Eric had stood when he called her. Gary picked up his trail from there and before long they came upon an abandoned campsite. The circle of stones for a fire was still in place.

Amy could make out Eric's footprints in the dirt here and there. Then she saw what Eric had told her about over the phone, the footprint of a child. She took a knee and looked closely at the print. She touched it with her fingers. She felt something flash inside her. Was she losing it? This track could be from any child. But than why was she there? She was there because her gut told her different.

Amy stood up and looked at Gary. "Let's track them down."

They followed their trail to the river bed and found Eric's canteen still hanging from the tree. Why would Eric leave behind his canteen? They found the handmade fishing pole in a sandy spot by the river and another set of prints that did not belong to the child or Eric. They were large prints from a large man. Amy found drops of blood on the ground. Why would there be blood? Gary saw it too and looked around with a little more caution.

When he saw the fear on Amy's face he tried to calm her.

"People cut themselves fishing all the time. Let's not panic."

He was right. Here she was, an E.R. doctor, freaking out at the sight of blood.

They followed the trail into a small grassy clearing in the trees. There were tire tracks, which were out-of-place here. Gary looked around; he spotted a shell casing and searched farther until he found the bullet hole in the ground.

"Amy, come look at this."

He dug into the hole and pulled out the lead.

"A bullet?" Amy was worried now.

"It's from a hand gun, 9mm."

Gary was getting worried. *No hunter would be in these woods poaching with a 9mm hand gun, unlikely anyway.* He thought to himself.

After scouting about Gary had another revelation.

"Both Eric's trail and the tire tracks lead that way," he said pointing north. "Did Eric say anything about meeting someone out here?"

"No, just the child he was tracking."

"We should call the police, this seems suspicious to me."

Amy pulled out her cell. There was no service. Gary nodded his head in understanding.

Amy was not about to abandon her husband's trail to climb back to where they had started.

"You go call the police, Gary. I would just slow you down. I'll wait right here. Maybe they will come back."

Gray knew her better than that. The minute he left she would be following Eric's trail.

"Young lady, I brought you into these woods and I'm not about to leave you here alone in them. We either go to make that call together or we follow their trail together, you got it?"

She gave him a smile.

Amy followed the vehicle tracks where they went into the woods. In the first tree she found another bullet hole. Gary found two more shell casings. Someone was shooting and someone was being shot at.

"OK girl, it's time to decide. Do we keep going or do we call for help?"

"I need to find Eric; I just can't turn away now. He may be in trouble. He may be wounded. I'm a doctor. I'm his wife."

Gray pulled out a .44 Colt revolver from his backpack, loaded it and strapped on its holster.

"OK, let's go."

Eric built a fire right there on the shore. Both he and Benjamin needed to get their wet clothes off and dried out before nightfall. They stripped down to their underpants and hung their clothes on overhanging branches close to the fire. The sun was going down and the river mist felt cool. Eric tried not to stare at the scars and burn holes on Benjamin's body. But as he saw for the first time the evidence of

Benjamin's abuse a flood of emotions threatened to make the grown man break down and cry. He turned away to wipe the tears from his eyes. What had his son been through over the last five years? Eric felt like a complete failure as a father. How could he ever make up for this? What concerned him even more was the damage done to the boy's soul. He needed to win his trust. He needed to help him. Eric got a hold on his feelings and tried making some conversation with the boy.

"Running away from them was a brave thing to do. I think you must be a pretty smart kid to pull that off."

Benjamin was not sure how to take that. He was not used to anyone saying he was brave or smart.

"Harvey was taking me to location D. We always stopped at the same gas station on the way there. It was out of the city. I liked all the trees, no houses, just trees! I thought it would be a good place to run away. I always wanted to climb a tree and live in a tree house. I snuck out the back window in the bathroom," Benjamin said sheepishly.

Eric wanted to ask him so many questions. Could he remember the gas station if he saw it again? Could he describe location D? But now was not the time. Instead, Eric decided, he just needed to be a friend. There was already something the two had in common. Eric decided to build on that.

"I love to climb trees. I'll tell you what! Tomorrow we're going to find some trees to climb."

Benjamin looked up at Eric. "Really, you like climbing trees?"

"I have been climbing trees since I was your age. I'll teach you what I know. We'll find the biggest coolest tree in this forest. What we need is an old wide-leaf maple tree. They make the best climbing trees."

Benjamin smiled. That would be fun.

Chapter 3
The Hunt for Benjamin Savage

Harvey sat in the specially outfitted helicopter with the two police officers sent from Chief Hobbs. They were all heavily armed with automatic weapons. He did not know the officers. That was not uncommon in the judge's operations. The fewer people you knew the better. They were, no doubt, on Judge Hurst's payroll.

After flashing their badges and getting the information they needed from the pilot who had taken in Amy and Gary, they set out for the same landing spot. From there they just needed to get within range and they could follow the tracking device to the rest of the Savage family and wipe them all out at the same time. At least, that is what Harvey was told. The two officers had different orders. They were to track down the Savage family and allow Harvey to take the lead. Judge Hurst wanted Harvey killed, by the police, trying to recapture Tiny Tim, in front of Noland Savage if possible. The police would save the day and if Tiny Tim remembered too much he could be handled later.

Gary Holland knew the sound of a chopper when he heard one. It was in the distance, back near where they had landed. Everything about this little adventure did not set well with his gut. He was no stranger to these mountains. It was something else. Something he couldn't put his finger on. The 9mm handgun he discovered laying empty on the ground with the smell of powder still detectable just added to his concerns. There were small amounts of blood on the gun and with all the signs of activity in the area he could only imagine what had taken place there. He carefully put the handgun in a plastic bag and into his pack. It was late in the day and they needed to make camp while they could still see.

Night fell on Eric and Benjamin and the stars came out. The sound of moving waters and the reflection of their campfire had a calming effect on Benjamin and he seemed to relax a little. Benjamin couldn't explain it but he felt safe for the first time in a long time. The feeling was alien to him and he wondered how long it would last. They both put back on their dried out clothes and were glad to feel warm again. Eric made a bed of fern leaves for them next to the fire. He found some eatable shoots growing close by and being hungry, they both eat without complaint. Eric washed out his injuries and wrapped his cuts with leaves he knew had healing properties. Benjamin started asking questions about the leaves and shoots. Where could he find more? What other plants could he eat in the woods? It was obvious this was something that concerned him, so Eric asked him about it.

"Why all the interest in forest plants?"

"I need to learn how to find food so I can live in the forest. I'm never going back. I like it here," Benjamin replied matter a fact like.

It was so simple. He liked it here. Who could blame him? Eric wasn't about to argue. He liked being out in nature too.

Eric told him about clover, dandelions, and watercress. All of which he could eat. He also showed him some blue elderberry and explained how it was used as a medicine for generations by people native to the Pacific Northwest.

The two stared up at the bright stars. Benjamin was amazed at how clear and beautiful they looked out there compared to in the city where they were hardly noticeable.

Just out of habit, Eric started talking about the names of the constellations. He talked about how far away the stars were to earth. He pointed out the big dipper to Benjamin. He talked about the galaxies. He talked about planets and moons. He talked about Mars and the mission being planned to go there. He talked about the speed of light. What did the kid know? How much had he missed?

Surprisingly, Benjamin had a lot of questions. He had been allowed to watch movies and had picked up on quite a bit of information. Eric was proud of him. What a little soldier. He was smart and brave and every bit a Savage.

Deep in the heart of Mexico City Noland Savage moved silently along a building's outer edge avoiding the bright security lights. He stayed in the shadows and timed his every move. His camouflage blended with the night. Even the blade of his knife was black. He saw the shadow of the north guard walking to the northwest corner of the complex. He waited until the shadow turned. For three days he had watched and gathered information before making his move to rescue Benjamin. There would be fewer guards today because of the soccer game being hosted by the country of Mexico just miles away. Many had gone to the game. He counted in his mind's eye the location of every person in the complex and then swiftly ran around the corner and up the stairs. The guard at the top of the stairs would be heading his way. If things went as planned, this guard would be the only casualty. He took no pleasure in taking a man's life, even if he was a slave trader.

Noland crouched low and ready like a mountain lion would. He did not need to think or plan his next actions. His mind and muscles knew what to do. His knife punctured the guard's vocal cords; his life's breath blew silently away in the wind. He took the keys he needed and moved toward the cells. The one factor he could not control was the boy's reaction to him. Noland's face was black with camouflage and he hoped the boy would not scream or call out when he saw him. He was prepared to drug him if necessary.

He opened the cell door as silently as possible. The small room was bare, save for the sleeping body of a ten year old boy covered in a mangy blanket. Noland placed his hand on the boy's shoulder to wake him. His body was cold. Noland ripped the blanket to the side and started CPR, but it was too late. Noland prayed. He took a needle out and thrust it into the boy's heart. The medicine was designed to kick start life.

"Come on, Benjamin."

There was no response.

All his life Noland Savage had been a fighter. He was a man that believed he could do anything if he put his mind to it. When his grandson was kidnapped he knew he would find him. If it took the rest of his life he would find him. When he uncovered the possibility that the police had ignored some evidence that lead to Mexico City, he thought he had finally found the break he was looking for. He did not think it would end like this. He lifted the back of the boy's shirt and saw the birthmark.

In a blind rage Noland cried out from a broken heart. The guards came running from all directions. They would have guns on him in less than a minute. But he would not abandon the body of his grandson to these swine. He was prepared to fight his way out of there, carrying Benjamin with him if need be. At 53 years old Noland was still strong and fast and lethal at his craft. To him, age was just a number. Someday, time would catch up to him, but not this day.

Noland quickly threw Benjamin over his shoulder and strapped their bodies together. There were two stairways leading up to the cell. They would discover their companion's dead body at the top of the stairs to the right and sound the alarm. The sight of death and the threat of real danger would slow them down, make them cautious. They would group up and move together, guns ready, toward the cell.

Noland pulled the pins on two grenades and tossed them

down the hallway balcony, one in each direction. He heard the rush of retreat and a course of profanities in Spanish as the two grenades rolled into view. They detonated as one, sending lethal fragments of medal casing at the attackers and providing cover for his next move. He retreated into the cell to get a running start and then rushed straight out of the door, leaping over the edge of the third story balcony railing and out into empty space. He turned his body back toward the building as the cable caught and swung him back down to ground level. There was an open walkway that cut the building in two. He appeared suddenly, out of nowhere, from above to the three armed men running down the hall. They were too slow to react; Noland fired three muffled shots with his sidearm and ran passed their fallen bodies, detaching the cable on the move.

The garage was in the southeast corner of the complex. It held two transport trucks parked side by side. Breaking open the locked door, Noland located the keys for one of the trucks and planted a timed explosive device on the other. He carefully laid the body of the boy in the back of his truck, strapping him down. The guards were now cautiously approaching the garage doors outside. Noland started up the engine and gunned the vehicle forward. The truck smashed through the old wooden double doors and into the courtyard coming under fire from the startled guards. He did not take off for the heavily fortified front gate but rather toward an unguarded location of the security fencing, which he had strategically cut the night before. The remaining guards jumped into the second truck and started to follow. Noland saw the exploding fireball in his rear view mirror. He felt no sympathy for the bastards. They had kidnapped and killed his grandson. As he drove away his thoughts turned to Eric and Amy. How would he tell them Benjamin was dead?

Eric was determined to keep his promise to Benjamin. Today they would climb a tree or two. So when they came upon a grove of old wide leaf maple trees on their way back to safety, he couldn't say no. The trunks were twisted and thick. The branches spread out in every direction. One tree had grown almost sideways and then curled up. It made an almost natural stairway leading to its higher branches. Perhaps a strong wind had knocked it over when it was young and then it had just grown that way. Benjamin was climbing all over that tree like he had found an old friend. Eric joined in, laughing and hanging and climbing higher and higher through the interlocking limbs of the Maples.

Benjamin followed Eric through the branches of the trees, but finally came to a spot were the next branch was just too far for him to reach. Eric stopped and held out his hand for Benjamin to take. Benjamin looked down at the forest floor far below and then at Eric's offer of help. Tiny Tim slowly backed away. He went back down the way he had come and the game was over. Eric just watched him go and wondered how long it would take before he would trust him. But he would not pressure him. He would not expect too much too soon. Eric jumped from the high branch and ran for another tree. A few seconds later he was delighted to see Benjamin joining in once again.

It was upon this scene that Amy Savage and Gary Holland suddenly emerged. Benjamin and Eric were both hanging upside down by their legs. Father and son were covered in dirt, leaves, and twigs. Amy's heart skipped a beat at the sight. It was Benjamin. He looked older, but it was her Benjamin. Eric dropped from the tree at the sight of Amy. Amy just started to cry. Benjamin swung back up into the tree and backed into the branches. He climbed high and hid in the leaf covered camouflage. He did not like new people.

Amy looked at Eric with the question in her eyes.

"Benjamin?" She was looking up at the tree where the boy had disappeared into the branches. She was so afraid she was just seeing what she wanted to see.

Eric nodded his head and said the words slowly to give her time, "Yes, it is our Benjamin." But then he added. "He doesn't remember me. I haven't told him yet. He seems like a very hurt little boy. I don't know how much he can handle yet but I do know he needs you."

Amy took a moment to let that soak in. She looked at her husband covered in dirt and leaves with a few twigs here and there and then up the tree where Benjamin was hiding. Eric explained to Amy that he had promised Benjamin the night before to climb trees with him today.

"In that case, I think you were doing just fine, a promise is a promise, but I'll join in."

Amy walked to the tall strong tree and looked up through the branches for her son. Through the thick maze of wide leaves and warped branches she spotted two eyes looking back.

Amy smiled. "Hey there! I hope you don't mind but I like to climb trees too and this is like the best place on the planet to find climbing trees."

Amy looked to Eric. Eric walked up beside Amy and put his arm around her.

"She's ok," Eric said, looking up to Benjamin. "And now that there are three of us, we could play tree tag."

Benjamin lowered himself just into view. "What is tree tag?"

It took everything in Amy not to start crying again. She tried to reply but choked up.

"What's wrong with her?" Benjamin asked

"She just cries sometimes," Eric replied holding his shaken wife up with one arm around her waist.

Benjamin came down from the tree and looked at Amy. "It's ok to cry sometimes. I cry sometimes. But climbing these trees helps me feel better." He took Amy by the hand.

"Come on, you can play with us."

Amy let herself be led up the tree by her long lost son. She so wanted to just hold him in her arms but it was apparent he had no clue who she was. Would he ever remember her? If he did, would he blame her for not protecting him the way a good mother should?

Eric looked over to Gary who had stayed back. He signaled with two fingers to his eyes and then to the surrounding area. Gary understood and disappeared into the forest to keep watch.

"I'm it," Eric said looking up at the two in the tree. "I have to try and catch you both. You can run, hide and climb anywhere in these maple trees. But If I tag you that makes you it and I get to run and hide. I'll count to twenty and then I'm coming after you."

Benjamin was pleased. He grabbed Amy by the hand again and said, "Let's go!"

Just a few miles away from the grove of maple trees Harvey was growing suspicious as he stalked through the forest. He noticed the others were letting him take the lead. Did they think him an idiot! They had fallen back as the trail had gotten hot. They stayed behind him, one to his right and one to his left. They were alert and ready for Noland Savage no doubt. But there was something else, something not right.

Harvey remembered the fear in Judge Hurst eyes at the name of Savage. He would want to pin this whole thing on someone else. He would want Noland satisfied and to come out looking clean himself. There was only one way that could happen. Harvey realized he was walking into a death trap. He suddenly stopped and put one hand up, like he had spotted something. He held the tracking device.

The two men in police uniforms were ready. Harvey motioned for them to circle around. He would take the lead.

He made hand signals indicating they were to wait for his move and then close the circle on the Savage family. They were more than willing to give the OK. That would work nicely.

Harvey waited until they were out of sight, and then back tracked behind the officer on his right. He first had to even the odds. He took aim and pulled the trigger!

"Tat,tat,tat…" Three shots to the head and he was down.

He fired a couple more shots just to add to the confusion. The second officer restrained himself, unwilling to fire at unseen targets; he had his orders from Judge Hurst.

"I got him!!" Harvey said out loud, "I killed Noland Savage."

At that, the second officer stepped out from his cover and into Harvey's crosshairs.

"Tat,tat,tat…"

"Sucker!!" Harvey was proud of himself.

Eric and Amy froze at the sound of the gunfire. It was close, to the south. Gary Holland came running out of the woods.

"I saw two police officers gunned down through my binoculars. I was too far away to help."

"Harvey!" Benjamin said in fear.

Eric put his arm around Benjamin. "Maybe?"

Benjamin was panicked. "You need to leave me here! He is after me! He will kill you if you stay with me."

Eric and Amy took a knee to looked Benjamin in the eye. "Family doesn't leave each other."

Benjamin didn't understand. Everyone left him.

Amy pulled an engraved stone out of her pocket and

showed it to Benjamin.

He looked down at the stone and stared for a moment.

Then pulled the "Courage" stone out of his own pocket.

Eric and Amy couldn't believe their eyes. After all these years, how did he hold on to that?

Amy spoke, "I'm frightened Benjamin. It looks like you have what I need and I have what you need. Will you trade me?"

Benjamin took the stone out of her hand and ran his fingers over the letters.

It was engraved with the word family.

"You want me to be part of your family?" Benjamin questioned.

"As far as we are concerned, you already are," Eric replied.

Benjamin handed her the stone of courage. "Don't lose it."

Amy laughed. "Not a chance!" She hugged Benjamin and he did not pull away.

Benjamin was smiling but at the same time felt concerned. "Harvey will not be happy with you two taking me into your family."

Amy knew in her gut who Harvey was and for the first time in her life was ready to harm another human being.

"I'm not concerned about making Harvey happy," Amy said as she stood up.

Gray Holland knew just how out gunned they were. "We need to move, far and fast."

Gary handed one of the back packs to Eric and the four of them took off running north with no trail to lead them.

Harvey took the extra ammo off of the dead officers. It

was possible that he could blame their deaths on Noland Savage, but it wouldn't take much for Judge Hurst to figure out the truth. It was time to just disappear. The smart thing to do would be to just walk away. But it bothered him that someone like Tiny Tim had caused him so much trouble. He did not take his defeat at the hands of Eric Savage lightly either. This was personal. He would find them. Kill them. Then he would write a letter to Noland Savage telling him all about it, signed Judge Fredrick Hurst. The idea pleased Harvey.

They couldn't be far ahead. They probably heard the gun shots and took off running. But that wouldn't help them. Harvey flipped the switch on the tracking device to find Tiny Tim's location. He then flipped on the thermo imaging tech on his rifle and spotted them across a small valley running up the opposite hill side. The judge always believed in having the best equipment. The night vision setting was also state-of-the-art. He would find them. There was no doubt in Harvey's twisted black mind. He would find them soon.

Chapter 4
Family on the run

The judge was holding a slave auction at a very upscale hotel ball room. His best clientele from all over the world had come to Seattle, Washington for the bidding. It wasn't like the low class southern slave auctions of the 1800's. He demanded that it look like a Hollywood fashion show. The participants on stage had long ago had their wills broken with mind altering drugs. He was relishing in some twisted prestige hosting such an event brings to a depraved mind. It was well known that he did not like being interrupted at times like this, so the messenger was reluctant. He stood nearby hesitating for longer then was comfortable. The judge finally gave him a look that demanded an answer.

Realizing that was his que, he hurried to the Judge and whispered into his ear, "Sir, Savage attacked the Mexico City base. We had dozens of casualties. The body of the boy was taken."

"Are you sure it was Savage?"

"Everyone who got close enough to identify him is dead, but who else could it be?"

Hurst wanted to explode, but not in front of his international guests. So Harvey had lied to him and Savage had been gifted wrapped for them in Mexico City. Couldn't they do anything right. How long would it take Savage to figure out that the boy wasn't the real Benjamin?

"How many men did Savage have with him?"

That question made the messenger take pause, because he knew the judge would not like the answer.

"Just Savage, sir," the man confessed.

The judge's fist instinctively hit the table, turning a few heads. "I told them to double the guards, how could one man…?" The Judge stopped himself. He would deal with this later. This was not the time or the place. But heads would roll.

The messenger had no intention of bringing up the soccer game. He knew the old phrase, don't kill the messenger, wouldn't hold weight here. But there was another issue he couldn't avoid. "There is more sir…..we haven't heard from our team in the cascades. They have not checked in as planned."

Fredrick Hurst forced himself to smile at his guests.

"So what you are saying is two police officers are missing in the Cascade Mountains while on assignment. Consequently, it sounds to me like Police Chief Hobbs he has a problem. Any responsible Police Chief would send half the force to find these guys. You tell him to eliminate Harvey and the whole damn Savage family! Get out the dogs! Send out the choppers! It's time to take the gloves off. Go tell him that, NOW!"

The messenger hurried away.

Chief Hobbs was a man who liked to hear the sound of his own voice, usually barking orders. He fancied big guns and was able to amass a large arsenal under the guise of police activity. This would be a chance to flex his muscle. Three choppers would deploy one dog team each. Each team would comprise of four heavily armed men and one attack trained dog. He would pull some loyal men from the force and others from the factory. The choppers would have .50 caliber guns off one side. This was probably over-kill, but why miss out on having a little fun. He would be in the lead chopper himself behind one of the big .50 caliber machine guns. Someone should bring a camera.

Offing Harvey would be satisfying. Hobbs never liked the way the big man looked at him. Harvey probably didn't know about the chip they had implanted in his back. He was an easy man to get drunk and drugged. The three police helicopters lifted from their platforms amid a swirl of wind and dust. The predators soared above the city of Seattle and headed into the Cascade Mountains.

In an un-noteworthy, poverty stricken barrio, somewhere in the heart of Mexico City, Noland Savage looked again at the birthmark on the body of the boy, but this time through a high powered magnifying glass. The small room felt like a furnace and he had to wipe away the sweat from his eyes several times. But the body he examined was immersed in ice. What he had hoped and suspected was confirmed. The boy resembled what Benjamin would look like at this age but this was not Benjamin. This was the first mistake they had made in five years. Now he had a trail to follow. He would start by visiting a few of the men still alive from the Mexico City Complex. He would visit them in their homes at night where they could relax and have an adult conversation. They would tell him where to find the man who faked the birthmark. He would light the fuse leading back to whoever gave this order and ultimately back to the real Benjamin. Someone must be growing worried. He wondered what had happened to cause them to put such effort into baiting him into a trap.

Noland felt compassion for the dead boy used by these villains. He was not Benjamin but he was a human being. Who was he? What was his name? Where was his family? These men and woman buying and selling people like they were cattle were lower than insects. What kind of person could be so selfish? Slavery had gone on for thousands of years on planet earth. The Romans, the Greeks, and the Egyptians were all steeped in the filth of it. Then for just a brief moment, a light had shown in the darkness. An Army went to war to set other men free. Why did that generation differ from most all the generations before it? What motivated them? What was the driving force behind the end of slavery? Whatever it was must now be fading because slavery was growing again. We must have been naive to think it gone forever. Those who live in the sunshine of what others have done often foolishly abandon the ideas and principles that won them such happiness.

Did this generation have the moral courage to stand up and fight for others? Or was this truly the "ME" generation, only concerned with self gratification? Noland had been in battle with good men willing to give their lives for the man standing next to them. But he had also seen the cowards. They were often the big talkers who always had something to prove. One thing Noland was sure of, selfishness was at the root of being a coward. No man or woman walked into danger without first loving something outside of themselves more than themselves. It seemed to him a selfish generation could pave the way for a generation of do nothing cowards to arise.

On the other side of the United States a little girl named Abigail stood there with her social worker like unclaimed luggage. She was going to another foster home. The couple seemed nice enough, but so had the last couple and the ones before that. Maybe if her hair wasn't so red, or if she was a boy or if she was still a baby, someone would want her for keeps? But she could read people now. She could tell you who was in it for the money. She overheard the fights and sometimes would have her things packed before they broke the sad news. It took more than background checks and good intentions to protect a child. Abigail was in the system but after today that system would lose track of her. The smiles, the nice talk and the hugs stopped faster than usual with this new couple. She was told to shut up and sit still before they were even two blocks down the road. She wondered if she would ever be loved.

Gary Holland knew how to evade an enemy. As a United States Navy pilot, he had gone through survival training in case he was shot down behind enemy lines. They had changed direction several times and made their trail hard to follow by walking in a river for miles and covering their tracks at the exit point. The dense forest was also in their favor. So when they made camp that night he felt confident Harvey was long gone. They still would have no fire. They still would take turns keeping watch, but they all needed rest.

Benjamin was the first to fall asleep, almost as soon as he hit the ground, he was exhausted.

Gary took the first watch.

Eric and Amy just sat together over Benjamin as he slept, still in shock over having him back.

"What has he told you?" Amy looked to Eric questioning.

Eric did not want to say the words, knowing what they would do to his wife's heart. But she had a right to know.

"He told me that he was forced to work hard, treated badly, and fed little. They told him that we threw him in the garbage. He was made to believe that he was unwanted. They changed his name to Tiny Tim and told everyone he was two years older than he really was, and then they made fun of him for being small for his age."

Eric hesitated, but realized that Amy needed to know the whole story.

"Under his clothes his body is covered with scars from beatings and burn holes from cigarettes. He told me it was mostly from this guy Harvey. He made Benjamin call him dad," Eric said with a broken heart.

Amy walked away, unable to control herself any more. She cried with great sobs. How could she ever make this right? It was her responsibility to keep an eye on her son. She had lost him to a monster.

After some time she walked back to where Benjamin slept. The doctor in her went to work. She needed to do something. She tried not to wake him but did an examination right on the spot. She felt his arms and legs. They had been broken in two places and reset badly. Amy Savage snapped at that moment. She wanted to find Harvey and hurt him. She wanted the gun from Gary. She walked away from Eric without saying a word and went into the woods after Gary.

Automatic gunfire erupted into the night.

Amy was shaken to her senses as she saw the bleeding body of Gary Holland fall to the ground. She ran to him and tried to help him but he was shot full of holes and bleeding out fast. He was like a second father to her. Without thinking she picked up the gun she had come for and started firing in the direction she hoped Harvey was hiding. Eric tackled her to the side half a second before the ground she was standing on danced with the impact of countless bullets. Eric tried helping Gary up but he waved him off. "Get out of here!" he ordered in a fading voice.

They scrambled back to Benjamin.

"How can we just leave Gary?" Amy was torn. She wanted to help him. It was not in her nature to abandon one of her own. She hesitated not knowing what to do.

Eric realized Gary was done for. "If his sacrifice is to mean anything we need to move now!" He felt just as torn but there was no helping their friend.

Eric flung Benjamin over his shoulder and the three were off, running for their lives. Eric didn't understand and his mind kept asking the same question! *How did he find us*? He was afraid. And Eric was not a man who was often afraid. What had he missed? Harvey was a dangerous man but was he that good of a tracker?

Harvey stood over the body of Gary Holland. It was his third kill of the day. He was on a roll. He let the others run. He wanted them to feel afraid before it was over.

Half the night long they struggled through the dark forest. Over fallen logs, across rivers, into deep gorges and out again. Their arms and legs were cut up from brier bushes and devils clubs that grow naturally in the northwest. Finally, Benjamin could not go on and neither Eric nor Amy had the strength to carry him. They flopped down together hidden under the shelter of an evergreen tree, everyone fell asleep.

Eric was the first to awake early the next morning. He looked around as quietly as possible. There was no sign of Harvey but Eric had no doubt that he was on their trail. But how? Amy woke up next and checked Benjamin. He was not as strong as they were, but he was a determined little boy.

"We have a real problem," Eric spoke softly to Amy being careful not to wake Benjamin. "Harvey must be a talented tracker or he would have never found us. Gary knew how to lose someone in the forest and yet this creep somehow tracked us down."

Amy and Eric loved Gary Holland. But they had no time to grieve.

"What would your dad do?"Amy asked him.

At that moment Eric wished his hard as nails Navy Seal father were with them. But without a doubt he knew what his dad would do? Stop running and go on the offense. He would use what he knew about his enemy against him. What did they know about Harvey? Harvey had kidnapped Benjamin and wanted him back. No, wanted him dead! He would follow Benjamin to the ends of the earth to find him. It seemed like he always knew where Benjamin was. But how? It came to Eric like a revelation.

"Amy, check Benjamin for a tracking device."

She worked over his clothes and then remembered the hard bump she had felt on his back the day before. She looked at Eric with concern.

"I think it may be implanted under his skin?"

She felt for the spot on his back and showed Eric.

Benjamin started to wake up.

"What's wrong with my skin?" he asked still half asleep.

Eric gave Amy a look. "We may need to remove something from your back that is under your skin Benjamin. It's a tracking device. Harvey is using it to find us."

"Will it hurt?" Benjamin was awake now and worried.

Amy looked at him.

"I'm a doctor; I've done lots of surgeries a lot harder than this. But the truth is, yes it will hurt. I don't have medicine out here in the woods to numb the pain." She said hoping he would trust her.

Benjamin did not like that idea one bit. But Harvey was out there too.

"Will Harvey find me again if you don't take it out?"

Amy answered, "I think so."

Benjamin was a tough kid. "Go ahead and do it," he said. "Take it out so he can never find me again!"

Eric and Amy both hugged Benjamin and he even hugged them back a little.

Amy went through what they had on them. They were down to just one backpack that Gary Holland had packed for their trip. She found a few energy bars and handed them to Eric and Benjamin and opened one for herself. She found a clean knife, some hand sanitizer, fishing line and a needle. She had water but it would need to be boiled. That would mean a fire. The spot was too close to the spine to risk infection. They set out in search for a good place to make a fire that could not be easily seen.

A determined elderly lady walked up the steps to the police station with a look of resolve in her eyes. Her name was Rose O'Reilly and she was sixty seven years old. She lived in a small house in a not so wonderful part of town. Her husband had died eight years ago leaving her on a fixed income. The neighborhood was going bad back when Robert O'Reilly was alive and they had talked about moving but it had never happened. Now the drugs and the bars and the clubs had taken over. The little church she went to was all that was left of the community she once knew.

She was there today because she had seen things going on at the old water heater factory, people coming and going at all hours of the night. One night a covered truck rolled right passed her house. She saw a hand reaching out of the back, through a hole in the canvas. She called the police and gave a report but nothing happened. Next time she saw that truck the hole was stitched up.

Her house was almost broken into the night before but the two men stopped to have a smoke outside her window. She overheard them talking about the factory. One man said it was where all the slaves were kept. He said some other nasty things she would never repeat. He said the police knew all about that place but did nothing. When she had heard enough she gave her double barreled shot gun one good pump and the two would be thieves lost their gumption.

She sat down with a young officer. He seemed new to the department, just a child in her eyes.

"What is your name?" Mrs. O'Reilly asked.

Officer Daniel Lane was fresh out of the police academy. He had been with the force for only three months.

"I'm Officer Lane, how can I help you?" he smiled.

"I need an officer who still has some sand," she said while looking him over.

"I don't follow," Officer Lane replied.

"My father cut his teeth storming the beaches at Normandy in World War II. My husband fought in Vietnam. They both faced some difficult things in those wars. They didn't talk much about it but what they did say I'll never forget. That generation had sand. They had courage. They were willing to sacrifice their own lives to set others free."

Officer Daniel Lane nodded his head in agreement.

"I agree with you and I thank you for your father and husband's service."

Mrs. O'Reilly pointed a finger at him and poked him in the chest.

"Would you have fought the Germans? A lot of people back then wanted to stay out of it."

Daniel didn't know how to take this feisty old lady but he liked her spunk.

"It's hard to say what a person would do in a different time and place. I'm not afraid to put it on the line if I think the cause is just. I'd like to think I'd have had the guts to do what needed to be done."

She looked at him again, sizing him up, and then made the decision to give him the chance to prove it

"OK then, young men we shall see? I live over on N. 4th street, 2309 N. 4th St in uptown. Do you know where that is?"

"Yes I do."

Mrs. O'Reilly lowered her voice then and said, "What if I told you slaves were being held in the old water heater factory down on 3rd?"

"Slaves?" he was not expecting that.

"Sex slaves, worker slaves, ransom prisoners, I don't know exactly, people being held against their will. And what if I told you I think that some of the officers who work around here were in on it."

She had caught him completely off guard with that one. He was at a loss for words.

"Don't just dismiss me as a crazy old lady and don't go putting this on some report. If I'm guessing right, you are new around here. So all I ask is for you to keep your eyes open. Don't talk about this to anyone. My house was almost robbed last night so I'll fill out a report about that. That is why I came in, if you are asked. You said you would put it on the line if the cause was just. Did you mean it or are you just all talk?"

She filled out the report about the two men snooping around in her yard and left.

Officer Daniel Lane was deep in thought as he watched her leave. She was a brave woman to do what she did, defending her home in such a bad area of town. Her father was a WWII vet. She obviously admired him and that whole generation. He remembered his dad talking about the greatest generation. That group of men and women unlucky enough to come of age when a mad man threatened the world. They somehow found the courage to take a stand and instead of fading to grey they rose to the challenge.

He walked the report to the proper office for recording but was stopped on the way by assistant Chief Walker. "What was that about?" Walker questioned.

"Just some senior citizen who lives down on 4th, she ran off two guys with a shot gun last night." Daniel liked the elderly lady.

Walker wasn't impressed. "People that old should not be

allowed to own guns. She could hurt herself or someone else on accident. Did she have it registered?"

Daniel didn't like his attitude but knew his place. "I didn't ask, sir, she probably has owned that gun forever; I doubt it's required to be licensed." But then he had an idea. "If you like, I can pay her a visit and see how many guns she has? Like you said, she is getting old and if her house was ever broken into we wouldn't want all those guns falling into the wrong hands."

Walker gave a nod. "Ok Lane, see what you can do."

Officer Daniel Lane stood there for just a moment thinking. He would put it on the line. Not only because this old lady had dared him to but because for the last three months he had turned a blind eye to what his gut instincts told him. Something fishy was going on in this police department.

Eric held Benjamin still while Amy cut as straight as possible. The capsule came out easy. The incision was small and would heal nicely. Amy gave him a few stitches and cleaned up the area. They were both impressed with Benjamin. He clinched his teeth but he did not cry out.

Eric held the small tracking capsule in his hand. They finally had an edge in this fight. It was time to stop running. It was time to go on the offence.

"Harvey will be following the signal from this capsule." Eric looked at Amy

Amy finished his thought, "I still have Gray's Colt .44 with three shots left."

Eric remembered the look in Gray Holland's eyes as he selflessly ordered Eric to leave him to die and felt no remorse for what he needed to do next. "We don't have time for any fancy traps. We just need to get him out in the open where he has no cover and I do. I won't miss if I can get close enough."

Amy agreed but needed to make one thing clear. "I'm not leaving you. Benjamin and I can stay at a safe distance but we are not splitting up."

"Ok, but at a safe distance and hidden. If this doesn't go well, do not move until Harvey wonders off."

If this doesn't go well, we'll go together as a family. Amy kept the thought to herself.

Eric found what he was looking for a short time later, an island of trees and dense brush surrounded by a clearing on all sides. It looked like a great place for an ambush. Harvey would have to cross the open area to get to it. Eric placed the capsule in the center of the grove and then hid back across the clearing. A fallen tree over a nature dip in the ground provided Eric with the perfect hiding place. He had a good field of fire covering about ninety percent of the possible approaches to the capsules location. This was as good as it was going to get. Amy and Benjamin hid farther away but still within view of the unfolding drama. Eric wondered if that was wise, but it was too late now. No one could move for fear of giving away their position. Harvey could already be close. They had to wait him out.

It was Sunday morning and the little community church looked empty. Mrs. O'Reilly was there and the pastor was there. Where were the Millsap's and the Dun families? They always made things seem a little alive with their children running around. Mrs. O'Reilly loved children. It was good for her old heart to see them playing with all that energy. It helped make her feel young again.

Pastor Markus Johnson was a tall lanky African American. He had been a history professor before his conversion to Christianity. Mrs. O'Reilly loved his preaching, it was always filled with historical facts and stories. Pastor Johnson didn't believe in blind faith. He taught that you had to give the reasons for your faith and that rang true with Mrs. O'Reilly.

The pastor looked ominous as he made his way over to where Mrs. O'Reilly sat. He put on a smile as he greeted her but she could see his anguish.

"It looks like it's down to just you and me now," Pastor Johnson started.

"Are the Millsap's kids sick?" she asked.

Pastor Johnson shook his head not knowing how to break the news.

"We could pray for them if they are sick and Mr. Dun has been working nights lately, it must be hard to get up on Sunday morning after working all night. His family will be back after he adjusts to….."

"That's not it Mrs. O'Reilly," he said as softy as he could. "I'm sorry to have to tell you this but the Millsap's have moved away. They were in trouble with the bank and lost their house. They were embarrassed about it and so kept it to themselves."

"Oh my, I'm sorry to hear that!" Mrs. O'Reilly felt her heart breaking. She reached for the candy in her pocket that she would always give little Kate. She would never see that smile again.

"That's not all." Pastor Johnson looked for a way to lighten the blow but didn't see one.

"The Dun family is moving away as well. I met with Mr. Dun about it yesterday. The neighborhood just isn't a safe place a raise a family anymore. They have had their home broken into three times in the last year. How long before it happens with the kid's home. I can't blame him."

Mrs. O'Reilly held back the tears. What would that help? All things change! She of all people should know that. But this felt more like an invasion than just a change of season.

The signal on Harvey's screen told him that Tiny Tim had stopped up ahead and was hiding in a thick grove of trees. He approached the clearing that surrounded the grove but hesitated, cautious of crossing open areas. He decided to circle around. Eric couldn't see him but could hear him off to the left somewhere. Harvey stayed just inside the tree line looking for any movement in the cluster of trees ahead. Nothing moved. He would have to cross the exposed patch of grass and smoke them out or wait where he was for them to move. Ultimately he got tired of waiting, but just as he made the decision to step out into the open, the sound of a helicopter came thundering over the treetops. Moments later there were three choppers circling above with the words, Seattle Police Department, clearly written on their sides. Harvey grinned at the sight of the .50 caliber machine guns aiming into the tree grove; this was going to be entertaining.

Eric was relieved to see the police arrive. It was about time this nightmare ended. Police Chief Hobbs was visible through the open side door of one of the choppers. He would have to thank him later. Their relationship had gotten strained over the years but this time he had really come through for them. The .50 caliber machine guns looked intimidating, he had no idea the police force had those but they were a welcome sight against Harvey. Amy stood up from her hiding place with Benjamin.

"We have both signals now, weapons hot!" Chief Hobbs ordered.

One of the helicopters broke off and hovered with its gun facing Harvey while the others trained their weapons on the signal of Tiny Tim. Harvey immediately understood and ran like a madman. Suddenly, all hell broke loose. The three big guns opened fire. One aimed at Harvey and two at the grove of trees. An invisible hand of destruction followed Harvey through the forest as he ran. Branches and brush disintegrated into sharp airborne splinters. The sheer power of the .50 caliber rounds pounded the ground behind him. The path of ruin pursued the wake of his every step. He could not get away from the harvest of his ways. It overtook him fast and he was shot to pieces.

The tree grove exploded with flying wood. The thick dense patch of forest was being put through a shredder. The thick trunks of Hemlock blow apart in the middle. A huge tree fell, then another and another. All three guns were at it now. The helicopters circled the grove like dragons spitting out demon fire. In minutes the grove was gone, reduced to toothpicks.

Amy held on to Benjamin in horror. They were firing at the exact location where they had hid Benjamin's tracking capsule. Eric couldn't believe his eyes. What were they doing? Why? He was about to wave them down but stopped short. He caught sight of the grinning face of Chief Hobbs behind one of the big guns firing into the capsules location. They knew! They had to know! Eric didn't want it to be true. He did not want to face it. But the evidence was pointing to the painful truth. Keeping out of sight, he made his way back to Amy and Benjamin. They all stayed low and hidden from the three hovering predators.

Eric looked into Amy's frightened eyes. "They were out to kill us. They were part of it. They were tracking Benjamin. I saw Chief Hobbs face behind one of the guns. They have been playing us for fools all these years. They knew where he was because they took him!"

Amy looked down toward the carnage of trees blown to bits. "Why?? Why would Chief Hobbs do this? What is going on Eric? I can't do this anymore. Who do we trust? Where do we go?" Amy was afraid, really afraid.

Eric didn't have an answer for her. They watched the three police helicopters circle several times but with no safe place to land they flew away.

Benjamin stared at the fallen body of Harvey. He felt nothing. That was strange to him. He wanted to feel good about it. But he was more worried about Eric and Amy now. They were the first two people he had ever started to trust. He reached into Amy's pocket and pulled out the "Courage" stone. He held it out in front of him. He just ran his finger over the letters and stared at the word. At the same time he held out the "Family" stone for Amy to take back.

"It's ok, I understand if you want to leave me. You don't have to do this anymore. If it wasn't for me you wouldn't be in danger."

Amy pulled herself together. She realized that it was up to her to be strong for Benjamin's sake. "Benjamin.... this is not your fault."

She gently took the "Courage" stone back from him and said. "You told me not to lose it, but I guess I did... I'll pull myself back together. There is one thing I can promise you; no matter what happens we are going to face this thing together. This is hard! But that doesn't mean we give up. Got it?"

Benjamin was still worried. He didn't want to be the cause of their deaths.

Chapter 5
A Light in the Darkness

Mrs. Rose O'Reilly never went out at night after dark but tonight she was going. It was not a spur of the moment decision. She had thought this through long and hard. She knew what she knew and she felt responsible for what she knew. If she could get into that factory she could help in some way. She did not have a very complicated plan. The front gate would open when the trucks came. She would do the unthinkable and just walk right in after them. Once inside, they would either have to kill her or keep her. Either way, it would cause them problems.

She started out the front door just as Officer Daniel Lane pulled up in front of her house. He gave her a questioning look as he stepped out of his patrol car and up to her front steps. Mrs. O'Reilly quickly hid the rolling suit case full of cook books and clothes in the front coat closet.

"This is not a very safe neighborhood at night Mrs. O'Reilly. Do you need a ride somewhere?"

Mrs. O'Reilly felt like she was caught with her hand in the cookie jar.

"The night air is good for these old lungs?" It was all she could come up with.

Officer Lane wasn't buying it.

"I came by to talk with you about your statement. Do you have a moment?"

She was so set on what she was about to do that she

almost refused him but then decided it would be best to talk to the man before she disappeared.

They sat down together in her kitchen. She offered him some hot tea with honey and after they both had a few satisfying sips Daniel started the conversation.

"I drove by the factory on my way to your house and didn't notice anything unusual, just a few homeless men wondering about."

Mrs. O'Reilly did not want to make him feel young and naive but she was going to lay it out for him never the less. He seemed like a good man to her. He just needed more time and experience.

"Those men are not homeless. They are the lookouts. If you watch closely you'll see that they change shifts every four hours. The raggedy clothes they wear will be the same but the faces change."

She led him over to a telescope she had set up in her living room. The curtains were closed so that just the end of the scope looked through the window in the direction of the factory. Officer Lane looked through the scope. From the location of her home it had a commanding view of the front gate of the Factory and about five hundred feet on each side. At one time it had been a thriving business but now it sat empty and unproductive. The main brick building housed the old factory floor, a huge commercial kitchen and the offices. There were loading docks and storage rooms all under one massive roof. The parking area had to be large enough to accommodate the semi-trailers. Surrounding it all stood a tall chain link fence with privacy blinds and barbed wire. The City of Seattle forced the present owners to secure the property after the community complained that the vacant building had become a beehive of gangs and drugs. The factory looked dark and empty but the street lights gave off enough light to see what looked to be a homeless man walking toward the gate. He stopped at the gate and looked around and then continued down the street. Daniel got a good look at the man's face so that he could recognize it again.

"So when does the next shift take over?" Daniel was curious.

Mrs. O'Reilly was glad he wanted to help but wished he realized more.

"The shift is over at midnight but the first truck would normally get here in about ten minutes, but that will not happen tonight….unless they…" she had a thought.

"Why… how would you know that?" Daniel asked.

"You have a marked police car parked in front of my house Officer Lane. Don't you realize they've been watching you? I hope you have a good story for why you are here tonight," she said.

"I told them I would try to get you to give up your guns, you know, like the shotgun you used to scare away those men. You are a little elderly to be handling a shot gun safely, at least that is what I told them," he replied with a wink.

"Oh, smart thinking young man." That gave Mrs. O'Reilly an idea. "Now you tell them I would have none of that! You tell them I quoted the second amendment of the constitution to you, the right to bear arms, and threatened to shoot the next officer that came to my door trying to take my guns."

Daniel did not think that was a good idea. "Why would you want me to say that, they'll think you're crazy?"

"Never mind that, just tell them what I told you to say."

But she would share the obvious with him.

"My guess is that you are about to get called away on…." Before she could finish a call came out over his police radio.

"All units in the area, we have a 211 at the shopping mall on Broad Street and Denny Way." It was only a few miles away.

Officer Lane responded to police dispatch that he was in the area and was on his way.

"So you think they are getting me out of the area so their truck load of slaves can be delivered?"

Daniel was having a hard time believing they had that kind of control over the police. The truth was, it scared him.

"You just go and respond to that call and see if it isn't just a wild goose chase," Mrs. O'Reilly replied.

"I'll be back," he said as he left. "Don't do anything unsafe tonight Mrs. O'Reilly."

She just smiled and waved goodbye.

As soon as Daniel was out of sight she retrieved her suit case and started back down the road. She heard the truck coming and picked up her pace. The gate was about a city block away, with the suit case in tow, she was not going to make it in time.

Mrs. O'Reilly pressed forward. *Come on you old lady!* She thought to herself.

The front gate started to open revealing nothing but darkness inside. The truck would have its lights off as usual. Mrs. O'Reilly had purposely dressed in dark clothes so as not to be noticed. The covered truck arrived at just the right time, the moment when the gates were open enough for it to drive right through without slowing down. But when its back bumper cleared the entry the gates started to close.

Mrs. O'Reilly was moving as fast as her legs would carry her. It would be close. She risked being crushed by the closing ends of the gates as she made one last leap into the darkness. She fell inside breathing heavily and exhausted.

The two guards inside where startled. They both trained their high powered assault rifles on the fallen old lady. She put her hands up at the sight of them. "Don't shoot!" she said and tried to look as surprised and helpless as she could.

Just miles away, Officer Lane looked over the little shopping mall carefully. There was no sign of anything out of the ordinary. Was it just a prank call-in or a purposeful distraction? He was about to head back to check on Mrs. O'Reilly when he got called back to the station to fill in at the front desk.

Pastor Markus Johnson felt like the right thing to do was to turn the church building into an outreach center for the neighborhood. God knows, it was needed. He started out by just feeding the homeless on Saturday mornings. He was surprised at the number that showed up, not just the homeless, but families as well and many immigrants who spoke little or no English.

One Saturday a distressed looking man approached Pastor Johnson.

"I come on boat with wife and daughter! Understand?" he said with a strong Russian accent.

"I understand," Pastor Johnson replied.

"They say we owe money but I pay money. They take my wife and daughter." The man was crying now and started speaking in Russian.

"Hey, hey, hey, slow down. I want to help you. I.....will......help.....you." Pastor Johnson said it slowly.

"You help me," the man gave him a hug. "No one cares." He pointed everywhere.

"Where are your wife and daughter now?"

"No one help us." The man did not understand.

"Do you have a picture?" Pastor Johnson pulled out a picture of his wife and kids.

"Oh, yes, yes, yes....I have." The man pulled out a picture of his beautiful wife and daughter. "They come with me here for job, but no job, all lies!!" He was angry now and started speaking in Russian again.

Pastor Markus Johnson was a student of history. He knew that taking advantage of immigrants was as old as time. This man was lost and scared and if ever he needed a friend it was now.

"Do you have a place to sleep?" Pastor motioned with his hands and closed his eyes.

"No. I sleep in street."

"Tonight, you can sleep in the church. Tomorrow, we'll go down to the police station and talk to them."

"No police," the man sounded scared now.

"Don't you want to find your family?"

"No police, just you help me!"

Pastor Markus Johnson wasn't going to push the issue. This man may have come to America illegally and was afraid to be sent back before he found his family. He was going to help him anyway. Maybe his wife and daughter were being forced to work in some shady factory somewhere in Seattle, someone had to know something.

Noland Savage listened to the message from Amy. It was four days old and there were no follow up messages. If she had found Eric the first thing she would have done is call him back to tell him everything was ok. He tried their cell phones, no answer. He then tried calling Gary Holland's cell, no answer. Finally, he decided to call the police department back home to see if they had heard anything.

"Officer Lane here, how can I help you?"

"This is Noland Savage, can I speak to Police Chief Hobbs please?"

"I'm sorry sir, the chief is out of town at the moment, can

I take a message?"

"Well, maybe you can help me? I need someone to check up on my son and daughter. My son, Eric, went hiking in the Cascade Mountains about a week ago but did not check in on schedule. So his wife Amy and a friend of mine went looking for him about three days ago. Now I can't reach any of them. Has anyone called your office about this?"

"Let me check." Daniel looked through the recent missing persons reports.

"Sorry sir, I don't see a report about any missing hikers but I'll file a report for you if you'd like and I'll keep your number in case I hear something."

"Yes thank you, but it really isn't like them to just disappear like this. Could you also have someone drive by their house and just check on things?" Noland was concerned.

"Not a problem, if I can I'll do it myself. What's their address?"

Noland gave Officer Lane Eric and Amy's address and Ben Holland's as well. Daniel gave Noland his cell number in case the missing persons showed up. It would take Noland about twenty-four hours to get home from where he was in Mexico.

Daniel Lane hung up the phone and looked up from his desk surprised to see assistant Chief Walker.

"Did I hear you say the name Savage?"

"Yes sir, I just took a call from a Noland Savage," Lane replied. But in his mind he knew he had not spoken the name out loud. How could Walker have known who called unless the phones were bugged? Officer Lane was beyond suspicious.

"What did he want?" Walker asked like he didn't know.

"He says his son and daughter and a friend of his are

missing. He wanted to see if anyone called in a missing person report. No one had so I was going to file a report and drive by their homes to check on them." Daniel's mind was working fast. He looked down at the report and quickly committed the names and addresses to memory.

"I'll need to take that report from you; Chief Hobbs will want to know about this. The Savage family has a long history of sending this department on wild goose chases. You don't need worry about it, I'll handle it." Walker's hand was already out.

Officer Lane shrugged his shoulders and handed him the report like it was no big deal. But in his mind he was planning his next move. When Chief Hobbs left town so had some of the officers that seemed to be in his inner circle. Whatever was going on, Walker was in on it, but was left in charge. Obviously, not everyone in the department was a rotten apple. Officer Lane looked around at the busy police station. There were good men and women working here too. How could he know who to trust? To do what they were doing would take people in key positions, someone in dispatch, someone in accounting, some officers on the street. He needed an ally he could trust, but who? From the way that call was intercepted Daniel could guess Hobbs and Walker had a bone to pick with this guy Noland. Maybe he could find some allies among the Savages.

While it was fresh in his memory Daniel wrote down all the information he had just gotten from Noland Savage. He folded up the page and stuffed it in his pocket. He had a few days off coming up and while his patrol car was sure to be tracked his personal car was another matter.

Back in the woods, Eric retrieved some necessary items from the dead body of Harvey. Amy and Benjamin stayed away from the gruesome scene. Eric did his best not to hurl. The .50 caliber machine gun didn't leave much. The high powered tech heavy rifle Harvey carried was damaged beyond repair but his 9mm sidearm was in good condition, loaded and with two extra magazines in Harvey's pack. He headed back to Amy and Benjamin with the much needed supplies.

Eric was sure Chief Hobbs would want confirmation of their deaths. When they realized they had been fooled and the tracking capsule removed, they would come looking for them with more men and resources. The problem was where to hide? There was no way they could go home. Hobbs would never take the risk of being exposed. He would probably just shoot them on sight and concoct some story to cover himself. It was all out war on them now. With the tracking device removed from Benjamin it seemed to Eric that the best place to hide and come up with a plan would be in these mountains. They just needed to find a place to hold up with clean water, food, and shelter. How long would it be before dad got Amy's message? Eric needed his father now more than ever and Benjamin needed to meet his grandfather.

Eric, Amy, and Benjamin dragged themselves through the forest. Their strength was gone and they were making slow time. They had not traveled more than one mile from where the police helicopters had ambushed them when they heard the dogs. Eric had to assume they were trained police dogs. They did not have much time now. With what little strength they had left, the small family struggled ahead. They stayed together, helping each other along. They were bleeding, cut, muddy and exhausted.

The attack dogs were on their trail now and closing in fast. The cruel men that followed the beasts were having trouble keeping up with their German Shepherds. They finally gave them their freedom and the three huge shepherds took off way ahead of their handlers. If the dogs got there first and did their jobs for them they could be back to Seattle before dark.

Basic instincts took over; the dogs were in pack mode

now, working themselves up into a hunting frenzy while chasing down their prey. Eric looked back and could see the three k-9s closing in. Up ahead there was the sound of a river. They had to get there or risk being torn apart. But it was too late. The three shepherds had amazing speed and agility. Eric and Amy pulled out their hand guns and put Benjamin behind them. The dogs spread out and stayed behind cover as they got within shooting range. Then, suddenly, they charged forward together ready to tear into the family.

Eric and Amy took aim and were about to fire when Benjamin unexpectedly pushed passed them both and got between them and the dogs.

"Stop! Don't shoot!" he screamed. "These are my dogs!"

Benjamin walked forward without fear as the three shepherds closed in around him still snarling.

Eric and Amy held their fire afraid to hit Benjamin who had put himself in the way.

Benjamin held out his hand right into the teeth of the lead Dog. "Timber, you stop acting like that right now!" he said it with an authority that amazed Eric and Amy. What surprised them even more is what happened next.

All three dogs changed right before their eyes, first the lead dog that Benjamin called Timber, followed by the other two. They actually started wagging their tails and licking Benjamin with apology as if to say sorry, we didn't know it was you. Please forgive us!

Benjamin hugged the three beasts with the biggest smile on his face. Then, turning to his parents explained, "I've taken care of these guys from the time they were just puppies. It was my job at the factory to feed and clean up after them. The men would beat them to make them mean but I would sneak in their cages after dark and pet them and talk nice to them. They are my friends."

Eric and Amy were shaking with adrenaline but finally lowered their guns and smiled with wonder. "That is incredible Benjamin, simply incredible."

Timber the dog looked back where the men were sure to be coming and gave a concerned growl. He then tugged on Benjamin's shirt in the opposite direction as if to say, you need to get out of here, now!

Eric was amazed and had an idea. "Benjamin, how smart is Timber. Do you think he would understand if we asked him to help us?"

Without waiting for Benjamin to reply Timber stood at attention and barked twice at Eric.

With Benjamin's help Eric removed the GPS tracking collars from the other two dogs and placed them around Timber's neck.

Eric explained his plan to Timber hoping he could understand, "The bad men that want to hurt us will follow you. Lead them away for us." He pointed back southeast and said it once more, "Lead them away."

Benjamin hugged Timber. "Don't let them catch you boy! Just run away like I did."

Timber backed away from the group. He gave two last barks of command to the other dogs as if to say, look out for them while I'm gone, and then darted away to the southeast barking as he went as if in hot pursuit.

The tired family turned to the Northwest and pushed on with new hope, lead by two energized dogs. After awhile it was clear to Eric and Amy that Timber had done his job. The men had not found them.

Eric turned to Benjamin. "Timber saved our lives."

Benjamin was concerned for his dog. "Do you think they will find him and be angry with him?"

Eric thought about that for a moment. "I think Timber

would lead them in circles and never let them find him, tracking collar or not. That is one smart dog!"

Benjamin called the other two German Shepherds to him, "Maverick! Axel! Come here boys!" The two dogs came right to him.

Amy sat on the ground next to her son and let the two shepherds get use to her being there. "Thank you both for being there for Benjamin." She said as she scratched under their chins. "You are part of our family now." Eric joined in, sitting next to Amy and letting the shepherds get his scent.

"What about Timber?" Eric asked. "What is he like?"

Benjamin smiled and raised both eye brows. "Like you said, he is one smart dog!"

Mrs. O'Reilly was tied to her chair. The men in the room were uninterested and bored with the idea of having captured an old lady. She knew the kind of men these were and felt grateful that she was not a young girl in their custody. They were weak evil men that lacked the courage and strength to be anything else. Her plan had worked. She was on the inside and alive for now. A tall sour faced man walked into the room and looked at her with cruel contempt. The others stepped a little back from him. He was obviously in charge.

"I don't have time for this gentlemen. Can't you handle a little old lady?" he asked coldly.

The three men woke up a little. "Not a problem, we just thought you always wanted to be notified when...." He cut them off as he turned to walk out.

"I have bigger things to worry about right now. We have new orders to capture and hold Noland Savage when he returns shortly."

That woke the men up. One man even put his hand on his

gun for some reason.

"Do whatever you want with her, kill her, drop her off a bridge if you like, or put her to work," he said as he walked away.

The youngest of the three spoke first, "I want a piece of that Navy Seal. Hand to hand or just knifes. I'll bet all the stories are just smoke and mirrors. He's just an old man now, a dinosaur."

The others looked away from him and laughed, but it was a nervous laugh.

Then they looked at Mrs. O'Reilly again as if they almost forgot she was there. "We could just shoot her right here." One suggested.

"Yah, you do that and clean up the blood and the body yourself," the oldest of the three replied.

"We could drive her to the river?"

"And miss out on going after Savage?"

Mrs. O'Reilly spoke softly, "I can cook the best tasting food you three will ever have. Do you have a kitchen around here?"

The three looked at one another considering it.

"Truth is we need a good cook, hell I'm sick of Mike's cooking," one said.

"And with Tiny Tim gone there is a lot of work around here to keep her busy," another spoke up.

"Ok, lady. You saved your life. But you're nothing but a slave here. Do as you're told or you'll be burned alive, you hear me!" the man warned.

Mrs. O'Reilly humbly nodded her head but inside she was smiling.

Officer Daniel Lane was dressed in his street clothes and

driving a Ford Mustang when he pulled up in front of Eric and Amy Savages home. The amount of news papers in the front driveway told him no one had been home in awhile. The call from Noland Savage that was intercepted so quickly had to be important but how did it connect to the illegal actives down at the factory. Noland Savage was concerned about his missing kids. He said his son had gone hiking in the mountains. It just didn't add up to anything yet.

Daniel decided to take a walk around the house just to see if anything looked out of place. He opened the little front gate and noticed an engraved stone just beside the walkway that read, "Keep moving forward". It was surrounded by flowers and had an original flare to it. He walked toward the house. Nice landscaping, he thought to himself as he saw the flower garden. Someone took the time to really make things look beautiful. He looked down and saw another stone with the word "unforgettable" engraved in deep letters. As he walked he saw more stones here and there with words and sayings written into them. "Be the Change", "Forgive & Forget", "Find a way"!

I guess it was their thing? Daniel thought.

In the back yard he saw a swing set but no other kid toys laying around. That was odd. Do they have a child or not. Noland said nothing about a grandchild missing. Next to the swing set there was a larger stone that caught his eye, just because it seemed out of place where it sat. It read, "Act while there is time." Daniel tried the back door but it was locked. He walked around the other side of the house and back to the front. There was nothing there that told him what he needed to know.

As he was getting into his car he looked up the street about three houses and stopped cold. The homeless man he saw down at the factory was coming out of the front door of a home. He was dressed normal now and carrying a garbage bag out of the house. Daniel got into his car and pretended to be on his phone. After the man left, Daniel waited to see if anyone else would be coming or going. After a while, he walked down the quiet street toward the house. Here was a connection between the factory and this area but did it have anything to do with the Savage Family? Daniel decided to find out. He walked around to the back of the house and tried the back door which was locked. He looked for windows and found one that he could reach. Slipping the blade of his knife through to the lock between the top and bottom window frames he unlocked the mechanism and opened the lower window. He was inside moments later shutting the window behind him.

The house was poorly decorated, bare and filthy. Not much on the walls or much of anything really. He went to a desk that had a stack of bills.

"Harvey Benvenuto," Daniel read the name off a water bill from the month of June.

There was a waste basket next to the desk full of receipts. One was from an outdoors store in town. It looked like this guy purchased a sleeping bag and a tent recently. Someone was going into the woods. That made Daniel think of Noland's lost son and daughter. Was there a connection?

Suddenly, he heard someone working the front door lock. Daniel looked around for a hiding place but there was nothing. He ran for the bathroom and stretch out down in the bath tub, closing the shower curtain behind him. The smell was horrific and the tub was gross. Daniel had to control his gag reflex. Who lived like this? He was a bit of a clean freak.

Two men walked into the house talking to each other. Daniel could hear them clearly because he had left the bathroom door open.

"Hobbs never did like Harvey. He probably enjoyed gunning him down with a 50cal," the first man said.

"The guy was an idiot anyway for letting Tiny Tim escape. He deserved what he got!" the second man answered.

It sounded like they were at the desk loading everything into trash bags.

"You hear about what they got planned for Savage? Hobbs finally got the green light to take him down," one said

"Capture him alive, is what I heard," replied the other.

"Why would they want to do that?" the first man asked.

"To find out what he knows and who he's told. But also to get the rest of the Savage family to come out of the mountains, you didn't hear this from me, but Tiny Tim is really Savage's long lost grandson."

"No way! Where did you hear that?" the first man asked surprised.

There was a silence for a moment and then the second man spoke.

"I didn't say anything about it and if you say that I did I'll kill you just like Hobbs killed Harvey, you understand!"

"Calm down, we were just talking. I'm not a snitch."

There was silence after that little exchange save for the filling of trash bags and the sound of footsteps.

Daniel Lane's mind was racing. Chief Hobbs was a murderer. The Chief of Police was the head of some kind of organized crime ring. But then why would he need the green light from someone else to go after Noland Savage. There was someone higher up the ladder here, but who? Harvey was one of them but had lost Tiny Tim, who was really the grandson of Noland Savage. They were going to capture Noland and hold him to get to the rest of the family. Daniel knew he was in way over his head now. He needed help. Fast! But first he had to call and warn….

"Ba…Ba…Ba…Bad, Bad to the Bone!" His cell phone sang out through the house. He scrambled to his feet in the bath tub as he tried to get it out of his back pocket.

The curtain was thrown back and two guns were on him.

He held his hands up high!

"Don't shoot! You got me, I give up!" Daniel pleaded. But he had already seen that the call was from Noland Savage and pushed the green answer button. Noland was hearing what was happening now.

"Who the hell are you?" one asked

"I'm officer Daniel Lane, I work for Chief Hobbs. He sent me here. My ID's in my back pocket. Can I get it?"

They were not taking their guns off him.

"Slowly, and if you make any other moves, Hobbs will be one officer short."

Daniel got his police ID out and gave it to one of the Men.

"So do you work for Chief Hobbs or do you work for Chief Hobbs?" the lead man asked with emphases.

Daniel was hoping this wasn't some coded question that demanded a specific answer.

"I work for the factory down on 3rd," Daniel answered calmly.

"Why were you hiding from us?" the Man asked suspiciously.

"I was sent here to keep watch for Noland Savage. His son's house is just a few houses down across the street. This is a great place to keep an eye out for him. But I was up all last night at a party and well, I fell asleep in the bathtub here. That was my alarm going off. Don't tell Chief Hobbs or he'll have my hide."

"And you expect us to believe that?"

"Call the Chief if you like, but don't tell him I fell asleep and I won't mention how I know that Tiny Tim is the grandson of Noland Savage."

"Haaaa, I never said...."

"Loose lips sink ships." Daniel had him.

The man just wanted to change the subject. "So you fell asleep on the job while looking for Savage. You should be shot. Don't you know how bad Hobbs wants this guy?"

Daniel was fishing for more information, hoping Savage was listening on the phone just in case this didn't end well. "At least I'm not the one who lost Tiny Tim."

The two thugs lowered their guns, "Falling asleep is almost as bad. The thing that really makes Harvey an idiot is that the boy had a tracking device installed and Harvey didn't have a receiver with him when the boy ran off into the woods."

"What an idiot!" Daniel agreed

The two men went back to their duties. Daniel stayed in the house watching the Savage home through the window for effect. He was trying not to show his anxiety. At any moment the gig could be up. Hobbs could walk through the door. They could call his bluff and check out his story. What had he gotten himself into? Thank God these two were not the sharpest tools in the shed. One look in that filthy tub would have told them he was lying about purposely taking a nap in the slime.

After the two men left, Daniel stayed put for an additional twenty minutes just in case they were waiting down the street watching. Then he got into his mustang and started driving. He had no idea where to. He needed to do some thinking and come up with a plan.

Noland Savage had listened carefully to every word of the conversation between the two thugs and Daniel Lane and read between the lines as well. Officer Daniel Lane was a friend. There was a place called the factory on 3rd. Benjamin ran off into the woods. Amy said Eric was tracking a lost child in the woods when he disappeared. If Eric and Amy found Benjamin and Benjamin could be tracked, they were in big trouble. Gary Holland was with them but if this crime ring was local and had police resources ....Chief Hobbs was a dead man.

Noland had called from SeaTac Airport. He was at baggage claim waiting for his luggage when he made the call. He grabbed his bag and headed for the exit door. He had taken only five steps when an officer stopped him and asked him for ID. Out of the corner of his eye Noland spotted the others closing in from both sides.

In his mind, the safety locks were being removed. He was not a civilian at an airport in the good ole US of A. The situation on the ground had changed. They were not concerned about waiting till he was alone. They were not concerned about witnesses or news coverage. That told him they had power. This was war, but WAR is what he ate for breakfast.

The officer took his ID but without even looking at it reached for the outside pocket of Noland's luggage. When he unzipped the pocket a small .22 caliber handgun dropped to the floor.

"What have we here Mr. Savage, is this gun yours?" the officer asked glancing to the right and left with a nod.

Noland smiled back at him and pushed his thumb into the handle of his luggage. The bag burst open revealing a small arsenal of high powered automatic weapons.

"That's not my gun. These are my Guns!!"

Suddenly, the air was filled with flying lead. Savage was a fast moving target and an expert marksman on the move, the men were taken by surprise, they should have killed him while they had their chance. They were shooting civilians who ran into their line of fire. Noland knew their type, they were ruthless but not effective. Noland made every shot count.

The alarms at the airport were pulled. In minutes, he would be overrun. Noland had no desire to engage the many good officers who would just be doing their duty. The bad apples were down but he would not be free to help Eric and Amy if he let himself be captured. He ran for the baggage ramp and through the opening where workers were unloading the luggage. He was a flash, a ghost, a blur. He flew over and under, through doors and down hallways. Moving, moving, moving! But it was not enough. He stopped in a mop closet just in time as a troop of airport security headed toward the baggage claim area. He needed to disappear. The airport would be in lockdown. All exits blocked all flights cancelled. Nothing coming nothing going,...... except for the wounded.

He found some gloves and a kitchen apron and put them on. The mop and bucket came out of the closet with him. He left his weapons in the closet, save one hand gun. There was no getting around what he needed to do. Fake blood wouldn't fool anybody. He knew just where to place the bullet to cause the least loss of function. It wouldn't be the first time he'd been shot. Just the first time he shot himself.

Bang!! The shot rang out down the hall. He tossed the gun into the closet, closed the door and fell to the ground.

As he lay there in his own blood his thoughts turned to Benjamin. He was alive. Thank God, he was alive. He remembered taking the little Savage fishing with him. He hooked a big one and had a fight on his hands. But the five year old didn't want papa's help. He wanted to show papa what he could do. Noland could understand that and it made him proud.

"We have a man down in the west hallway next to the staff Kitchen." Noland could hear an officer talking into his radio.

The new training on active shooters demanded that the officer leave him there and keep looking for the shooter. But soon after others would come and he would be on his way to the hospital.

Chapter 6
A Cabin in the Woods

"I don't care if the dogs have taken off! You and your men are not leaving those woods without the confirmed death of Tiny Tim and the Savage family!" Chief Hobbs barked.

There were some questions coming from the man on the receiving end of the orders that Hobbs didn't like.

"It's summertime in Washington you wimps, you don't need tents, sleep on the ground! I'll air drop food, water and ammo and that's it!" Chief Hobbs was infuriated.

"You'll stay out in those woods as long as it takes. That is all you need to know!"

He slammed the phone down so hard everyone at the police station would have heard it if not for the sound proof walls and glass he had installed.

The fact that Noland escaped their first attempt at capturing him came as no surprise. He disagreed with Judge Hurst on this point. They should not waste time trying to capture Noland to bait the others. They should focus all their resources at getting Noland's family and use them as their leverage against him. But that was not his call. Now that Noland had shot up an airport, accused of killing police and civilians in the process, he was public enemy number one. The news was eating it up. "X Navy Seal goes berserk at SeaTac Airport killing eight and wounding dozens... He is armed and extremely dangerous." The FBI and some special military unit called and wanted Chief Hobbs' full cooperation and all files on Noland Savage. Hobbs was more than happy to help them.

Now if his men in the Cascades would just do their jobs and find Tiny Tim! He was just a boy, an escaped slave, and Eric and Amy were tired scared parents. Hobbs liked the power he had over others. It covered up his insincerity well. Behind the barrel of a .50 caliber machine gun, he was a man. In uniform barking orders, he was a man. When the lady he was with had no choice, he felt powerful. But take away all the show, all the props, all the pretending and he would boil down to nothing. The idea that a slave like Tiny Tim could put one over on him was not acceptable because it messed with his fantasy of strength. Someone might see the truth that he wasn't so *Bad Ass*, but rather,… just an ass!

Special Operations Commander, Thomas Troy, watched the recorded footage from the airport over and over again. Many things became clear to him as he observed Noland Savage in action. The idea that he had gone crazy was not one of them. He looked again at the specially designed suitcase they recovered from the mop closet. It was loaded with weapons and explosives. Noland could have left the airport in ruins and cause quite a bloodbath, but he didn't. The news had got it all wrong as usual. Five officers were involved in the initial attempt to apprehend him and five shots were all that were fired from Noland's weapon. Save the one shot from his side arm splattered with his own blood. He knew Savage was resourceful but shooting himself to get out with the wounded; that would be added to the text books and the Savage name already came up a few times.

The cabin looked abandoned. It sat in a small clearing surrounded by Fir, Cedar and Hemlock Trees. The solar panels on the roof and the outside propane tank gave the idea that whoever built this place wanted to be off-grid. Maverick and Axel scouted around the place as Eric tried the front door. It was locked. They were all so tired and the sun was going down.

"Look under that wooden carved bear thing," Amy suggested, desperate for a roof over their heads. "That's where I'd hide a key."

Sure enough, Eric reached out and got the key that looked like it had not moved in ages. He held it up for Amy to see.

"Good call, honey," Eric said sleepily and opened the door. They were too fatigued to do anything but lock the door behind them and fall asleep. Eric took the couch. Amy and Benjamin collapsed onto the one bed in the nearby room.

The next morning came and went. They all slept in until around noon.

It wasn't much of a cabin but it was homey. It had one great room with an eat-in kitchen and living area. Off of the great room was one bedroom and a full bathroom with tub and shower. What made the whole house feel right was the stone fireplace with the stacked wood off to one side. There was a kitchen table and chairs. The living area had a couch facing the fireplace. The bedroom had a twin bed and a dresser.

"I'm gonna take a shower," Amy said as they all finally started moving about, she felt like a filthy pig and had found some half full bottles of shampoo and soap she was ready to put to good use.

"You don't feel a little odd, walking into someone else's home and just......" Eric stopped short.

Amy gave him a look like, people are trying to kill us and you're worried about property rights?

"We'll send them a check,... later,.... if we live. See if they have any food in the fridge," Amy ordered.

Under the circumstances Eric wasn't going to argue and thanked God when he opened the pantry. They were into canning. Looking at the dates on the glass jars it seemed they were all from last year, which in canning terms spells fresh.

He popped open two jars of peaches and handed one to Benjamin. They found some forks and dove in.

Benjamin's eyes lit up at the taste. "Wow, this is good!" he exclaimed.

Eric had to admit they were exceptionally flavorful and nodded his head in agreement.

Eric walked around the house eating his jar of peaches, taking inventory. Whatever reservations he had about making himself at home were gone now. *Me casa sue casa*, he thought to himself.

The pantry was stocked with peaches, apples, pears, and what looked like Mount Rainer Cherries as far as canned fruit. They also must have had a garden somewhere because there was a whole additional shelf of canned veggies. He found a couple of fishing poles in the back mud room area. Hanging from a nail in the wall was a compound bow. Searching around a little more Eric found a bunch of arrows in the corner of a closet.

"Hey, Benjamin, do you want to learn how to shoot a bow....." Eric just then noticed that Benjamin was asleep on the couch still holding his jar of peaches. The little guy was out cold again.

Eric took the peaches from him and lifted his legs up on the couch. There was a blanket on the back of the couch that he covered him with.

Amy came out of the shower smiling. "You are not going to believe this. This place has hot water somehow; it must be heated by solar power."

Eric handed Amy the jar of Mount Rainer Cherries knowing that they were her favored. Her eyes lit up the same way Benjamin's had. *Exactly the same way*, Eric thought looking from Amy to Benjamin. Amy read his thoughts.

"What?" she asked with her mouth full of cherries.

"Benjamin has some of your expressions," Eric said as he tried to dip his fork into her jar of cherries.

She pulled them away with a smile. "He is our son. Get a shower, you stink! I'll keep watch over the cherries."

After all three had been in and out of the shower Amy found a first aid kit and went to work treating their wounds from days on the run. Eric wondered if they were feeling a false sense of security in this setting. But they needed this. They had been in a state of panic for too long. The dogs would warn them if someone was approaching. They would stay put for the day and if it seemed safe enough they would all sleep there again that night. Tomorrow was a new day.

The next morning Eric was up before dawn scouting the area a little better. He would plan out a few escape routes for the family. Having a plan was half the battle his dad would say. If they had to separate they would need a meeting place. If they had to run at night they would make better time if they knew the layout of the land. He also used the time to prepare bug out bags of essential survival supplies. Some of the bags where hidden in the woods others where with them in the cabin. But Eric was not satisfied. They needed a place to run to. A second hiding place, beyond where they would meet up.

Eric was preparing to go on a little exploration when Amy walked up to him.

"Take Benjamin with you," Amy said, surprising Eric.

"You think so?" Eric asked.

"He needs to be with a good man. He needs to see you and learn from you. He needs his dad." Amy walked closer to

Eric so only he could hear. "Did you see him flinch when you reached for me this morning in the kitchen? He thought you were going to hit me."

Eric did see it and it hurt to think about the abuse Benjamin had witnessed as a slave.

"Ok, I'll take him with me." Eric looked at the hurt in his wife's eyes.

"Don't just take him with you, teach him. He is so hungry to learn from you," Amy said.

"What about you? You'll be here alone," Eric said concerned.

"I'll hold down the fort until you get back, Axel and Maverick will stay with me in the cabin," she said with confidence.

Eric and Benjamin took a deer trail from the Cabin. It sloped down a ridge and crossed a creek. Eric explained to Benjamin what they were looking for and why. They traveled up to the top of another ridge but stayed in the trees. Eric pointed to the high point and explained to Benjamin that you never expose yourself at the top of a ridge. The cowboys of the old American west called it "sky lining". A body could be seen for miles if it was lined up against the blue sky or white clouds, but if you stayed in the trees you were hidden. He also talked about checking ones back trail. The land would change greatly in appearance when they traveling back to the cabin. If they didn't look back and study the look of the land from that view point they would think themselves lost on the way back.

Eric made a game out of walking through the woods without leaving a trail, no footprints could be left, no broken tree limbs, no sign that anyone had ever passed that way. Benjamin was eating it all up. He didn't just play along; he asked questions and came up with ideas of his own.

"So if I jump from rock to rock and then climb that tree and go from tree to tree and then into the creek bed and downstream…" Benjamin was really into it.

Eric made the game even more interesting by letting Benjamin go ahead on the trail and then try to track him down. Later he switched places with him and let Benjamin track him. He showed him how to identify the tracks of several different animals, deer, elk, coyote, rabbit and let him help set some snare and dead fall traps. Eric showed him what he knew about eatable plants, picking up where he left off on that first night by the river. What amazed Eric was how much Benjamin remembered. He was like a dry sponge soaking up information.

They stayed out all day and finally found what Eric was looking for. A cave about three miles from the cabin. It was perfect, with a small entrance that opened into a large room. Water was close by and several wide evergreens hid its entrance.

They both returned late that evening to the cabin. The next day they all took a load of supplies to their fallback hideout by a different trail. Amy liked the cave and made sure she could recognize the way there by landmarks. On the way back, Benjamin found a track he could not identify. Eric stooped down and looked at the print of a mountain lion.

"Amy, come look at this."

Amy came over and did not like what she saw. "Is that what I think it is?"

"What is it?" Benjamin wanted to know.

"A mountain lion, a big cat!" Eric was looking around. Axel and Maverick didn't seem upset and that was a good sign. Maybe the cougar was long gone. "The track has lots of bug trails through it and the sides are falling in. It's an old track. Nothing to worry about," Eric said to ease his own nerves as much as Amy's.

The next day Amy took Benjamin for a walk. She wanted to know her son more. She wanted to listen to him. Would he open up about the last five years of his life? Could she handle it if he did? Amy was smart enough to know that this could not be rushed. Benjamin would talk when he was ready to talk. For now it was enough for them to converse about her being a physician. He seemed interested in that.

"I get to help people when bad things happen to them. When they get sick or injured and they need a doctor."

"Is that why you left me that day when the bomb went off? Did you go to help?"

Amy choked down the tears. So he did remember or had Harvey told him? Did he blame her somewhere deep in his heart? "I'm so sorry Benjamin. I didn't mean to leave you. Yes, I was going to help someone who was hurt."

"I know that you would never leave me on purpose. It wasn't your fault. It was Harvey's fault and the bad men like him at the factory. You don't have to feel guilty anymore. I love you."

Amy felt like the weight of the world was just lifted off her shoulders by a ten year old little boy. This time Benjamin hugged her first.

The sunrise on their fourth day at the cabin was brilliant. Beautiful colors filled the eastern sky, violets, crimsons, and golden light shined through as if heaven had broken open. From the cabins location three mountains were visible, Mt. Rainer, Mt. Saint Helens and what Eric thought was Mt. Adams, but he wasn't sure. The smell of highland fields of wild flowers filled the morning air. Amy found someone's stash of coffee hidden in the back of a top shelf and all three sat on the front porch with a hot cup of Joe and took in the splendor of the morning.

Benjamin surprised them both by taking his cup black. "It was the only way they would give it to me at the factory. They said they weren't about to waste sugar and creamer on me."

Amy's head dropped but the guilt she felt was no longer as sharp as it was before.

Just then Maverick and Axel came bounding up the front steps. They were all over Benjamin. Amy took his coffee just in time. Eric remembered seeing a ball on the floor in the back closet of the cabin. He set his coffee down to go retrieve it. "Do they know how to play catch?" he asked Benjamin as he appeared back on the front porch with ball in hand.

"Maverick will!" he said with anticipation.

Benjamin took the ball from Eric and threw it. Maverick was on it like it was a running rabbit. Eric stepped down from the porch and joined in, throwing the ball as far as he could. Amy sat on the porch with Axel beside her watching the two men in her life play. She realized what a treasure it was to be here with them both. They had a lot of catching up to do as a family. If only they were here on vacation and not running for their lives from an insidious crime ring.

Amy decided to try and make some breakfast. She found some dry waffle mix that said; just add water and a nice waffle maker that beeped when done. The canned fruit would go on top to add some flavor.

This would be their first special breakfast all together as a family in five years. Amy found some plates and set the table. She placed the engraved courage stone in the middle of the table next to a little vase. There were wild flowers growing out back. She went out the back door of the cabin and picked a good sized bouquet. Why was she getting all emotional about this? It was just breakfast. She went back inside and put the flowers in the vase. It was a cool morning. A fire would be nice. She could hear Eric and Benjamin outside having a time and didn't want to bother them. She found the matches and paper to start the dry wood that was already cut and stacked. She stopped herself just in time. What was she thinking? The smoke would have been seen for miles.

"Remember where you are girl," she said to herself.

Putting it behind her she started thinking about how long the coffee would last. What she would give for orange juice right now. Dry milk was all she could find to set out for drinks with breakfast.

Amy stepped back from the table when it was all ready. A hot pile of waffles sat on a platter with fruit toppings she had mixed up next to that. There were three tall glasses of milk and a beautiful bouquet of wild flowers adding some color to the table. The smells must have drifted outside because just then the front door swung open and two hungry faces stepped into the kitchen.

"Time to eat," she said as if it was nothing.

Eric hugged her and looking around said, "This is really nice, honey."

Benjamin sat down and forked a waffle.

"Hey mom, can I have two?"

Amy caught her breath; he called her mom.

The gift shop section of the plant nursery always had a good selection of engraved garden stones. The young college student was trying to find one he hadn't seen before. He was buying a gift. Finally, he spotted one that read, Phoenix. He remembered from his comic book days that it meant, risen from the ashes. It was one he knew they didn't already have. As he placed the stone on the checkout counter the casher looked at his hand. He was missing one finger and the others were stitched together as best modern medicine could manage. He was lucky to have a hand at all. He paid for the stone and headed home. He would stop by the Savage's place on his way.

As he pulled onto his street he was surprised to find a

crew of city workers surrounding Eric and Amy Savages house. They had the whole thing barricaded off and a large wrecking ball crane in place. What were they doing? A small group of neighbors were milling about. Some were auguring with the crew.

Steve Mills parked his truck as close as he could. Leaving his gift behind, he approached the scene.

"What is going on here? He questioned. "This home belongs to some friends of mine!"

"Get back kid, I've already verified with my department head twice. This is the house. I have all the paper work right here." He held up some official looking notice. "My men have checked and double checked, no one is in that house."

Steve was on his cell calling 911. "We have an emergency on East Crescent Drive, some misinformed workers are about to demolish a perfectly fine house that....."

He was interrupted. "You're the fifth call we've had on this. The crew is at the right house. It's nothing to worry about."

Bull, was the word that came to his mind.

"Sir, sir…" Steve spoke to the man in charge at the scene. "Just look at that house. Just look at it for a moment. Does it look abandoned to you?"

The man hesitated for just a second. The white picket fence, the front garden, the Seahawks mailbox, and the craftsman style little house all looked cared for enough. The grass was a little long and the news papers had piled up but…….But what was he thinking, he needed this job.

"Let's start hoisting the ball back." He walked away from Steve.

Steve jumped over caution tape, "Wait, wait! Can I get some of their things out of the house first?"

"Orders are that no one takes anything from the house."

The man felt bad about it but he was just following orders.

Steve looked around at the crowd of neighbors. "What about the stones?"

"What stones?" the man asked as the wrecking ball got higher and higher.

"Outside, around the house, they collected engraved stones, can we take them?"

The man looked around at all the people nodding their heads ready to help gather the stones.

If it'll get this mob off my back! He thought to himself.

"Ok, take the garden stones, but nothing else."

About ten people stepped over the line and helped Steve retrieve the engraved stones they loaded them all into the bed of his pickup truck.

The Savage family sat having breakfast together in the little cabin in the mountains miles and miles away.

The ten thousand pound wreaking ball was at its full height and ready to go.

"We have the cabin surrounded and are ready to move in." the whisper came over the phone to Chief Hobbs.

Eric heard the dogs start barking.

The steel cable holding back the weight of the ball was released.

Eric rushed to grab the guns. The windows on all sides of the cabin shattered with the impact of flying bullets.

The huge concrete ball smashed through the front porch and into the decorative front door of the Savage home sending it flying back through the house. The entire front wall of the house buckled.

There was an explosion on the front porch of the cabin,

blowing down the door and collapsing the log timbers supporting the porch. Amy heard the dogs yelp in pain.

The ball was on its way back up for a second strike.

"Come out now! All of you or the next explosive will come through a window."

Eric was down with one bullet to the shoulder and one that grazed him in the back of the head. He was knocked unconscious and was bleeding. Amy was putting pressure on the wounds but.....

The wrecking ball was released again, this time it destroyed the entire inside of the home, crashing through the kitchen, bouncing off the side wall and back through the living room.

Amy and Benjamin drug Eric into the back bedroom as the explosive came through the window. Amy kicked the door shut with her foot just before it exploded. The whole cabin shook.

The little house could not stand another hit. With its insides revealed it was plain to everyone that Eric and Amy were given no chance to remove their belonging. Pictures fell off the walls, family heirlooms lay destroyed, a china cabinet somehow still stood in one corner. But the ball was ready again.

"Help me! Please someone help me!" Amy was trying to keep Eric from bleeding out the same way Gary Holland had.

The men outside were callous to the cries of a women. They had heard it all before. They were cowards, every last one of them.

Benjamin stepped out of the smoking house with his hands over his head.

"Please help my dad!" he pleaded looking from cold face to cold face.

A man flung the boy to the ground and was preparing to

bind up Benjamin's hands behind his back.

The rest of them surged into the cabin from all sides.

Out of nowhere Timber came leaping through the air at the man who had Benjamin. Long canine teeth clamped down around the man's neck and penetrated into the windpipe. Benjamin was free but hesitated, looking back to the cabin.

He could hear his mother's voice urging him to move, "Run Benjamin, run NOW!"

The mammoth concrete wrecking ball came like an unstoppable force. This time it smashed right through the house causing the whole structure to fall in on itself. It was over. The bulldozers would push what remained into piles and haul it all away to the dump.

Judge Fredrick Hurst felt like a celebration was in order. They had Eric and Amy Savage in their custody. Chief Hobbs and assistant Chief Walker had moved this game of chess with Noland Savage in the right direction. They would never be seen together, but he would reward them for a job well done.

Daniel Lane walked into the police station and went right to his desk. He had been watching the news about Noland Savage. This was getting bigger by the minute. They were still looking for him and that indicated he was still alive. Daniel was taking a risk coming back to work. If the two men from Harvey's house asked about him it would be all over. But he needed evidence, hard evidence, before going to the FBI. He had a hunch the place to find that evidence was in the private files of Chief Hobbs. The door to his office had a coded lock and it was never just left open. But he had an idea.

He stood his cell phone up on his desk recording what

was happening behind him in the direction of Chief Hobbs office. After a while he checked on what he caught and adjusted his aim. It took hours to get it just right and he had to look busy in the process. Hobbs' secretary was coming and going all day but would normally block the view he needed. But once when she got distracted she punched in the numbers with her hand extended and in full view of his cell camera.

Hours later Daniel was at home on his computer watching the video on the big screen. He had the code. That was step one.

"Don't make any sudden moves Officer Lane," a voice that sounded dead serious came from behind him. Daniel's gun was still strapped in its holster.

Mrs. O'Reilly had never been treated more appalling in all her life. But she had met those brave women who survived the Nazi concentration camps of WWII. This was much less horrific than that. If Corrie Ten Boom could help others while suffering like she did, Mrs. O'Reilly was determined to do no less here.

The girls were being moved through the factory like cattle and then separated into groups by evil men who sat like judges of their level of beauty. Some were gone the next day. Others sat in cells. Mrs. O'Reilly did her best to speak words of encouragement to them as she brought them what these animals called food.

At night Mrs. O'Reilly was locked into a small room with just enough space to lie down and have a chair to one side. There were some old blankets and some writing on the walls from past occupants. She asked for her suitcase every day and one night after working in the kitchen, it was waiting there for her in her cell. Someone had searched through it but must have done a half-hearted job because her lock picking set, two small pieces of long flat metal, were still right where she had hidden them. Her husband Robert O'Reilly was a lock smith in his later years and she had learned a thing or two from him about picking locks.

After picking the lock on her room, she carefully opened the door and dared to poke her head out and look both ways down the hall. No one was there that she could see. She closed the door and locked herself back in her room. She would have to think this through before just wondering off into the night. Her goal wasn't to escape anyway. She was there to be a little light in a very dark place. That next day she watched closely where things were, how the factory was laid out and how the place operated. The first good thing she could do was get extra food to some of the girls that looked in the worst condition. There was a little thing brought in that next day that looked half starved to death. Mrs. O'Reilly noted where she was held and took her some food that same night.

"What's your name sweetie?" Mrs. O'Reilly asked as she handed her some plain bread rolls through the bars of her cage. The young girl took the rolls but did not reply.

"Where are you from?" Mrs. O'Reilly tried again.

The girl was not in the mood to talk or maybe didn't understand English.

"Ok, you don't have to say anything if you don't want to. I just wanted you to know that I'm here for you. I'll bring you more food tomorrow night." Mrs. O'Reilly wished she could do more but that was all she had to offer. The little thing had beautiful red hair and Mrs. O'Reilly wondered if they shared an Irish heritage. Maybe she could get her to talk a little tomorrow.

Noland Savage sat in the living room of Daniel Lane. The

doctor at the hospital told him he was the luckiest man alive. The bullet had amazingly missed all vital organs, tendons and muscle groups.

"As a matter of fact, if I ever had to be shot, I'd want it in just the same place," the doctor said shaking his head in amazement.

Noland slipped away soon after he was treated. He needed a safe place to lay low and the one man who he knew was on the right side of this was Officer Daniel Lane. Neither man had ever seen the other so there was a little tension in the room as Daniel turned to face the voice behind him.

Daniel sat with his hands up in front of a very fit man in his fifties who wasn't ashamed to go grey. Military was written all over him. He had steel blue eyes that never looked away. The gun in his hand was steady and pointing right at Daniel.

Noland had one clarifying question that only Daniel Lane would know the answer to. If he gave the right answer, they'd be friends, if not; the man he faced would be dead.

"So do you work for Chief Hobbs or do you work for Chief Hobbs?"

Daniel remembered the question from the conversation in the bathroom with the two thugs. If this was Savage and he was listening on the phone he would want him to answer the same. But if he didn't catch that part of the conversation he would hate the chief and probably shoot him dead if he replied the same. Daniel had the feeling his life depended on his next eight words.

"I work for the factory down on 3rd," Daniel replied with the thought of, *please don't shoot me,* written all over his face.

Noland put the gun away and held out his hand. "Noland Lee Savage."

Daniel took the hand. "Daniel Lane." The older man had

a grip like a steel vise.

They had a lot to talk about. Both men were full of questions that only the other could answer. It did not take long for each of them to recognize the quality of the other. It was the beginning of a friendship.

Chapter 7
It's all about what's for dinner

Eric and Amy were taken to the factory and placed in a cell and held under constant guard. Eric was in and out of consciousness. Amy did what she could but was not given much to work with. She was a good ER doctor and had him stable, but there was still the risk of infection. A little old lady with a smile of gold was allowed to bring them food and water. She looked as out of place as anyone could in such a place.

When she saw how bad Eric was she gave Amy an understanding look and said in a low voice, "What do you need?"

"Something to keep infection away, antibiotics," Amy whispered back.

"I'll see what I can do." Mrs. O'Reilly left with that.

She smiled at the guards as she walked by and then stopped and said, "I've been ordered to bring you men dinner. What's your favored food?"

The question caught them both off guard. She talked to them like they were her grandsons coming over to grandma's house after church not two hardened criminals working in a slave factory.

When they didn't answer she made a suggestion, "How about some big juicy bacon cheeseburgers with homemade fries on the side?"

The two men looked at each other thinking, *what the hell!*

Sounds good to me!

"Ok lady, make mine a half pounder with lots of bacon," one finally said.

"Me too," said the other.

Mrs. O'Reilly walked away toward the kitchen. Now she just needed to get into the medical supply room. She already knew where to find the hamburger and bacon. Cooking was her strength, food her weapons, she had no problem recruiting accomplices in the kitchen and those who ran supplies, no one liked eating the plastic tasting meals Mike dished out anyway and no one saw her as a threat.

That evening she came around the corner with a meal cart carrying two plates of large oversized burgers covered in bacon and dripping with flavor. The wonderful smell filled the ugly cell area. The two men took their plates and sat down on the floor to eat. From under the cart she pulled out a two liter of coke and poured them each a cup over ice.

"Wow. This is good!" one man said while holding the oversized burger with both hands.

The other guard just nodded his agreement, unwilling to pause his fest for comment.

"Well, I'm glad you like it," she said as she reached beneath the cart for one last distraction.

The guards were not prepared for what came next and she knew it. She had purposely kept it hidden until just the right moment. It was her weapon of choice and of a caliber that would even penetrate the armor vests they wore.

Homemade double chocolate cake!

The two men stood to their feet as she placed the cake on top of the cart and began cutting out two large slices.

"OK, Mike is soooo fired!" one said.

She waited until they were seated again with both burger and cake to keep them busy. Then she simply put the food that came from Mike's kitchen on top of the Cart and asked, "Can I feed the prisoners now."

The first guard looked at the appalling glob of food on the two plates and opened the door. He did not bother to check the cart. Once inside and alone with them, Mrs. O'Reilly smiled and handed the medicine for Eric to Amy.

Amy whispered a grateful, "Thank you."

They were able to have a hushed conversation while the guards ate.

As she left their cell and headed back to the kitchen one of the guards spoke up with a question, "Can you make real homemade pizza?" Mrs. O'Reilly smiled.

Like fish on a hook, she thought to herself.

"I make my own crust from scratch and build it up from there. But I have one condition. I get to feed those two in there whatever I want. No more of Mike's slop for them either, if you agree to that, you'll have your pizza once a week"

They didn't have a problem with that.

Daniel told Noland everything he knew about the factory, Mrs. O'Reilly, working for Chief Hobbs, the house that belonged to Harvey, the conversation he had with the two men, what he saw in the house. Noland asked questions. He asked for Daniel to tell the stories again. It wasn't that he didn't believe what was being said but rather that he wanted to glean every last detail out of the mind of Officer Lane. New details that Daniel considered trivial would cause Noland to stop him and ask for clarification.

"Did you ever see Mrs. O'Reilly again, after that night?"

"No"

"Did assistant Chief Walker take the report from you using his right or left hand, try to remember."

"He used his right hand."

"How much was Harvey's water bill?"

That question made Daniel think, "Come to think of it, it was like $745.00. I just thought that maybe he was behind or something."

Noland stopped him. "Are you sure, for water?"

"That's what I remember."

"Did you see any late notices on the front door, any sign that the water had been shut off?"

"No, as a matter of fact, I washed my hands several times while I was there, the water was on."

Noland had a look in his eye. "No water company is going to continue service to a house that owes $745."

"Where is the water company for that area located?" Noland asked

"Down on 3rd next to the factory!" Daniel was impressed.

Noland grinned. "The devils in the details my friend, never forget that."

Daniel already liked Noland Savage and was glad that he was on his side in this fight.

"So what now?" Daniel asked. "Are you going to go into the Cascades to search for your family?"

Noland considered his answer for a moment and then said, "No, I don't think they are in the mountains any more. You said Hobbs and the other officers came back to the station, right?"

"Right."

"You said Hobbs looked angry at the world when he first got back but then things changed and he started acting a little too happy, a little giddy even."

"Ya, he did."

Noland stood to his feet and paced the floor, thinking as he walked.

"The odds are that they are holding Eric, Amy, Gary and Benjamin down at the Factory. You said this lady; Mrs. O'Reilly had a house not far from the place in a good spot to observe."

"That's what she was doing." Daniel worried about what had become of the feisty old lady.

"I need to get into her house and from there into the Water Works."

Noland looked at officer Daniel Lane. He seemed like a good man but could he handle what was about to come his way. Noland had to ask this young man to do the one thing that went against everything he stood for.

"Daniel, we need somebody on the inside of this. Would you consider being a mole? Getting on the inside through your connections at the police station would be a start."

"How would I do that?" Daniel asked a little afraid of the idea.

"It's risky to tell you the truth. If things don't go well, at best, you'd lose your reputation and career as a police officer and at worse they would kill you." Savage wanted him to know the score.

"But how would I go about it?" Daniel wanted to know.

"You have an evidence storage room at the station right? A place where drugs and drug money and hot guns and such are stored as evidence, you could start by stealing from the pot. Take a lot of money and go buy yourself a boat."

Daniel was following him, "And they would find out

about it but instead of turning me over to the DA's office they would make me an offer I couldn't refuse." But was there an easier way? "I do have the code to Chief Hobbs' office, why not just sneak in there, get the evidence we need and take our case to the D.A.'s office ourselves."

Noland understood Daniel's desire to take the fast track to victory but his own instincts and experience warned him.

"Because we don't know who all the players are yet. I could get my family out of the factory but unless we take this weed out from the root, we would just be buying time. There is someone bigger than the Chief of Police calling the shots here. I want to know who he or she is. We need a list of all the players. This is a game of chess and to win we have to think ahead, position our pieces and then strike hard and fast."

Daniel liked Noland's way of thinking. How long had it been since he'd heard someone talk like that, straight about a situation, with no political correctness considered. Then Daniel remembered who Noland Savage reminded him of. His father had talked with that same no nonsense attitude.

"Ok, I'll do it. God help me, I'll do it." Daniel sat back in his chair deep in thought.

Benjamin sat in the cave hideout with his dog. He was less afraid because he had Timber with him. The big lug was a comfort to him there in the lonely mountains, just as he had been at the factory. This was the place his family was to meet up again if something happened at the cabin. Benjamin knew that if his mom and dad where able; they would come here looking for him.

When he ran from the attack at the cabin, he did not travel directly to the cave but led the men in the wrong direction for awhile and then, stashing the three tracking collars from Timber under a fallen tree and using every trick his dad had taught him about not leaving a trail, made his way to the cave.

He had shelter, food and water. The weather was good. The summer nights could get a little cold but they had prepared the cave with bedding from the cabin. Eric had supplied the place with a stash of rope, a fishing pole and the bow with arrows. Benjamin knew how to fish but never got around to learning to shoot the bow. But Eric had worked with him on how to set up a line of traps and he had what he needed to do that.

Benjamin tried to pull the string back on the bow but he was not strong enough. The arrow would just fall to the ground a few feet in front of him. He picked it up and tried again but he was off balance and the tip went astray while the back end of the arrow stayed notched. He decided to make a spear. He went out and found a fallen branch about the size he needed. Then he took out his red Swiss army knife with his name scratched into the side and started cutting away at the point.

Suddenly, Timber was on his feet and alert. Benjamin held his unfinished spear in his hands. They both went to the mouth of the cave and looked around. Coming slowly out of the woods were two wounded exhausted dogs, Axel and Maverick. They were in bad shape. The explosion on the front porch had trapped them under the collapsed roof. No one bothered to help them after the attack. But they finally struggled free.

Benjamin was happy to see them. "Come here boys, are you ok?"

They came to him but just dropped down to the ground with fatigue. Benjamin brought them food and water.

"It's going to be ok," he said encouraging them to eat.

Timber went out with Benjamin the next day to set up some traps. Axel and Maverick lifted their heads to look as they left but had no energy to follow. Feeding himself and three dogs would exhaust his food supplies fast. He needed to make his food last and if he could get a rabbit it would really help. He hiked along the creek and looked for tracks.

Animals need water just like people do. He recalled Eric saying.

He set up five snare traps and four dead falls beside the creek right in the path of a small game trail. He was not that good at getting the deadfall traps to work at first and it took him all morning to get them right. On the way back to the cave he found some wild blackberry bushes weighed down with plump juicy berries. After eating what he wanted he carried what he could back to the cave.

"Look what I found!" He hand fed Axel and Maverick the blackberries.

Benjamin then took the fishing pool from the cave down to the creek but didn't see any fish. But he remembered from Eric that if he following the creek downstream it may lead to a larger stream with fish. After following the creek for some time with no luck Benjamin wondered what to do. It started to get dark and he headed back to the cave empty handed. That night he ate the saltine crackers and the peanut butter from the cabin.

The next day he went out to check his traps. There was nothing in the first three but the forth trap had been tripped. But whatever tripped it had gotten away. The deadfalls had fallen but it was because they were poorly set up and the wind set them off. Benjamin tried again but this time did a better job.

The next day he caught his first rabbit in a snare trap. He killed it by knocking it over the head with a large stone. Eric had showed him how to gut a rabbit but watching and doing were two different things. Benjamin did the best he could but in the end decided to just give the rabbit to Timber. Timber seemed pleased with that and ate the whole thing fir and all.

Benjamin decided to build on his success. He would become a trapper. He had lots of rope and could follow the creek in both directions. Over the next three days he set twenty-five traps and caught himself two more rabbits. He did a better job of gutting these but gave them over to Axel and Maverick because he was not out of food from the cabin yet. But that day was coming and Benjamin was thinking about how he would cook his rabbits.

A fire can be seen for miles. If you have to build a fire, build a small one in the cave at night so no one can see the smoke or the light. Eric had told him.

Noland Savage came through the back window of Mrs. O'Reilly House in the dead of night. The place was empty but far from bare. There were family pictures on the walls, old love letters in the closet, and a purple heart proudly displayed on a mantle top. The furniture was dated but well cared for. Noland was a man keen on observation. He saw their story unfold with every door he opened and every aged box he went through. It was the tale of a strong man and brave women who loved each other and loved their country. They never had much. They didn't have it easy. But they had each other.

Noland knew he was being a snoop. But he needed to know who she was. What she was made of, this Mrs. O'Reilly who dared to poke Officer Daniel Lane in the chest and challenge him to be a man. There were many women out there who wanted power over a man, who knew how to manipulate a man, or shame and devalue a man but few who could bring out the strength in a man. If Mrs. O'Reilly was where Noland believed she was, he would need her help.

Hidden up in the attic in an old dusty box he found all he needed to know. He placed the lid back over the certificate of recognition and sat down. So, she was *that* Mrs. O'Reilly. He laughed when he thought of it. Now he knew he could count on her with his life if need be.

He departed the house by a different route. One never developed a pattern one's enemy could watch and learn to anticipate. He made his way silently through the dark shadows toward the water plant. From the lack of lights and activity the place look to be down to just the night crew and not as heavily guarded as the factory next door. Noland was able to scale a pipeline up to a fire escape and into the third story vacant office area. From there he used the stairway to go down to the lower underground level of the building. He had no desire to be challenged by the gangsters who ran this operation. But if he did meet someone whose time had come, he would not stand in the way of their destiny.

Noland searched the basement of the building; he was looking for a way across to the old water heater factory. The City of Seattle was build on top of the old city. There were secret passageways all over the place. They gave tours of the known areas but there were pockets that got walled in and forgotten. Noland recognized brickwork old enough to hide a few secrets. His work would be slow and quiet. He made the opening through the old bricks just large enough to squeeze through and hid it from view with wooden pallets. Once inside the forgotten passageway between the two buildings he found the wall that was part of the factory and went to work there in the same slow quiet fashion.

The courtroom was close to empty save for those who had to be there and those waiting for the next trial to began.

"The Smith family vs the Seattle School District, his Honor Judge Fredrick Hurst presiding."

The judge sat in his seat of power looking out over his domain. The Smiths were a divorced couple who each had a record of neglecting their responsibilities as parents. They were filing suit against the school district for providing medical information and guidance to their fourteen year old daughter which led to the abortion of her unwanted pregnancy. The school never informed the parents of their daughter's pregnancy or of her decision to have an abortion or of their assistance in driving her to the clinic. The daughter ran away from home soon after the abortion. It was the investigation into her disappearance that led to uncovering the information about the school's role in her private medical decisions.

"Why would the school not let me know my daughter was in trouble? She was only fourteen years old. They never said a word to me." Her mother was unhappy with the way things were going. It made no common sense to her no matter how many big legal words the attorney for the school district used to describe it.

"The law protects the privacy rights of your daughter and the rights of the school district to provide health counseling." The judge was looking down his nose at the ignorance of this emotional plea.

"She was barely fourteen! She can't go on a field trip without parental permission but she can go have a potentially risky medical procedure without us knowing and the school can drive her to the doctor's office?"

The face of the judge was stone cold. "Yes, that is the law."

"If I had known, I could have helped her through it, supported her. Maybe, she would not have run away from home." The mother was crying now. The father was there next to his ex- wife but they were anything but a united front.

The judge opened a file with a picture of the girl paper clipped to the upper right hand corner. The file had nothing to do with the case against the school. It showed the judge just how much the girl had sold for at auction and the place in China where she was now owned as a slave. Parents of this caliber were his bread and butter. The more irresponsible parents became the more the schools and government would have to step in and protect the children. That made the judge laugh to himself. The system was so full of holes and red tape; kids were easily lost in the process.

"The school was responsible to give the child a safe ride to the clinic. The doctors were professional, and highly trained. There were no complications with the abortion. You should be thanking the school for stepping in and giving your daughter a good, safe option. It takes a community to raise a child these days and we are all just trying to do what is best." Fredrick Hurst tried not to let his sarcasm show.

This was a great case because it would set precedent for future cases, widening the schools wall of protection around children against their parents and opening the door to grant privacy rights to even younger children. The judge was always amazed how much bull shit people could believe. His contacts at the schools and clinics were a gold mine of information. A young girl estranged from her family and indoctrinated in her right to privacy was a sitting duck for his operatives.

The mother and father left the courtroom going in different directions. They were devastated but not truly changed. Change takes courage. They would depend on the police to do what they could to find their daughter but take no real risks themselves.

Mike's anger was white hot, his wolf like face, red from the neck up. If one more person told him what a horrible cook he was compared to Mrs. O'Reilly he was going to cut them up and serve them with the next meal. The men were always looking for a weak target to be the butt of their jokes and Mrs. O'Reilly made him look weak and unfit. Like sharks to blood these men would keep coming at him until he was the next Harvey.

Tonight, he would take care of that! No old lady was going to get the better of him. She was weak and about to die anyway. He could do it in such a way that no one could prove anything. They would all suspect him but no one would cry for justice, not in this place. He may even gain a little respect as someone not to be played with. The more he thought about it the more his mind was made up. Mrs. O'Reilly would die tonight.

Mrs. O'Reilly was in the kitchen kneading a batch of dough for a pizza crust. The secret to her homemade pizza was in the crust. It had just the right mix of crisp outer texture and inner depth of hot soft flavor. The sauce was from her time spent in Italy, but it was really Sicilian in origin. It was so good she had been offered ten thousand dollars once by a business man for the rights to it. But it wasn't for sale. It was to be passed down to her children like it had been passed down to her by a close friend of the family.

Mrs. O'Reilly stopped and rested against the counter. Looking around at the kitchen she asked herself the obvious question.

"What are you doing here? Is it because you have no one? Is it because… "

Just then a frail looking girl came slowly into the room. Her eyes were big and green and her hair was red and disordered. She looked about nine years old. It was the quiet little girl she had been feeding at night.

"I was told to report to you in the kitchen," the little thing said just above a whisper.

Mrs. O'Reilly had asked for help in the kitchen for her special project meals. When they laughed at her request she thought she was on her own. But who was this little bit.

Mrs. O'Reilly smiled at her and in a kind voice asked "OK, child. What is your name?"

The girl dropped her head as if ashamed. "Abigail."

"Abigail," Mrs. O'Reilly said it with love. "That is a beautiful name." She truly did like the name.

"My name is Rose O'Reilly, but you can call me Mrs. O'Reilly." The girl was wearing a filthy blue dress and so needed a bath but Mrs. O'Reilly was careful not to make her feel rejected.

"Well, I am so happy to see you. I need your help. But first let's get you up to the sink and wash those hands. After that we will get you something to eat and get to work."

The girl obeyed and came to the sink. Mrs. O'Reilly helped her wash her hands in the hot soapy water.

"I'm making homemade pizza. You can help spread out the dough into a circle shape."

Abigail did what she was told but did not say a thing after that. Mrs. O'Reilly didn't ask questions that would make her feel uncomfortable. She made the extra dough into bread sticks and handed a hot one to Abigail. She put some sauce into a bowl and set it beside her as well.

"Dip the bread into the sauce and see what you think," Mrs. O'Reilly said.

Abigail smiled the moment the flavorful treat hit her taste buds. Mrs. O'Reilly enjoyed watching her eat.

A memory stirred in Mrs. O'Reilly's mind. It was a photo of a vulnerable little girl walking between the tall uniform men of Hitler's SS. They were not walking her to the school playground, but to her death. It was that image and others like it that stirred young men like her father to lie about his age and join the fight against the Nazis. Would others do the same today if they could see this girl? She had to hope there were those who still had the heart to love and the guts to fight. That hope made her recall Officer Daniel Lane. She wondered what that young man was up to since she last saw him.

Officer Daniel Lane was stuffing stacks of hundred dollar bills into a black mangy backpack. His heart was beating a million miles a minute. They could be back at any minute. He wanted to get caught but make it look like he didn't want to get caught. If he could get away with it a few times first it would add credibility to the deception. He quickly changed the ledger that would lead to an accounting of the missing money and stuffed a smelly sweat shirt into the top of the pack. He left the backpack partly unzipped and walked back to his desk dropping it on top and leaving it in plain sight.

Assistant Chief Walker just happened to be walking by, "What's up with that?" he asked looking at the pack.

"Evidence being released to the parents of the kid caught breaking and entering into that Chinese restaurant. It smells wonderful." He held it out into the face of Walker. It smelled like something had died in there.

Turning his head away from the smell, Walker was not impressed. "You watch yourself Lane and show a little respect around here."

"Yes sir! Sorry sir." Daniel acted humbled as Walker focused his attention elsewhere.

Daniel had an advertisement from Basspro Shops open on his desk. He would be sure to wear his uniform when he went in to pay cash for his new boat and ATV. Maybe someone would start to ask questions and maybe not? It was a dangerous game he was playing. They could just as easily turn him over to the DA as to invite him into their club, or kill him outright if they suspected him a spy.

Abigail was helping Mrs. O'Reilly push the food cart toward the cell of Eric and Amy Savage to give the homemade pizza to the guards there. Mike came around the corner walking toward them from the other direction. Mrs. O'Reilly pushed the cart to one side and put Abigail between herself and the wall. She knew that Mike hated her and would try something soon. But now that she had Abigail to protect, Mrs. O'Riely was wishing she was a little younger and a little stronger.

"Well, well, well, if it isn't grandma Mother Teresa and her little helper." Mike had murder in his heart.

"Did you make me some pizza?" he asked sarcastically

Mrs. O'Reilly knew better than to say anything to this man. He knew who the pizza was for and she doubted he had the guts to cross them.

Mike looked quickly to see if anyone was around and then in a low voice said, "This is not some church social lady, you think your safe here but you're not. People die in here all the time. I wouldn't go making any promises to carrot top here either. You both are going to end up where you don't want to be, understood."

Mrs. O'Reilly said nothing. The fact that she did not show fear made Mike even angrier. He walked away but only because he knew that within hours he would have his hands around that old neck of hers and that alone consoled him for now.

That night, Mrs. O'Reilly left Abigail asleep in her room and snuck out to the kitchen. Abigail was now her responsibility. Never-the-less, she needed to make her nightly rounds, bringing extra food and medicine to the worst of the worst. She had been seen by some of the men but no one stopped her. There was no compassion in it, just apathy mixed with a little self-interest. The factory was its own world with its own rules. If you had something to bargain with and played your cards right the rules bent in your favor.

If you were weak and seen as a drain on the system, you would find yourself at the bottom of the food chain.

From the kitchen she had to walk down several long dark hallways to get to the medical supply room, which was a large square room with boxes of various necessities. Walking in the dark of the factory was a lesson in courage all on its own. There were too many threatening blind turns concealing frightening characters, likely to be intoxicated. Suddenly, there were heavy footsteps coming from behind her. She hid herself behind a large group of pipes and willed herself into the wall. The drunken man stumbled passed her and continued on his way. She made it to the supply room but stopped at the door and turned around looking into the darkness. Nothing was there but she could feel eyes on her back. If she went into the room and was cornered inside there would be nowhere to run.

But what difference does it really make anyway? She thought to herself. *If I screamed would anyone come to help me, I doubt it?*

Mrs. O'Reilly opened the door and went into the room. She could find what she needed in the dark having already memorized the layout and planned ahead. Her wits were all she had left. Mrs. O'Reilly knew that someday her mind would fade and that worried her but it also made her want to live life while she still could. Was it wrong that her old soul got a little rush out of living in this danger zone?

After gathering what she needed she turned to go but was immediately startled by the sight of a man standing in the doorway. He stepped into the room and closed the door behind him, flipping on the lone hanging light bulb. The glow revealed the long wolf like face of Mike with a glare of revenge written into his yellow eyes. Mrs. O'Reilly looked for a way out. But saw none. She could plead and promise but she saw no angel that would make a man like Mike change his mind. She decided not to give him the satisfaction.

"Scream if you like," Mike teased.

Mrs. O'Reilly stood proud and brave. She turned her thoughts to the life she had lived and those she loved.

Mike came at her with hands out stretched eager to fulfill his lust for murder.

Smash! The single light was shattered.

A force collided into Mike's face, breaking his nose and opening a flow of blood down his shirt. Mike was in the air now, two powerful hands griped his clothes tight and body slammed him to the ground. A follow up blow to the head rendered him unconscious.

Noland Savage would leave him alive only because his death may cause too many questions.

"It's OK, Mrs. O'Reilly; I'm a friend of Officer Daniel Lane." There was no answer

"Your safe now, no one is going to hurt you. Can you tell me about my kids? Eric and Amy, and my grandson Benjamin, are they here?"

Mrs. O'Reilly tried to compose herself in the darkness. What had happen? She still wasn't sure. Someone else was in the room but how? His voice was kind and he had saved her from Mike.

"My name is Noland Savage. Are my kids being held here?"

"Yes,….. Amy is very nice and thank you," she replied still in shock. "Thank you for coming when you did."

Noland needed clarification. "Are they all alive? Is Gary Holland being held here with them or somewhere else"

Mrs. O'Reilly sat down on a box and took a deep breath.

"OK, I'm Sorry, I just need a moment."

Noland realized she needed time to get her thoughts together. He went to the door and listened for any movement from outside but heard nothing. He popped a glowing stick that gave the room a little light.

"I have seen Amy & Eric." Mrs. O'Reilly tried again. "Amy is well, but Eric was shot in the shoulder and grazed in the back of the head. I have been smuggling in antibiotics to Amy who seems to be doing a great job of caring for him." Mrs. O'Reilly was starting to calm.

"She's an ER doctor and a good one at that." Noland was in deep thought.

"They are allowing me to bring them food and I have been able to distract the guards enough to sneak in a few other things that Amy has requested."

"So Benjamin is not with them?" Noland was reading between the lines.

"No, just the two of them. I'm very sorry to have to tell you this but they said Gary didn't make it out of the woods. He was shot several times and that's all I know." Mrs. O'Reilly could feel his grief.

Noland feared for his long time friend. Gary was a good man. He held on to hope that he may have survived. Being shot is not always a death sentence. Noland thanked God for Eric and Amy being alive, and for Mrs. O'Reilly. He was almost afraid to ask his next question.

"What about Benjamin, was he killed, are they holding him elsewhere?"

Mrs. O'Reilly remembered the hushed conversation she had with Amy. "Amy said they were hiding out at a cabin in the Cascade Mountains. They were suddenly attacked and Benjamin got out and she told him to run. But she doesn't know if he got away or not. If he did get away, they had a cave prepared as a fallback hideout. He would be there."

Noland could hear voices down the hall, they were coming their way.

"Do they have any alcohol in here?" he asked Mrs. O'Reilly.

"Yes, there is a box of imported wines." She pointed.

Noland quickly retrieved a very expensive looking bottle of wine and almost fainted when he saw the brand and year. *What a waste*, was all he could think of as he opened the bottle shielding the sound as best he could. He poured it over the body of Mike and put the bottle in his hand. He helped Mrs. O'Reilly behind some boxes and hid the glow stick. Mike started to wake up just as the door opened and a group of men entered the room. They had flash lights glaring at the fallen man and as Mike awoke with the bottle in hand he was still in fight mode. He came at them with the bottle ready to strike. Without warning two shots rang out. Mike took both of them in the chest and went down, dead on arrival.

"Who the hell is that?" questioned a man in the back of the group, surrounded by guards.

"One of our own, sir, drunk and in some kind of fight from the looks of him," a man said in a very professional tone.

"Get some light in here!" the one in charge ordered.

The room became lighted with a few lanterns and Noland and Mrs. O' O'Reilly prayed not to be seen.

"Damn, that bastard was drinking my best wine."

Why did Noland feel like he knew that voice?

"OK, clear out this room as well, we will need the space. Put up some temporary tent shelters outside to house the supplies. This next shipment of slaves will be the largest ever, even the slave ships from West Africa never trafficked these numbers. This whole operation at the factory needs to be revamped and expanded. If this is any indication of how things are run around here...", he was pointing at Mike's dead body. "...new management is needed!"

"Yes sir!" came a unison of voices.

Thankfully, they all left together, ignoring the dead body of Mike for others to clean up.

After the sound of their footsteps faded away, Mrs. O'Reilly turned to thank Noland Savage for his help but he was already gone, vanished like a ghost.

The international slave auction in Seattle had been more than a success. The world's lust for unshackled satisfaction was growing and the demand was driving prices up. Fredrick Hurst sat at his desk and looked over orders from all over the world, Brazil, China, North Korea, oil rich Middle Eastern nations, Europe, and the US. He had to act now or his competitors would seize these opportunities. His empire was expanding on all sides. He was gobbling up his competition in the United States and buying off others in Mexico and the Far East. He was careful to cooperate with others from a position of strength.

Hurst rested his gaze on an antique set of shackles from the hay days of slavery in America. They sat on his desktop to stir the imagination. The rusted iron was still strong, still stained with the dried blood of a slave. He never wanted it cleaned. They were part of his elaborate collection of authentic memorabilia on slavery. His office was filled with framed documents from the old south along with a stone tablet from ancient Babylon. A leather whip with a handmade wooden handle sat under glass with a written description below. He justified his collection to visitors by proclaiming his commitment to justice for the oppressed and admonishing them that we must never forget the past.

The truth was he believed in slavery like others believed in democracy. Look at what the Pharaohs of Egypt accomplished with slaves. For him it wasn't about race or economic class, it was about trust. He didn't trust others to do what he wanted them to do. So he didn't give them a choice.

The Savage problem was a fly in his ointment. But his reach was growing and with it, his abilities to deal with men like Noland Savage. He had a certain amount of respect for a man of Noland's abilities but Hurst despised his old-fashioned out of date values. He himself had suffered from those ethics. He would not delay fulfilling the world's cry for sex-slaves, worker-slaves, servant-slaves, slaves forced to fight to the death like in the days of Rome, just because of Savage. The money he would acquire from these transactions would fund his next move. Soon he would be out of reach, even for a man like Savage.

Around the United States the word was being put out through various criminal channels. The money to be made was huge. Pimps sat with accountants trying to decide the value of those under their influence. Affiliated crime rings in all major cities gathered in shock over the numbers they were ordered to fill and the amount of money they would make for filling them. Transportation, logistics, communications all had to be taken to the next level. There wouldn't be enough milk cartons to put the missing faces on.

The government had a special unit that was activated for men like Noland Savage and Commander Thomas Troy was the leader of that unit. They were aware of his training, briefed in his tactics, like him, they were men from the varying branches of the Special Operation Forces. They had commandeered the use of the police station's parking lot as a make shift command post. Commander Troy was instructing his team about the man they had been ordered to apprehend.

Chief Hobbs saw himself as a big man. It made him feel even bigger to have one up on these so-called élite soldiers. He knew what they didn't. They were being played, used to bring down one of their own. His men had apprehended Eric and Amy Savage and now held them as leverage against Noland. They had put Noland Savage on the run and would soon find Tiny Tim as well. But to out maneuver and eliminate Noland Savage they needed men like the one's renting his parking lot.

Hobbs walked away from the window overlooking the parking lot and passed Daniel Lane's desk on his way into his own private office. As the door closed Daniel could see a fellow officer sitting there in Hobbs' office. He had seen it all before; the meeting with Hobbs, the promotion, the privileged access. What made men take the easy road that promised so much but in the end delivered so little. Maybe that was it, because it was easy? It was challenging to make it through life the honest way, overcome setbacks, not let bitterness and anger take over, find a way through seemingly impossible odds and not let hope and faith die in the process. And you needed all that just to hold a family together in today's world. Daniel remembered his father.

Chapter 8
Matters of life and death

Gary Holland's wife gave Noland the GPS location he needed. She trusted Noland no matter what the news media was saying. She asked him about Gary. Noland would only say that he was in a very dangerous situation. Until he confirmed his death or survival personally, he could not be sure. He also told her others may come from the U.S. Military seeking information. She understood and burned the paper with the global longitude and latitude numbers. As Noland was leaving she asked him to please bring Gary home to her alive. Noland felt a deep sorrow in his heart but said he would do his best.

Noland discovered the damaged cabin on his second day in the mountains. After carefully examining the evidence he was fairly confident that Benjamin was still alive. While cautiously evading Hobbs' men, he took the time to find and observe Benjamin's sign, the length of his stride and way his prints walked beside Eric's larger print. In his mind's eye, Noland could see the two walking together. He could see that they had been at the cabin for days and Eric was teaching Benjamin how to walk through the woods without leaving a trail and how to set snares. Amy had spent time with Benjamin as well. Noland knew that Amy blamed herself for Benjamin's disappearance and he wondered how she was holding up. There were two large dogs with them and another one that circled the area and watched from a distance. For that reason Noland started calling that third dog by the name, Distant.

He found the cave, but no Benjamin; something had warned the boy away. But he did find two graves. Noland respectfully identified the deceased. One was marked with an AX and the other MvrK. Benjamin had taken the time to lay a circle of stones around the graves with words scratched on them like, strong, friend, courage, and family. Noland was pleased with the thoughtfulness his grandson had put into the burial places and thanked the two animals for whatever friendship they had showed him.

Noland looked at the dark sky in the west and realized a strong summer storm was coming. Benjamin was already doing a good job of concealing his trail but the rain would wash away all sign of him. Noland circled the area in ever widening arches until he found Benjamin's trail again, leading southwest. He was about to head that way but stopped. Something wasn't right. Looking closely at the print he noticed that the depth was wrong. Benjamin walked on his toes, leaving a deeper impression in the front. These prints were deeper in the back. Noland couldn't help but smile; the boy had tied his shoes onto his feet backwards to throw off his pursuers.

Noland had to admit, Benjamin was getting along fairly well on his own. He had to think tactical. He could find the boy or work to distract those who hunted him. In his heart, he just wanted to see him alive. But Noland knew that he himself was the subject of a manhunt that would include the Special Operation Forces. He dare not bring that fight to Benjamin. But if he could get Hobbs' men off his trail long enough, the boy had a chance. On the other hand, there were dangers in these mountains that Benjamin was not prepared to face. There were bear and mountain lions to worry about. Summer would not last forever and it could get cold in the Cascades as early as September. A young boy without proper clothing and shelter could freeze to death at night.

As much as it pained his heart, Noland decided he would catch up to Benjamin later. Timing and strategy told Noland what his next move needed to be. Nothing halted a search for someone faster than finding that someone dead. So he would lead Hobbs' men to the dead body of Tiny Tim.

Hobbs men were tired of living in the forest. They were city boys. They liked things to be over fast not dragged on and on like this. The victory of catching Eric and Amy had worn off. The thrill was gone. The storm had left them wet and miserable. So when Noland gave them a clear trail to follow the next day, they took the bait. It was Benjamin's trail copied to the last detail.

He led them to a high cliff overlooking a rocky area of sharp jagged boulders, one false step and the plunge would be deadly. Looking over the cliff, they would see the lifeless form of a child. They would think Tiny Tim had slipped there in the wet mud and fallen to his death.

Noland looked at the body of the boy and felt true compassion. In a way, this was the boy's revenge against those who sought to use him. This was his way of fighting back. Noland had frozen the body immediately after the rescue in Mexico City. Now he made him look like he had been living in the woods for a long time. The body would thaw in the heat of the day and by the time they found it; it would be the cold dead body of Tiny Tim and their ticket out of the woods.

Hours later the call was made to Chief Hobbs. They had found Tiny Tim and he was already dead. Hobbs called Judge Hurst who asked for verification.

"Check for the birth mark on his lower back." It was confirmed. Tiny Tim was dead.

In a way, they were right. Tiny Tim was dead. But Benjamin was very much alive.

Just miles away from Hobbs' team of searchers,

Benjamin and Timber rested under the branches of a large Douglas Fir Tree. They had spent the night of the storm in its dry under belly. Copying the actions of his mom and dad, he had prepared this place as his fallback hide out just in case the cave was discovered. The branches shed the rain to the outside. In a pocket of dry soft needles Benjamin was almost warm with Timber snuggle up next to him. Timber was hunting now. He would disappear into the forest and return with a rabbit in his mouth. Benjamin was hungry and tried making a small fire with the dry needles of the fir and then feeding the fire slowly with the dry twigs under the tree. He cooked the rabbit meat over the fire. As the smoke rose through the branches it was spread out and left no visible trace as it dissipated in the wind.

The next day Benjamin picked up his bow and arrows. He was getting stronger now. He could pull back the bow and when he released, the arrow would fly a little ways, but not far enough. He was determined to do better. Timber stood guard, watching Benjamin practice. Finally, one arrow barely stuck into the side of a tree. Benjamin was excited.

Noland watched Benjamin through a scope, judging how to approach the child and the formidable looking dog he called, Distant. He decided to make a bow and arrow out of what the forest provided. Noland, dressed in military gear, looked too much like Hobbs' pretenders. Benjamin would run from him and the dog would attack. So Noland hunted, killed a deer and made clothes out of the hide. He exchanged his boots for moccasins and took on a mountain man look that would hopefully disarm Benjamin and cause him to be curious.

Noland set a line of snares that Benjamin was sure to find, ones that were guaranteed to arouse his attention. The boy had a mind that liked to figure things out. Noland would use that. Benjamin came across one of Noland's snares while setting his own. It was designed differently than the traps he was making. He circled the snare inquisitively; wanting to view it from all angles. The knots were different, and the trap was made of something other than rope. He would not disturb it but studied how it was made.

Benjamin decided to follow the strange and unfamiliar trail of whoever made the trap, careful to let Timber know they were to stay quiet and hidden. Noland had made camp not far away and was testing out his new long bow. The deer meat was cooking over his smokeless fire and his shelter was a teepee made of overlapping fir tree branches.

Noland draw back the tension on his bow with powerful arms and shoulders and took aim at the distant target. He knew he was being watched and hoped the show would impress. He released his arrow between breaths and it soared straight and true. A 'THUD' sounded the report as the arrow penetrated the grass filled man and struck the wooden frame holding him upright. The target was made to look like the men Benjamin feared, Hobbs men and the men at the factory. Noland used his own fatigues and boots to achieve the right appearance.

It had just the effect on Benjamin that Noland was looking for. Benjamin hated the men that took away his dad and his mom, took away his life and then, just when he had it back, took it all away again. He was going to stop them. To stop them he needed to be stronger, like this man was strong.

"Teach me." The words were out of his mouth before he could stop them. With his hiding place revealed, Benjamin stood up.

Noland turned slowly to face his grandson not suppressing the intensity of his stare. His silver gray hair was longer now and so was his beard. He could only imagine what he must have looked like dressed in deer skins. If the boy ran, he ran.

But Benjamin did not run. He stepped out of the tree line into the strange man's camp.

"Teach me!" This time his mind joined his heart.

Noland smiled and quoted an old Chinese proverb. "When the student is ready, the teacher will come."

On the other side of the United States in the small town of Zion, Illinois two eighteen year old girls got into a SUV with a couple who had promised them a better future in California. They would never be seen or heard from again.

A group of prostitutes from New Orleans were told they were going to work a major sporting event in Portland, OR. They were loaded on a boxcar train without heat and sped through the country side.

A teenage girl thought she was in love with a boy she met on-line, he was her true soul mate. They had talked on-line for months about everything, he understood her. They were meeting for the first time today at a mall parking lot. She waited and waited, suddenly a van pulled up and a man grabbed her, throwing her in the back. With a knife to her throat he told her not to scream if she wanted to live.

At a large amusement park in Ohio a mom and dad had lost track of their twelve year old boy. They were not all that worried about him, he had wandered off before, but this time would be different.

A father in Dallas, TX was under pressure from his seventeen year old daughter to let her go to a party that all her friends would be at. He had already told her no. But the text messages from her friends kept coming. The movie that they watched as a family that afternoon painted the character of the father as an over protective idiot and the daughter as just wanting to be free from his archaic ways. The father felt guilty as the family laughed at the movie. Was he that idiot? Was he needed? Was he just in the way? He changed his mind and let her go. The party was held a little out of town at a county home. The daughter felt safe because she knew her friends were there. The three punch bowls were the only sources provided to get a drink. One hour later all twenty two teens were on the floor out cold, their bodies loaded carefully into a semi-trailer.

All major news networks reported on the increase in the number of missing persons but the agencies interviewed could not agree on the numbers or the cause. A politician running for office used the up -tic in abductions to attack his rival. Some angry parents filed lawsuits against several theme parks and in response, a law firm purchased air time to offer services to what psychologists had labeled a new victim group. Law enforcement was warned not to over react and reminded to play by the rules and respect the rights of all, even criminals. Some hip movie star proclaimed it all just a 1960's revival of runaways and slammed parents who pushed their kids to that point.

All the while the slave factory in Seattle Washington was filling up with human cargo, so much so that the water works next door had to be converted as well.

Daniel Lane sat wondering how long it would take these idiots to figure out he was stealing from them. He had a boat, ATV, a new gold watch and ordered his lunch delivered by some of the best restaurants in Seattle. He dropped his head one afternoon when he saw a privileged officer help himself to the evidence room. Then it hit him, it was like, their slush fund. If something was missing they would just assume it was one of their own. Maybe it would get their attention if he took it all? But when he was just about to give up on the whole idea Chief Hobbs walked out of his office and made a beeline for his desk. This was it, Daniel thought he was about to get busted.

"Lane, I've got a job for you." Hobbs had something to sell.

Daniel was all ears and ready to pledge allegiance to the crime family.

"Sure would like something that paid better!" Daniel hinted.

Hobbs ignored his comment. "I need an officer to represent the department on T.V. for that City of Seattle reality show. The mayor called and wanted a boy scout, someone who looked clean. That baby face of yours came right to my mind." The other officers were snickering in the background. "I sure can't send any of these animals."

Daniel wanted to pull out his gun and take him down right there.

"Ok, not what I was…." Daniel started to say.

"Thanks, that settles that!" and Hobbs was gone.

He left a business card from Reality Productions on his desk.

Daniel called the number on the card and made an appointment to meet with the producer. They wanted him to do an interview about being a police officer in Seattle. They would follow him around for a week in his patrol car and watch him in action with their camera crew. The timing could not be worse, or was it? If Daniel could get his hands on some real evidence he could give them quite a reality show. Would they go for it? If they didn't, the gig would be up. The evidence had to be convincing and the story a career changer for them to go rouge. He looked at the card again, it read; Reality Productions, producer and reporter Barbara Allan. Daniel looked her up on line. She started out as an investigative journalist and went on to produce reality TV shows. Maybe she missed the good old days. He was about to find out.

The next day he sat in the luxury restaurant at the top of the Seattle Space Needle. Across from him sat the career driven Mrs. Barbra Allen. The whole structure that housed the restaurant was designed to turned very slowly as you ate so that the view outside your window changed to encompass all of metropolitan Seattle and the water of the Puget Sound.

Barbra Allan was polite and professional but she looked at the young officer with some misgivings.

"So, how long have you been on the force?"

"Not that long really, four months now."

She was not happy with that answer. She asked to be excused and went out to call someone. Once she was safely out of ear shot and had the responsible party on the phone she expressed her concerns.

"This is not going to work. I asked for a veteran officer. How am I supposed to make an exciting, in -depth show with the new guy?"

The person on the other end explained that the Mayor's Office and the Chief of Police had approved Officer Lane and that if she had a problem with that she would have to take it up with them.

"Ok, I'll do just that!" Barbra was determined to get a good show out of this deal and Officer Lane just would not do. She called someone else and ordered them to start working on fixing the problem.

She came back to the table and grabbed her purse. "I am so sorry. This is not your fault but I asked for a veteran officer. I wanted to do a story that dug deep into the Seattle crime and justice system. I'm not just interviewing the police, but the courts and legislative branch as well."

Daniel was prepared for this. He dropped a bundle of hundred dollar bills on the table. "Not a problem, but you may as well stay for dinner, I'm buying."

She looked at the large bundle and then again at Daniel Lane.

Daniel pulled out another just for effect and dropped it next to the first.

"It is amazing what the city pays officers these days," he said looking up at her with raised eyebrows.

She sat down and took the first bundle and examined it. Was this some kind of joke? It took her all of two seconds to see the money was real. He had her attention.

"So what is this about?" she asked him. "And before you answer get that money put away before someone gets a picture and we are all over social media."

Daniel put the money away.

"This is about corruption, power, human trafficking, murder, misuse of government funds and a whole lot of other things that would make a great story." Now he was speaking her language.

Her phone rang and she answered, but her mind was absorbing the new information and taking a fresh interest in officer Daniel Lane.

The person who called was letting her know that their contact at the mayor's office texted and apologized for the confusion and would meet with them to work it out.

"That won't be necessary, I've changed my mind, Officer Lane is just the man I need."

Eric Savage had been in and out of consciousness for days. But something was calling him out of the dark pit he had been stuck in. It was time to return to the land of the living. He was needed.

"Eric, wake up!" Amy put the wet cloth on his forehead.

Eric Savage came out of the storm, out of the free fall; he was on the ground again. He was aware of a caring hand. Things slowly came into focus.

"There you are." Amy was beside him with a concerned look in her eyes.

Eric smiled at his wife. How long had he been out?

Where were they? Did he just dream they found Benjamin? He tried to ask a question but his throat was too dry. Amy put a glass of water to his lips and he took a sip.

"Don't try to move just yet, doctor's orders!" Amy gave him a stern look.

"I love you," he said in a weak voice.

"I love you too," she was happy to have him back.

"Benjamin?" he needed to know.

"He got out of the cabin when they attacked. I told him to run. I didn't see him after that. I think he got away."

Then she whispered in his ear, "Dad knows we are here. I got a message to him through a lady here named Mrs. O'Reilly, he knows about Benjamin and the cave."

Eric had so many questions but no energy. "Where are we?"

"We are at the factory, where Benjamin lived for the last five years." Amy couldn't hide her grief.

"Dad knows," Eric repeated. "It won't be long now."

Amy knew exactly what he meant. But Noland had made the right choice to leave them here for now and go after Benjamin. It was the choice she would have wanted him to make.

Suddenly, the door to their cell opened and four men walked in.

"You are being moved. Get up!" they ordered.

Amy pleaded with her eyes. "He is sick, he cannot be moved."

"It was not a request." The man grabbed Amy by the arm.

Eric lunged forward trying to defend his wife but was knocked down easily by one of the men.

"No, don't hurt him, we will go with you!" Amy cried.

"Of-course you will." He was not sympathetic.

They were both blind folded, led through the factory and put into the back of a van. Amy tried to keep her wits about her. She knew from Mrs. O'Reilly they were in old town Seattle. If she could pay close attention maybe she could figure out where they were taking them. But after the first twelve turns she started to lose track. Was it two rights, a left, another right, and then straight for awhile or...? It was no use. They were lost.

Benjamin sat across the camp fire from the strange man with the wild gray hair. He had never seen a man dressed in animal skins before. His arm muscles were hard and defined, his eyes blue and intense. He seemed like a beast of the forest more than a man. But for some reason his dog Timber liked the man and Benjamin trusted his dog.

Their camp was surrounded by tall old growth forest. Ferns grew up and around the base of the trees and soft moss covered the rocks. Little wild flowers decorated the areas between trees, Indian paint brushes, lupine, clover, and blue bells. The smell was intoxicating. Benjamin had never dreamed that such a place existed. There was something healing about the stillness and strength he felt here. In the distance stood the snow capped mountain called Rainier. Benjamin wanted to go there, he felt drawn to the mountain. It called to him deep in his soul.

The older man said little, but was watchful of the boy and moved about the camp with purpose. Sometimes Noland would not move for long periods of time. Benjamin would forget he was there, as he seemed to blend into the forest like a boulder, or a fallen log clothed with ferns and wild mushrooms, until he suddenly moved causing Benjamin to jump in surprise.

Noland made Benjamin a long bow matching his own and took him on a deer hunt. Benjamin proved a patient companion and Noland was able to successfully kill a young buck. He let Benjamin help him skin the animal and instructed him along the way. Benjamin's cheap city clothes were worn and torn and provided little protection for wilderness living. Noland measured his grandson for a new set of buckskins. When he was finished he handed the new outfit to the boy. Benjamin was delighted with the buckskins but hesitated to remove his tattered shirt in front of a stranger. He was aware of the unsightly scars that covered his back and didn't want to be asked embarrassing questions. Noland read his behavior clearly and removed his own shirt revealing a patchwork of scaring greater than the boys.

Benjamin looked at Noland's old wounds and wondered where he had been and what he had been through to get those. He no longer felt embarrassed about his own scars and took off his shirt. Noland saw the boy's back and understood more than most what the boy had endured. The two stood there together looking into each other's soul. There was a deep understanding that passed between them in that moment. Noland decided it was time to talk plainly to the boy.

"Benjamin, there's something I need to tell you. I'm your grandfather, Eric's father. When you were little you would call me papa."

Benjamin did not remember him and felt the loss in his heart.

"I'm sorry I forgot you, do you want me to call you papa?"

"I want to teach you to survive here in the forest. You may need to hide here for awhile. The men who were searching for you think you are dead for now. If they ever realize the truth they'll come looking for you again and you are not strong enough to defend yourself,... not yet. So I think it's best if you learn to live invisible in the forest. You have been a good student of what your father started to teach you. I can teach you more. Are you ready?"

"I'm ready."

The game was similar to the one that he had played with Eric but Noland would hide so well that it was like he could disappear completely until he would startle Benjamin by reaching out from nowhere and touch him. Benjamin liked the games and played to win but when it was his turn to hide Noland would find him easily every time.

"You'll get better with practice Benjamin, never give up!" Noland would encourage him.

Noland was also teaching him about plants and roots that where safe to eat in the forest, adding to what Eric had already taught him. Some could be used for medicines if he got sick. Benjamin learned to be mindful of the wind that would carry his scent to animals, both the ones he wished to hunt and the ones that would hunt for him.

"It's going to get colder soon and a fire will become your best friend. If you lose your matches or they get wet you need to know what to do. It's not easy but you can start a fire using a bow string looped around a stick," Noland explained and showed him how it worked.

The older man made it look easy but no matter how hard he tried, Benjamin could not get the flame to catch. His hands were blistered and bleeding and for the first time Benjamin felt completely defeated. Noland wanted to see how he would handle this setback.

"I'm not as good as you are, I'm just stupid sometimes. I can't do it!" Benjamin felt like Tiny Tim again.

Noland watched his reaction closely and could hear the voice of cruel men beneath the surface of his frustration.

"So they called you stupid?"

Benjamin was angry. "Yes, they said I was slow in the head."

Noland picked up his bow and notched an arrow. He handed it to Benjamin and pointed to the stuffed man target about fifty yards away. "I think I just heard him say it again, something about you being little and helpless, and how your mom and dad didn't love you. But he is a liar Benjamin and someone needs to shut his mouth."

Benjamin stood with the large bow in his hands. It was as tall as he was. He faced the target with new determination. Noland stood behind him and instructed his aim. Benjamin pulled back with all his might, Noland helped a little.

"Don't hold your breath; breath slowly, aim above the target for that black spot on the tree, release on the exhale, pull back just a little more, a little more....now nothing moves but the release."

Benjamin's fingers opened and the tension sent the arrow on its course. It cleared the bow and left the two standing together as if frozen in time. Nothing moved but the wooden arrow with feather fletching through the cool mountain air. The sharp flint arrowhead cut through the space in a long high arch. An eagle cried out from somewhere above. The shaft seemed to pick up speed on the down turn; the target came rushing into focus..."Thud"

Benjamin jump for joy. "I did it. I did it!"

Noland smiled at his grandson.

"Benjamin, the greatest battle is in your mind and your heart," Noland said to him getting on one knee and looking him in the eyes. "Do not let what they did to you or what they said to you stop you from becoming who you really are. I understand you've been hurt and healing takes time. But sometimes you have to move forward wounded and work around the pain."

"I'm going to keep learning papa; I'm going to keep moving forward." Benjamin felt better now.

That night the stars were so bright, Benjamin sat on his

back just looking up at the vast expanse. He felt a peace in his heart that he had never felt before in his life. Grandfather was a hard, strong man but not like the hard men at the factory. He felt love coming out from him even if he didn't say it, he showed it.

"There is a great battle happening Benjamin, between good and evil. Many people no longer believe in real evil. But they just can't seem to keep themselves from it. They call it by a different name but it's as old as sin. When things get difficult or complicated they abandon their values and reject all absolutes. They use half truths to justify living any way they want and hurting anyone they please. I believe God made the universe and everything in it. I believe he talks to us in our hearts and through his creation about what is right and what is wrong."

Benjamin had heard people pray at the factory and remembered how the men mocked them.

"Why doesn't God help the women who are kept in the cages at the factory, why didn't he help me?"

Benjamin did not question from bitterness or anger. He just wanted to understand.

Noland wasn't about to give the politically correct answer or some religious canned philosophy. He gave the answer that rang true in his heart. "For the same reason I didn't come to you, for a time you were lost to me, but not forever. I think the world is lost to God, for a season. It doesn't mean he isn't searching for us the same way I searched for you."

"Isn't God stronger than you?" Benjamin asked

"Yes, but so are the problems he wrestles with."

"Why did the men at the factory want the women?" Benjamin dropped the question.

Noland let out a sigh. Now he was in deep waters.

"That is a good question that deserves a good answer.

Did Eric say anything to you about that?"

"No, but I never asked him."Benjamin looked at Noland expecting an answer.

Noland prayed for wisdom. "Do you see our fire? It's a force of nature and like any force of nature it demands respect. My dad, your great grandfather used to say, *the same fire that warms the house can burn it down.* Most men have a strong desire to be with a woman. Your dad loves Amy and has a strong desire toward her. But just like our fire is surrounded by a circle of stones to keep it from running wild Eric's desires are surrounded by his love and commitment to Amy. Some men have no respect for the forces of nature. They light their whole world on fire with their own stupidity and then blame God."

"I respect fire," Benjamin said not really understanding.

Noland was ready to wrap up the conversation. "Let's get some sleep, tomorrow we're going to try to sneak up on a deer."

"Really, sneak up on a deer?" Benjamin was excited.

"Not to kill, just to see how close to touching one we can get."

Chapter 9
An explosive compassion

For the next week Noland did his best to teach Benjamin what he needed to know to survive on his own. Benjamin was a fast learner with an agile mind. He felt confident that the boy had mastered the basic necessities of survival; water, food, shelter, warmth, and staying hidden from and aware of potential enemies and dangers.

It was time for Noland to ask Benjamin to teach him about the factory and the different players and locations of this crime ring. He had been with them for five years and he knew more than anybody about their set up. Noland suspected that Benjamin could ID the major players behind the slave trade and that was why they had thrown so much effort into killing him and his family. That is also why the Cascade Mountains were the safest place to leave the boy for now.

Rather than hitting Benjamin with a million questions about the factory, Noland made a game out of it for Benjamin just like he had made learning to survive a game. They used sticks, rocks and grass to build a model of the factory. They used ammo to represent the guards and flat stones became the location of trucks. Benjamin started remembering things on his own and talking about them with Noland. All on his own, Benjamin made a road leading from the factory to location B and then two more going to location C and D. Noland asked questions when he felt it was necessary but let things happen as naturally as possible. Benjamin remembered feeding the seagulls at location B and the smell of the Ocean. So they put feathers down there to represent the birds and blue flower peddles for the ocean. He remembered the sound of a train at Location C and recalled playing on the tracks. Benjamin laid two lines of straight sticks to be the tracks. Location D was out farther than the others, Benjamin told of seeing a small airplane parked in a garage. They always stopped for gas at the same station on the way there. It was at that gas station that Benjamin found the courage to run away. Noland was making a map in his mind taking in every detail. Noland thought he was done and started writing it all down on paper.

Without saying a word Benjamin started building another location not connected to the others by any roads. Unlike the other buildings he used larger stones to build it up. He surrounded it with a forest of sticks and farther out a stone wall with a gate that opened and closed. He drew what looked like medieval shields in the dirt. When asked, he said it was the evil castle with the Iron Gate. A bearded dragon who dressed in a long black robe lived in the castle, he fed off the blood of slaves.

Noland wanted to know more about this dragon. He had a feeling they would meet someday soon.

Barbra Allen was on board if Daniel could produce some real evidence of corruption but she would not risk anything until then. She was one tuff cookie. If he didn't provide anything in the next three days she would turn him in herself. For all she knew he was the criminal. Bringing up the name of Noland Savage did not help one bit.

"You mean the crazy Navy Seal that shot up the airport? Don't tell me you're with him!"

Daniel told her the whole bazaar tale. She listened with interest and considered what a story like this would do for her career. She also considered what would happen if Daniel turned out to be a right wing nut. So he had three days.

Daniel was under the gun and needed to make something happen.

He came to work that next day determined to get into Hobbs' office. He needed a distraction or an excuse or both. He asked Chief Hobbs if he could snap a few pictures of him for the TV show, something official looking in his office in front of his wall of plaques. Hobbs liked attention if it made him look good. Once in the office, Daniel asked Hobbs if he wouldn't mind changing into his dress uniform reserved for special occasions. Hobbs had his own private bathroom in his office. As soon as the door to the bathroom closed Daniel started snooping around snapping pictures of everything. He pulled out files, open desk draws and prayed that Hobbs took his time. Some of the files were locked but Hobbs had left his keys on his desk. Daniel was trying keys. He found the right key and opened the locked files, Jackpot! But he was out of time, Hobbs was opening the door.

"Don't forget to wear the matching blue cap."

Hobbs swore and the door closed.

Daniel had time for one picture of the forbidden files and then rushed to close and lock and return everything just the way he found it.

Hobbs was feeling inconvenienced by now. Daniel took the pictures of Chief Hobbs and thanked him, assuring him he would look great for the show.

Daniel e-mailed the pictures to Barbra Allen who responded back by asking to see the file marked financial fronts in the last picture from the locked file. Daniel wanted to scream. He didn't have the file, just the picture. If she wanted that file she would have to help him. Hobbs would not pose for another picture without better bait. He told her what he needed.

Twenty minutes later he got the e-mail, it was one of his pictures of Chief Hobbs looking big and buff on the front cover of a prominent Seattle magazine. It came with a request for a few more pictures but this time with his gun drawn. Daniel simply forwarded that e-mail to Hobbs who was still in his office. Within minutes Hobbs was at his desk. He had printed the picture out on photo quality paper and was showing it off around the office.

"Lane you must have missed your calling as a photographer." Pointing at his picture he said, "That is one good looking guy."

"The producer said that they wanted a few more pictures," Daniel suggested.

"Yes, I know, I got the e-mail." He was already walking to his office. "Well, come on let's do this thing."

Daniel spent the next hour getting pictures of Chief Hobbs, first in his dress uniform and then in his normal working uniform. Hobbs opened his gun safe and was having a time posing with his weapons.

Every time the bathroom door closed Daniel went to work getting the whole damming file photographed and even some others that looked interesting.

"So when will this go to print?" Hobbs asked as Daniel walked out of his office with his camera.

"Well, the prison copies are always a few months behind." Daniel couldn't resist but said it too low to be heard.

"What was that?"

"The person who chooses the cover page is a few months behind."Daniel corrected

"Well, tell'm to send me some extra copies."

"Ok, will do." Daniel was smiling as he sat at his computer forwarding all the pictures to Barbra Allen.

One file caught his eye because it had his father's name in it. Daniel held his breath. Did he really want to know? Was his father a part of the corruption or the man of principle he had always believed him to be. The file didn't tell him much, just one name among many on a list. Daniel did not forward that file to Barbra Allen. He wanted to look into it himself or was he just hiding from the truth.

Mrs. O'Reilly was doing her best to keep up with the changes at the factory. It was overflowing with people now, more and more slaves were crammed into the cells. Greed turned a blind eye to their deplorable conditions. The old order of things, as bad as they were, had been replaced with an even harsher code of conduct. There were no more special meals or bribing the guards. She could no longer risk going out every night to feed the prisoners. The kitchen was a machine to be run and although she was placed in charge and given more help, she felt her ability to make any real difference was fading. Thank God she still had Abigail. They had taken Eric and Amy away weeks ago. It was time for her to leave and take as many with her as she could.

She had not planned on leaving at the beginning, but now she had Abigail. Of course, wanting to leave and leaving were two different things. When they emptied the old supply room they discovered the small opening in the bricks that Noland had used. They assumed it was one of their own men stealing supplies and sealed it up. So that exit was no longer an option. She would have to find another way. But things were so controlled now she could not think of how.

"You knew this was a one way ticket went you signed on," she said to herself. But now that Abigail had opened up to her, she had to escape to save her.

It was at night that Abigail started to talk to Mrs. O'Reilly.

"Mrs. O'Reilly," Abigail asked, "Is three thousand dollars a lot of money?"

"Why do you ask, honey?"

"Because that's how much they sold me for, three

thousand dollars. The man said I wasn't worth a penny more." Abigail wondered if the other kids sold for more than her because her hair was red.

"You are worth more than all the money in the world Abigail." Mrs. O'Reilly tried to console her.

"But my hair is so red and I'm so skinny and ugly." Abigail started to cry.

"You are not ugly Abigail, my hair was every bit as red as yours at your age. You are going to grow up into a beautiful woman someday and thank God for your red hair and Irish Heritage."

The next day Mrs. O'Reilly was passing by a long line of teenage girls held in dog crates; they were all crying their eyes out and pleading for her help. She was still determined to do what she could when she could. It would be so easy for her to just plug her ears in a place such as this, overwhelmed and exhausted. She looked around and saw that there were no guards watching her at the moment so she kneeled down and spoke to one of the girls.

"Where are you from?" It would be an awkward conversion no matter how she started it.

This girl was young and beautiful and in this place that was a bad thing.

"Dallas, Texas.....my name is Brittney Summers. Where are we?"

"You are in Seattle, Washington in an abandon water heater factory. My husband and I lived about a block from here," She pointed east where her house would be. "but now I'm stuck here just like you."

"Can you help me?" The girl was so afraid.

"I will do whatever I can, but right now that isn't much." Mrs. O'Reilly reached through the small openings of the wire dog crate and wrapped the girl's fingers in her own.

The girl wanted someone to talk to. "You know my dad told me not to go to that party. But I just made him feel like dirt until I got my way. My friends are here somewhere too. I think they drugged us all with something. I don't remember anything after feeling really light headed and sitting down on the grass. I tried to tell someone to call my parents but they were all sick too. I woke up in this wire crate."

Mrs. O'Reilly could feel her guilt.

"This is not your fault. Kids make mistakes, for sure, but when others take advantage like this….don't show them how afraid you are, they like that, try to be brave."

The lock on the crate was a key lock and Mrs. O'Reilly gave it a pull to no avail. She could pick the lock but what good would that do? There were guards everywhere.

"I have to go now but I'll be back if I can." Mrs. O'Reilly felt so angry, so ready to do something, anything. In that moment she wished she was strong and dangerous like Noland Savage.

She walked back to the busy kitchen where several workers were cooking up the evening meals. All the gas stove tops were ignited on the commercial sized ovens.

Natural Gas can be a dangerous thing, she thought to herself.

If she filled the kitchen with it, the explosion would probably blow an opening clear through the roof of the factory. If there was a way to save the innocent and light the rest of these perverts on fire, she would do it. So there it was, the beginnings of a plan. Something about Abigail lamenting about her sales price and seeing that other poor girl in a dog crate stirred it up. She was going to blow this hell hole back to hell.

Judge Fredrick Hurst had two appointments on his schedule for that afternoon. Both were made possible by the successful rise of his illegal operations around the globe. The money was flowing in and he was in a spending mood.

His first appointment was with Ivan Zanderwin. After ten months of negotiations Hurst had finally agreed to his outrageous price. He was notorious around the world as the man that never failed to deliver, weather it was an assassination or a government takeover or protection from a rival. His team could hold their own against the best and brightest. He would deal with the Noland Savage problem and a few other competitors Hurst was now ready to move in on.

His second appointment was with a local African American pastor, who was also somewhat of an historian. Hurst was purchasing an artifact from him that would be the crown of his American slavery collection. It was the actual sales receipt from a shipment of slaves purchased in 1807. What made it so valuable was the signature on the receipt, the infamous Mr. William Lynch. He is why we use the term lynch mob when referring to an angry mob bent on hanging someone. He was known for being one of the cruelest slave owners of his time. Hurst wanted his signature and was willing to pay to get it.

Pastor Marcus Johnson stopped his car at the large iron gate leading to the estate of Judge Fredrick Hurst. The cameras and the security guard came as no surprise. Judge Hurst had purposely circulated the stories of death threats on judges in the Seattle area to justify his security needs and raise sympathy for his reclusive nature.

Pastor Johnson was there because he needed to raise funds for his outreach center. He had prayed hard and long about selling this family heirloom. He did not part with it lightly. However, one hundred and fifty thousand dollars would feed a lot of hungry homeless and provide the funds to expand his dream to start a job placement program.

He was waved through security and drove down the long

tree lined driveway leading to the old mansion. The stone building was constructed like an English estate. It looked like a scene out of Pride and Prejudice. The grounds were beautifully cared for and adorned with large water fountains. A man dressed in a three piece suit was there to meet him at the decorative entrance. Another man took the keys to his car and parked it for him. He was escorted through the double entrance doors into a large hall with expensive art and elaborate crystal chandelier hanging from the lofty ceiling. To the right and through another set of double doors he finally arrived at a room intended to receive guests and was left there to wait. A maid was cleaning the room when he came in. She turned to look at him as she left and his mind had a flash back. He called after her but she did not turn to face him until he said her name, "Yalina Volkov?"

Yalina turned to face the tall African American Pastor. She was frightened that he recognized her.

Pastor Johnson was very surprised to find her here. "I know your husband, Leonid; he is looking for you and Anyah. He has shown me many pictures of you both." Something wasn't right; Marcus could see the fear in her eyes.

"I am not Yalina," she said in a strong Russian accent. "We Russian women all look the same to you Americans." Her English was better than Leonids but she was a bad liar.

Pastor Johnson was accustomed to not being trusted by the very people he was trying to help.

"I'm sorry ma'am, my mistake, but could you please bring me a glass of ice water and a paper napkin to wipe my sweaty forehead. By the way, could you write God bless America on my napkin in Russian. I would really like that. Thank you, ma'am." She gave him a questioning look as she went on her way not acknowledging his request.

Pastor Marcus Johnson was thrown a little off balance by seeing Yalina. It was clear that she did not want to be found.

But why, Leonid did not seem like an abusive man? Was she being held here against her will? That seemed foolish considering he was in the home of an outspoken advocate of civil rights, someone who championed education on the evils of oppression.

While he was still considering this, Judge Hurst entered the room, "Thank you for coming to meet with me Pastor Johnson. I have been looking forward to this." His hand was extended and Pastor Johnson had no choice but to respond in kind. He reminded himself that he was a guest in this man's home and it would be extremely inappropriate to question him on the employment arrangements he had with his help.

"Thank you for inviting me and your generous offer, you have a beautiful home."

Judge Hurst gestured them over to an empty desktop, "I am a history enthusiast and what you have is rare and amazing."

Pastor Johnson opened the specially designed tube that housed the document. He spread it out on the desk using approved weights to hold it in place, ones that would not damage the priceless receipt.

Judge Hurst produced a magnifying eye piece to examine the document.

"With your permission?" he asked.

"Yes, of course," Johnson replied.

Judge Hurst looked the document over taking his time on the signature of William Lynch.

"Amazing...simply amazing!" he was genuinely thrilled. "It was like he signed it yesterday!" he said almost too excited.

Pastor Johnson did not like the feeling he got from Judge Hurst. To him the document was a sobering thing.

"Thank God this kind of thing is not happening today,"

Johnson stated.

Hurst took his gaze off of the document and looked at Johnson. For just a moment Johnson thought he saw a wicked smile in his eyes but then it was gone.

"Thank God indeed!" he replied, "I understand you run a little outreach church in old town Seattle."

"I do."

"I would like to make a contribution to your work Pastor, outside of the payment for the document. We need people like you in our city. You can make a difference in the lives of people, help keep them out of trouble and out of my courtroom." He said in a flattering voice.

He open the desk drawer and retrieved a checkbook.

"First, for the amount we agreed on for the document…" He had that check already prepared.

"…and also a little something just for your charity work." He wrote out the check with sweeping strokes and handed it to Pastor Johnson with a smile.

Pastor Johnson looked at the check and almost fainted. Why did he feel so bad about this guy? The contribution was generous but the feeling of betrayal would not leave his gut. He felt like he was selling out, but why? He just stood there with his mouth open.

At that very moment the maid from before walked into the room holding two glasses of ice water.

Hurst was surprised and about to tell her to leave but Johnson reached for a glass.

"Thank you, ma'am," Johnson said and noting the awkward moment explained to the judge, " I saw her in the hall when I came in and asked her to please bring me some water." Johnson also took the napkin that she handed him and wiped his forehead.

The judge looked at the two suspiciously and rejected her

offer of water. She bowed her head and left without a word.

"I am a very powerful man, Pastor Johnson," the judge suddenly said out of nowhere.

Now Johnson's forehead really was sweating. Where was he going with this?

"A man with my connections could help you." Hurst decided to take the edge off.

Or crush me like a bug! Johnson thought to himself

"You have already helped me more then you know." Johnson lifted the checks up smiling.

Johnson did his best to keep his real feelings hidden as he discreetly stashed the napkin into his pocket.

The rest of the meeting was over fast. Marcus Johnson was driving himself out of the iron gate on his way home before he could really digest the whole strange encounter. He pulled over at a gas station and took the napkin out of his pocket. The words were in Russian and for all he knew said God bless America just like he requested. He would have to show it to Leonid to get a translation.

Barbra Allen agreed to meet Daniel Lane with a camera crew. They parked the satellite equipped news van behind Mrs. O'Reilly house and came through the back door. Daniel had not seen Mrs. O'Reilly in a long while but her house had the perfect view of the factory. Knowing Mrs. O'Reilly, she would not mind them using her house as a base. They set the cameras up in her living room to film the front gate of the abandoned looking complex. The trucks started coming and going just after sunset. Barbra Allen was not satisfied with what they were getting on film. She wanted something more exciting. This was her chance, her story.

"Do you want the world to know the truth about what is going on here?" she asked Daniel Lane in a challenging voice.

"Yes, of-course, that's why we're here," Daniel replied.

"People are going to see these trucks coming and going and think this is Willy Wonka's Chocolate Factory." Barbra had an idea brewing. "Evidence is one thing but nothing moves the wheels of justice like National Live Breaking News! We need to stop one of those trucks and see if they have a person being held against their will in there, otherwise the media isn't going to bite."

She was right, but how would they get it done. They couldn't call the police and the men driving these trucks were sure to be armed and dangerous.

Daniel shrugged his shoulders. "What we need is an army!"

From the attic of the home came a voice that made them all jump. The pull down stairs opened and Noland Savage dropped from the opening. "I have an army hunting me now. Let's put them to work."

Barbra and her crew were drawn to Noland Savage like bees to honey. But he would have none of it.

"First we bring the hammer down on this operation and get my kids back. Then I promise you exclusive rights to the first interviews. I'm sure I can speak for the rest of my family, you'll get your story."

"So what's the plan?" Daniel Lane was ready to rock and roll.

Noland had been listening in on their conversations for the last hour assessing Barbra and her crew, now he looked around the room at the resources at his disposal. "We'll need to do some fancy film editing." He looked to Barbra for that and then turned to one of the camera guys. "I heard you bragging about drag racing on the weekends, are you ready to show the world what you can do?" A plan was forming in his mind. "Daniel, do you have a spiked roadblock strip handy?"

Pastor Johnson showed the napkin to Leonid. Leonid recognized his wife's handwriting before he even started reading the words in Russian.

"Where? where you get this!" he asked in desperation.

"What does it say?" questioned Johnson, "In English."

"She says, they kill me if she talks." The Russian was angry now. He was ready to fight.

"We have to go to the police with this. The man who has her is a judge." Johnson said remembering the judge's words about being a powerful man.

"No police, in Russia we understand this. In America you trust too much!"

Pastor Johnson considered what he was saying. If the judge was not what he seemed to be then maybe he should listen to the Russian.

Mrs. O'Reilly found a safe place on the opposite side of the factory to hide Abigail. If anything ever happened to that little girl she would never forgive herself. Yet time was running out for so many others. The flow of human cargo was moving fast and it was time to blow a hole in this operation. She made it to the kitchen in the middle of the night and opened the natural gas values on all the large commercial ovens and removed all the shutoff knobs. Using wet towels she sealed the openings under the doorways and duck taped all of the air vents closed. She didn't want anyone smelling the fumes until it was too late. She locked all the doors from the outside using her lock picking tools and walked away. She had a lighter with her, it was only a matter of time now. The gas would first fill the kitchen and then slowly fill the hallways around. She had a lot to do and the clock was ticking.

The commander of the Special Forces unit, Thomas Troy, was awake and dressed in less than five minutes. Noland Savage had been spotted and teams were in pursuit.

"Do we have choppers in the air?" he asked strapping on his gun.

"Yes sir!"

"Where is he now?"

"He is in a news van sir and may have hostages."

Another man rushed into the room and grabbed the remote for the T.V. "Savage is not just in a news van, he is on the news, live!"

Everyone stopped as the live picture of Noland came over the TV screen. Barbra Allen was there with a microphone interviewing him from the passenger's seat as he raced thought town. The view changed to the pursuing vehicles hot on their trail and then back to Savage.

The commander quickly accessed the situation, "Tell our men to hold their fire."

"This is investigative reporter Barbra Allen with the fugitive and Navy Seal, Noland Savage! I'm reporting live from Seattle where thousands of Americans are being held against their will as human Cargo…."

The commander smiled. He had known Savage by reputation mostly, having only met the man once or twice over the years. Still, he had respected him and was hoping something like this would come to light. For now he had a job to do. He also had the authority to adapt to what the situation demanded. It was obvious to him that Savage wanted to be found and was leading them to where the real answers could be uncovered. He would play along. He wanted to find those responsible for trying to use his team against one of their own and make them pay.

Officer Daniel Lane placed the spiked strip across the road leading to the factory gate; it was almost invisible on the dimly lit street. The front tires blew out on the first truck that ran it over, causing the driver to lose control and hit a fire hydrant at the entrance, blocking the way. The truck loads of human cargo brought in from across the country started piling up at the entrance of the factory. Daniel was at the scene in seconds in his police car. The sudden appearance of a uniformed officer did not worry the drivers as much as the T.V. Camera crew that arrived out of nowhere.

Daniel walked up to the first driver who was not sure what had happened or what to do about the water spraying from the hydrant.

"You spread the word to the other drivers to stay put, keep the cargo in place. We don't need to make a scene here. I've already called Hobbs," Daniel said, "I gotta get the news media out of here, discreetly."

The man did as he was told.

Troy's men converged in multiple vehicles behind the speeding news van. It went airborne at the top of a hill, landed hard and bottomed out, sending red, yellow and white sparks flying. Another team was in pursuit from the air, spot lighting the news van from a helicopter above. All major networks started broadcasting the images now, Saturday late night shows were interrupted. It was all over social media, the mayor of Seattle was out of bed taking calls.

The news van came screaming over the horizon, speeding passed Pastor Marcus Johnson and Leonid, who were outside repairing some night vandalism from a local gang. The military vehicles appeared next, racing passed with choppers overhead. The two men ran into the church and turned on the news.

The news van zoomed past Mrs. O'Reilly's house and into the traffic jam of trucks at the entrance of the factory. The pileup blocked their path and the van braked just in time leaving two long sizzling skid marks on the road. It leaned forward on its front suspension before finally coming to a rebounding stop. It was instantly surrounded by the pursuing vehicles of the Special Forces. The whole area was also being converged on by a second wider circle of units. It was clear that no one was going anywhere.

Daniel suddenly took down the first driver, handcuffing him on the ground.

The man was indignant. "What are you doing man?"

"Getting my last Boy Scout badge, it requires me to take down a criminal operation."

Leaving him there, he turned his gun on the driver of the next truck.

The driver of the news van stepped slowly out of the driver's seat with his hands up. To everyone's surprise, it was not Noland Savage. The van was searched but there was no sign of Savage.

Daniel opened the back of the first covered factory truck. It was too dark inside to see anything at first but after flipping on his flashlight and pointing the aluminous beam of light, he stood there in shock, even though he knew what to expect. They were so young, little girls and boys chained together by their necks. They were all still wearing whatever they had on when they were abducted, superhero pajamas, Disney World t-shirts, play clothes, little cute dresses, and iron metal rings clamped around their feet. They were wide eyed and afraid to come to him at first. Slowly he persuaded them over and started helping them down and out of the truck into the view of the cameras, and the men and women of the Special Forces.

Some of the drivers saw what was happening and tried to make a run for it. They were quickly apprehended. Most could see the writing on the wall and just came out of their trucks with their hands in the air.

The line of trucks were being opened now, one after the other. It was a scene that would haunt the minds of all who were there for the rest of their lives. They were your neighbors, your friends, the kids who play in the park down the street. They were the forgotten ones. The street filled with them, the sound of their chains, the smell of their fear and the look in their eye.

America breathed in a collective gasp of shock.

Thanks to some fancy film editing Noland had long ago made his way into the factory. He was looking for Eric and Amy but was not having any luck finding them. With everyone distracted by the activity at the front gate he was able to make his way through the factory fairly easy. What was that smell?

Mrs. O'Reilly had successfully drugged the night guard's coffee and held the keys she needed in her hands. Picking the locks would have taken too long. She went down the long line of cages and larger holding pins, unlocking them and directing people away from the gas leak. A young lady offered to assist and she gave the job over to her. Others stepped up as well, helping the younger and weak ones. Mrs. O'Reilly urged them to run to the far outside walls and rooms, away from the center of the building.

Suddenly, a group of armed men were coming down the hall in their direction. They saw the flood of prisoners running free and shouted, "STOP!"

Mrs. O'Reilly lit the flame of her lighter and tossed it to the ground in their direction. The floor ignited in blue flame and the wave of heat rushed toward the thugs. They ran from the rising tide of hell fire, toward the gas filled kitchen.

KAAAABOOOM!!!!! The ground shook for three blocks in every direction with the explosion. A fireball shot into the night sky over the factory lighting up old town.

Every person eating at the Space Needle stopped and ran for the windows. The yellow, red and orange fire ball reflected in the waters of the Puget Sound, and off the sails of a hundred docked boats.

Noland was thrown back by the explosion. For a moment everything went silent, falling walls and flying debris were all around him.

Everyone at the front gate jumped at the deafening sound when it hit and turned to see the fireball. One camera crew caught it on film by accident. Barbra Allen thanked her lucky stars.

Mrs. O'Reilly made it to the relative safety of an outer room but fell to the ground with others when the blast reached them. She had one thought on her mind, Abigail. She forced herself off the ground and through the rubble. It was hard to see anything in the darkness and dust. Walls were half down, lights were flickering on and off, water and flame became strangely mixed dangers. She slowly made her way over, around, and through the maze before her. She needed Abigail to be alive, the explosion was larger than she had anticipated. What had she done?

When she finally made it to the closet hiding place where she had left Abigail, she was relieved to see that it was still standing. Mrs. O'Reilly prayed to the good Lord as she opened the door. Abigail sprang into her arms and would not let go for a long time.

"Can we go home now?" it was Abigail's only question.

"We are not out of danger yet, sweetie," Mrs. O'Reilly said.

The voice that followed was low and threatening.

"Noooo,.... you are NOT out of danger yet, sweetie." A group of bleeding vile men emerged from the surrounding rubble and recognized her and knew this must be all her doing.

"Gas from the kitchen was a nice move old lady." One man with smoking hair and burnt clothing commented as he pulled out a long knife.

Mrs. O'Reilly put Abigail behind her and made two fists with her old hands.

"I'm an old stubborn Irish woman and you may kill me but I'll go down fighting."

The lead man with the knife was the first to move but just as he did the flickering lights went completely dark.

There was the sound of impacting fists and breaking bones.

Flickering lights again illuminated the scene. Mrs. O'Reilly stood over the groaning broken body of the man triumphed, her two hands still balled into fists looking at the rest of them with a challenge in her eye.

Three rushed forward together this time. Again the darkness struck, she was not human, she was a beast, an avenging angel who had come to torment them. It seemed to them that she came at them from all sides, like she was one with the darkness.

A circle of light came from the chopper this time spotlighting Mrs. O'Reilly who stood over the four destroyed men on the ground all around her. The wind from the blades blew her kitchen apron up into the air behind her. To Abigail she looked like a superhero.

The last of the men hesitated, believing what they had not seen, their imaginations playing tricks on them. She suddenly looked powerful, invincible, the holder of some secret strength. They all turned and ran from her, chased by their own fears and fantasies.

Mrs. O'Reilly busted out laughing. "You can come out now, Mr. Savage. I saw you hiding there the whole time but didn't want to give you away."

Noland Savaged stepped out from his hiding place and thanked God for night vision tech and a good iron pipe.

Chapter 10
The follow through

"Please tell me that Amy and Eric were not in there?"
Savage asked as he pointed into the massive crater at the
center of the factory.

"No, no, no, Mr. Savage they were moved weeks ago,"
Mrs. O'Reilly said as if explaining herself. "But I did not
intend for the explosion to be so sizeable."

Noland was smiling. "You did this?" He was impressed.

"I'm afraid so," she replied.

The crater was still growing around its edges, feeding
upon the crumbling brick work of the factory. Unexpectedly
the center of the crater gave way, opening up a sink hole into
the ground, a black abyss swallowing up everything in an
ever widening circle. One villain who thought he had escaped
judgment was pulled into the hole by the waves of rubble.

Mrs. O'Reilly shrugged her shoulders. That man should
have changed his ways before it was too late.

Noland scrambled to help Mrs. O'Reilly and Abigail get
away from the sinkhole and out of the crumbling building to
safety.

Outside and around the factory Special Forces were
apprehending the filthy inhuman staff of what the news
media was already calling the largest slavery operation on
American soil in the last 100 years. The sheer force of the
explosion and the intimating presence of the American
Military caused most of the armed factory guards to simply

surrender. Others tried hiding among the prisoners but where easily spotted. A few managed to escape to the water company next door, before it too was raided and subdued.

Noland, Mrs. O'Reilly and Abigail found their way through the mess and out the front gate. Members of the Special Forces unit assembled for the purpose of capturing Savage had already received revised orders from Commander Troy and instead of detaining him, saluted him as he passed.

Noland leaned over and whispered in Mrs. O'Reilly's ear, "Funny thing is, they all think I blew up the building."

"I won't tell if you won't tell." She was serious.

Commander Thomas Troy spotted Savage.

"Noland." He held out his hand which Savage took. "It's been a long time."

"You are looking fit for a old man," Noland joked.

"I can still have you arrested," Troy was only half serous.

"I still have to find my kids commander." Noland pulled out a map with the other possible locations of the operation. "and I have information that will help you nab the rest of these…," he held his tongue in front of Abigail.

"Barbarians" Mrs. O'Reilly injected.

When the news broke, Chief Hobbs was sitting in a club bragging about some magazine wanting his mug on their front cover to whoever would listen. At first, when it was just Savage being pursued, he was thrilled. His mood grew somber as he realized where Savage was leading them. Then, as the truck loads of child slaves were unloaded and many angry patrons seated close to him called for the public execution of those involved, he quietly slipped away. He made one phone call to the necessary pilot, dropped his cell phone in the gutter and headed for the police station for a quick in and out the back door. Most of the officers would be in action at the explosion site along with other first responders, so it would be fairly empty. The other officers involved were on their own now. After picking up a few necessary items at the office, he was headed for the privet jet and mountain of cash at location D.

Hobbs was trying to be as calm and casual about it as possible as he walked into the station through the backdoor. He made a beeline for his office and after punching in the code, opened the door. The fist came at him so fast and hard he had no time to respond. He stumbled backwards trying to gather himself.

Daniel Lane stepped out of his office. "That shiner will not look good on your next picture."

Hobbs was about to go for his gun but Daniel tackled him, pushing him back into the desks of the open office area. He knocked his sidearm to the floor but in the process opened himself up for Hobbs to land a solid right cross. The few officers and staff who were there expected Daniel to go down hard. Hobbs was the bigger man and had made an image of himself as a fighter. No one had ever seen him in a real fight but believed what he advertized. Daniel never did buy into Hobbs tuff guy façade. Maybe he just didn't know he was supposed to go down or maybe he was just angry. But he came back swinging and landed a few good ones all over Hobbs face. Other officers were uncertain of how to respond to the fight until the name and picture of Chief Hobbs came over the large screen TV mounted on the wall. Hobbs and Daniel even took a brief pause to take it in.

"Seattle's own Chief of Police has been named as the mastermind behind the operation at the factory, water works and other locations in the greater Seattle area." Barbra Allen reported. And there was the picture of Hobbs holding his favored gun, complements of Daniel Lane.

Hobbs lunged at Daniel in a fit of rage. He was a strong

man and now he was blind with vengeance. Daniel was in trouble as Hobbs grabbed hold of him and threw him across the room. Daniel hit the wall hard and went down.

Chief Hobbs glared around the room at the questioning faces. Who were they to judge him? He stepped into his office but was tackled from behind and pushed into the outside window. His head was slammed into the glass causing it to crack and cut into his forehead. Blood flowed down his face. It was Officer Daniel Lane again.

Daniel jumped onto his back and got the big man in a chock hold. Hobbs backed up fast and slammed lane into some Cabinets. Daniel tightened his hold around Hobbs neck cutting off his supply of air. Without warning, a blow came from behind to Daniel's head and his world went dark.

Assistant Chief Walker stood over Daniel with his gun drawn. He had pistol whipped him.

Hobbs was gasping for air, Daniel almost had him, and if not for Walker it would have been over right then.

"I hope you weren't planning on going somewhere without me?" Walker questioned Hobbs with his gun still in his hand.

Hobbs was still looking at Daniel out cold on the floor with hate in his eyes.

Walker couldn't help but say what he was thinking, "Daniel Lane is a lot like his father." There was an accusing tune in his voice.

"He hits harder than his old man." Hobbs put his hand over his right eye. He wanted to kill Daniel like he had helped kill his father but the clock was ticking and he needed to move now.

"Guard the door while I grab what we need, we'll be airborne within the hour." Hobbs watched to see if he turned or kept the gun on him. Walker thought about it for a second but then turned to guard the door.

Hobbs was quick to gather what he needed and step over the body of Daniel on his way out.

"We'll take one of the choppers to location D and the plane from there," was all Hobbs said to Walker.

Fredrick Hurst sat comfortably in his estate and watched the news with interest while drinking his favored wine. He made no calls and had no plans of running away. He had prepared well for this day and would have a new site, larger and better staffed than the factory, up and running in no time. Hobbs would take the fall for him and that was always the plan. There would be nothing connecting him to the human trafficking operation, at least nothing that would hold up in a court of law, he had made sure of that. With Tiny Tim dead there would be no eye witnesses willing to testify. Noland Savage was not invincible. There were other men in the world with similar proficiencies and now he had hired just such a man.

Standing in the same room as the judge, but a universe of black operations apart, was Ivan Zanderwin. He was looking out a window at the grounds where his men lurked unseen. Ivan was two hundred and twenty pounds of TNT on a hair pin trigger. He had jet black hair and a chiseled hawkish look to his face. His hands were large and backed up by powerful arms and shoulders. Although he was proficient with all modern and historical weapons he was a master swordsman. Killing was no longer a thrill for him if it could not be done his way, a dual with swords is what got his blood flowing.

That is partially why Ivan was pleased to except this mission, not just because the pay was first-class, and he was expensive even to the wealthy, but because Noland Savage would be a respectable kill to bag. There were few men in the world that lived to the age of Noland and himself in their risky occupations. Ivan Zanderwin saw Noland Savage as the old sage buck in the woods with the ultimate trophy rack, and he was a hunter bored with lesser game.

In the far corner of the oversized office was something a little out of place even among Hurst's unusual collectables. It was a very decorative casket complete with an ornate cover and a set of golden candle sticks to each side. There were bouquets of beautiful flowers set about and a rug on the floor leading to a mourners' bench, a place to kneel and cry for the dead. The casket was not full sized but rather looked custom built for a child. It was closed, for by now the body was decaying even with embalming, but displayed proudly atop was a framed picture of Benjamin Noland Savage.

"I think we have kept our guests waiting long enough," Hurst spoke to the guard at the door.

The guard opened the door and Eric and Amy Savage were escorted in by their three handlers. They had been very well cared for after leaving the factory and as a result Eric was recovering. Amy had been given everything she requested to aid him. They were kept under constant guard but stayed in an extravagant room and were fed like kings. But whoever their host may be, he was no friend. Eric and Amy both realized that their first-class treatment was no sign of compassion.

Fredrick Hurst grinned in welcome as they stepped into the room. "Welcome Savage family, have you enjoyed your stay with us so far?"

Ivan Zanderwin had his mind elsewhere's up to this point but at the name of Savage he turned and observed Eric. *So this is the son*, he thought to himself. The judge had purposely kept this meeting as a surprise to Ivan. He liked the feeling of control. He was moving his chess pieces across the game board just where he needed them. He did not just want to win; he wanted it to be entertaining.

Eric and Amy made no reply but looked about the room and at the round bearded face of Judge Fredrick Hurst. It was Amy who spotted the small casket first. She did not move.

She did not cry out. She waited for Eric to see what she was seeing. Without asking for permission the two walked across the room to the casket area. The judge motioned for the guards to let them go. If not for the circumstances, the attractive display would have seemed honoring. Eric and Amy stood in front of the casket and amongst the trappings; they looked at the picture of their son and wondered. When was that picture taken? How old was he there? But they would not kneel at the bench and cry in front of these monsters, if their son was truly dead, they would not share this moment as part of some sick game. No words were spoken between them, they held each other's hands and that was enough.

The Judge was upset, impatient with them, where was the grief? Did they not realize that their son was dead! He wanted a reaction, anger, rage, cries for justice, something. They were not playing along. He had spared no expense to prepare this for them. They should at least pay their respects like decent parents.

"Open the Casket!" Hurst would force a reaction. "And make them look!"

The guards in the room surrounded them. They had no choice but to obey. Amy finally broke down and started to cry. She did not want the last memory of her son to be like this.

"If one of them closes their eyes, shoot the other." Hurst was determined to get what he paid for. One of the guards pulled his gun and stood at the ready.

Slowly the casket was opened, the young man dressed in a fine suit and although it was obvious he had been dead too long for an open casket the makeup was professionally done.

Amy gasped and held her one hand over her mouth careful not to close her eyes. Eric clenched his teeth and held

Amy's hand tight. They both realized it was not Benjamin at the same time and fell to their knees on the mourner's bench, Amy cried out loudly and Eric looked over at Hurst with a look of rage. If this man believed Benjamin was dead they wanted him to keep believing it.

Eric and Amy held each other and wept, they put on the best show they could muster and Judge Hurst seemed satisfied. Ivan Zanderwin was suspicious. He had seen the look of true grief up close and personal to many times to be fooled by amateurs. Yet he was a man who valued the power of information. If the judge was a fool, then the judge was a fool. He was being paid to assassinate a formidable foe not babysit every detail of his operation.

"I have taken the liberty of preparing a family graveyard right here on these grounds." The judge was enjoying himself now. "Being a judge I do have the authority to perform funerals and I believe it is time to put Tiny Tim......or whatever you called him....Benjamin, to rest."

The judge ordered the casket carried outside and to the edge of the woods where four open graves had been freshly dug. Large granite tombstones sat at the head of each cavity displaying the four names of the Savage family; Noland Lee Savage, Eric Gary Savage, Amy Marie Savage and Tiny Tim, as if that were his name. They had dates born and a dash followed by a death date, except for Noland Savage, his death date was still blank.

So dad is still alive. Amy thought to herself as she looked at his stone, no death date.

Eric looked at Amy's tombstone and his own. They both had the same death date, October 7th of that year, just two weeks away; he wondered what was so special about October 7th.

"You must be at least a little curious about your upcoming appointments." Hurst was pointing at their tombstones. "As you can see, I like putting on a show. Life can get so boring without a little theater to spice things up. Every year on my grounds I host, The Renaissance Festival. It's a spectacular event that celebrates the age of knights and kings, sword play and archery, jousting and catapults. We have a competition for the best knight of the realm. The winner of that competition gets a cash prize, an authentic medieval sword, and must also decide the fate of those who have betrayed their king. The choices include beheading, hanging by the neck until dead, or trampled by horses. We do this every year and the crowds love it. The executions are at such a distance from the crowd that the mannequins look real. This year they will be real. They will be you."

Amy and Eric wanted to vomit as they absorbed the information and were forced to stand there for the mock funeral of Benjamin.

Pastor Marcus Johnson and Leonid rushed to the scene at the old water heater factory. A large crowd had gathered, being kept at bay by police. Through the mob Pastor Johnson recognized Mrs. O'Reilly and called out to her. She saw her pastor and asked Commander Troy to let him come to them. He gave the order and Pastor Johnson and Leonid were let through to meet with Mrs. O'Reilly.

"Pastor Johnson, it is so good to see a familiar face." She gave the taller man a hug.

"What is going on here? We saw the police chasing a news van and went inside to watch on TV and then there was a large explosion, we heard windows shattering, the whole church shook."

"Imagine that?" Mrs. O'Reilly wondered if she would get a bill. "Pastor Johnson, this is Abigail."

Abigail was holding on to Mrs. O'Reilly like she was attached at the hip. Pastor Johnson looked at the child and for the first time noticed the other children. They were getting the chains removed from their necks and the clamps from around their ankles. Pastor Johnson's concern went from curiosity to compassion and horror. Who were these children? Why were they chained? His gaze once again rested back to Abigail. He saw the same wide eyed lost look in her eyes as the others.

"Hello, Abigail, my name is Marcus." The pastor got on his knees and looked her in the eyes. Abigail hid behind Mrs. O'Reilly.

"She was a slave pastor, like the slaves of Egypt, like your great, great, grandfather." Mrs. O'Reilly looked behind her at the others coming from the factory and the trucks. "They were human cargo, property kept for the pleasure of evil men."

Pastor Johnson had studied slavery, toured the old sites in America, but had never looked it in the eye. Even as he thought it, his mind flashed back to the look in Judge Hurst eyes and he knew. He knew who was behind this evil. The napkin! Leonid had been standing quietly behind Pastor Johnson.

"Mrs. O'Reilly this is Leonid, he recently came to America from Russia with his wife and daughter on the promise of a job and a better life. But he was lied too and when they arrived his wife and daughter were abducted."

Mrs. O'Reilly felt for the man. "Maybe they are here?"

"No, I saw his wife. She is a servant…I fear….a slave in the home of a very powerful man, a man who could be controlling things." Pastor Johnson wondered if anyone would believe him.

"Tell Commander Troy your story; he seems like a nice man." Mrs. O'Reilly was tired. She did not have the strength that she used to. She had done what she could. It was time for younger legs to take over.

Pastor Johnson could see the drained look in her eye. "Thank you Mrs. O'Reilly, I will, but first can I help you and

Abigail get home."

"They say we all have to be processed and taken to the hospital first." Mrs. O'Reilly was afraid that they would take Abigail from her.

The Commander walked up to them at that moment. "Stories are coming in from the..," he didn't know what to call them, "Captives,… stories of a brave old lady unlocking their cells, shooting fire out from her hands, single handedly fighting off groups of thugs."

Mrs. O'Reilly was embarrassed by the attention. "I did no such things!"

Abigail suddenly found her voice and popped out from behind Mrs. O'Reilly, "Oh yes she did! I saw it all, she put her fists up like this and said I'm an old stubborn Irish woman, and she fought off those men and the others ran from her and she blow up the factory with gas from the kitchen and she saved me and she is the bravest woman….."

"Hush child!" Now she was really embarrassed and a little worried about all the damage she caused. "Commander, this is my pastor, Marcus Johnson and his friend Leonid, they have information you need to hear." She was relieved to direct the attention elsewhere.

Commander Troy turned to face the two men. He would be fully debriefed later and would have time with Mrs. O'Reilly then. He shook both of their hands and they told him their story, starting in Russia, the abductions, the meeting with Judge Hurst, Leonid's wife, the napkin. Commander Thomas Troy listened patiently but was interrupted multiple times by pressing matters that demanded his attention. They showed him the napkin and he could read it in Russian. But in the end, he was honest with them.

"I hate to sound trite, but the chances of convincing a judge to issue a search warrant against another judge….."He shook his head just thinking about it, "you have a napkin; to put it bluntly your evidence is paper thin. Many illegal's land jobs with wealthy families as maids and such, her being there proves nothing."

Pastor Marcus knew this and he was sure that Judge Hurst knew this as well.

"I understand that, but look around you, sir. Look at the faces of these children, these young girls and boys. When the system that protects them becomes so inadequate, so full of red tape,.." He was searching for the right words that would strike a chord with the Commander. "When the rules of engagement protect the enemy and tie the hands of good men and women, isn't it time for decent people to take action,…" He didn't want to offend but he had to try and persuade. "Have you ever disobeyed an order Commander? My father was a good law abiding citizen but he believed in civil disobedience. If we do not act now, when we have the sympathy of the American public and the attention of the press, we may never have this opportunity again. Laws against slavery are not enough, if no one has the will to fight for the spirit behind those laws, we give unofficial, off the record, permission to the crazies to continue. If we allow slavery to arise again in America, we spit on the grave of every soldier that ever died for freedom!"

Commander Troy looked around him. Was this the America he wanted his grand children to grow up in? If he didn't fight, if he simply did what was expected of him, if he didn't follow up on every lead, history would someday look back with disdain.

"Good speech, pastor, I can see why Mrs. O'Reilly likes to attend your church." Thomas Troy had been a soldier his whole life. He had seen this all before in Asia, Africa, Central America, unfortunately human trafficking was a worldwide problem. But why police the world if you can't take care of your own house. This was his fight.

"I'll do what I can through the mayor and D.A.'s office but I would suggest, and you did not hear this from me, that you tell your story to Noland Savage."

"And how do I find this Noland Savage?" Pastor Marcus Johnson asked.

"Why don't you have a conversation with Mrs. O'Reilly about that? I couldn't find him when I wanted to, but from what she's told me, he seems to show up for her consistently," Commander Troy suggested while looking around and realizing that Noland was nowhere to be found.

The morning light was just beginning to illuminate the lower layers of hanging mist, shooting far reaching beams of brilliance among tall thick timber. It was not a white light. It was golden. And everything it touched seemed to come to life with a glowing presence. Benjamin was a part of it, not an observer, not an invader, he belonged to the forest, as if it was adopting a fatherless child, it seemed to love him.

He was camouflaged against the bark of a Douglas fir. You did not see the boy, just a growth, a swelling of bark like others you have seen. He was covered in mud with a layer of fir bark to the exterior. He was perfectly still and had been for a very long time. The big buck was walking closer now, closer than Benjamin had ever gotten to him before. He could feel his heart began to beat faster and suddenly he needed more oxygen. Just a little closer, ten feet closer and he could reach out his hand and touch the magnificent creature.

The wind shifted and the animal's head came up. He was looking right at Benjamin but did not see Benjamin. They had played this game before and always it was the same. When his nostrils flared the game was over. Benjamin had washed away his scent just like Papa Noland had taught him to, but even then, to get close enough to touch; one could spend a lifetime trying.

Despite all his efforts, the buck suddenly caught his scent

and bounded away.

Benjamin was about to peel himself away from the tree when some movement caught his peripheral vision. He remained frozen in place not even turning his eyes to look. He would wait and let whatever it was walk into his line of sight. The large mountain lion huntress came out of the tall grass less than a hundred yards away. From the tip of her head to the end of her tail was no less than seven feet. She moved with powerful grace, smooth and agile. The mountain lion went directly to the place where the deer had been feeding and sniffed at the ground, she was ten feet from the Douglas fir, ten feet from Benjamin.

Benjamin tried to control his heart and breathing, he must not give himself away. He had never seen a full grown mountain lion before. She was as magnificent as the buck but in an awesome, fearsome, deadly manner. He had no desire to reach out and touch her. The huge cat was looking in the direction the deer had gone and started stalking that way, slowly, methodically, without a trace of noise she glided through the forest, between the trees and among the ferns after her quarry.

What felt like an eternity later Benjamin finally stepped away from the tree and breathed heavily, he was afraid, and he hated being afraid. What scared him most was the way the creature moved without sound. He would never hear her coming.

Timber watched from a distance. He had been ready. He would have given his life for the boy. But even as formidable as Timber was, he was no match for the mountain lion.

Benjamin and Timber returned to their camp to find that they had been visited by the mountain lion earlier that morning. Noland had given him instructions before he left about what to do if he was forced to leave the mountains. At once Benjamin made the decision, it was time to leave. He packed up what little he needed, sure to include his long bow and quiver of arrows, and headed west toward the trail where he had first encountered his father Eric. From there he could hike out to the trailhead Papa Noland had told him about.

Chapter 11
All roads lead to Camelot

Someone had gotten word to the other locations of the human trafficking operation because by the time Noland and Troy's men arrived they had been cleared out. A cargo vessel was stopped by the U.S. Coast Guard bound for China with a hold full of slaves. Noland was able to get aboard and search for Eric and Amy. They were not there. The plane that took off from location D went off radar soon after takeoff but its last known direction was south toward Mexico.

Daniel lane was recovering from a blow to the head at the local hospital. Noland walked into his room feeling defeated in his heart but still grateful to his new friends for all they had done to help. Mrs. O'Reilly and Abigail were already there visiting Daniel when Savage walked into the room. Mrs. O'Reilly had been given temporary custody of Abigail until a family judge could hear the case. There were two other men in the room as well that Noland did not know. One was a tall distinguished looking African American gentlemen and the other a stocky well built man who had a particular Russian ethnic look to him.

Mrs. O'Reilly was the first to speak. "Well, if it isn't my knight in shining armor. It is good to see you Mr. Savage. Any luck finding Eric and Amy?"

"It is good to see you too, Mrs. O'Reilly and you too Abigail. No, I haven't found them yet." Noland hid his grief. "How is America's finest and best doing?" he asked looking at Daniel.

"Not feeling the finest or best, I almost had him Noland, someone hit me from behind." Daniel was not happy that Chief Hobbs had gotten away.

"You did good Daniel. Don't beat yourself up about it," Noland said it knowing he needed to take his own advise. "We hurt them, we won that battle, there will be others before this is over."

Mrs. O'Reilly spoke again, "Mr. Savage.."

"Please call me Noland..."

"OK, Noland, this is my pastor, Marcus Johnson and his friend Leonid Volkov. They have some information that you may find interesting."

Noland shook both their hands. "Good to meet you." To the Russian he said, "priyatno poznakomit'sya."

Leonid replied in kind and added, "Your Russian is good, have you spent time in the Soviet Union."

More than Moscow will ever know, Noland thought to himself. "Yes." Noland smiled. "It is a beautiful country."

Leonid told his story to Noland in Russian which was easier for him because of his limited English. When he was finished Pastor Marcus took over and shared his experience at the estate of Judge Fredrick Hurst. Things began to click in Noland's mind and he started asking some clarifying questions. The large iron front gate, the castle like home, the old stone wall, Noland could see Benjamin building its model with the sticks and stones of the forest. Pastor Johnson showed Noland the napkin and all doubt was laid to rest, not because of what was written on the napkin but because of the raised impression of the medieval shield on the napkin. Benjamin had drawn shields in the dirt just like the one on the napkin.

"Please describe Judge Fredrick Hurst for me Pastor,"

Noland Requested.

"Well, he is about the same height and build as Leonid here but with a beard and a rounded face."

The bearded dragon, Noland thought. "Does anyone have a picture of him?"

Daniel reached for his laptop on the table beside his hospital bed and started typing. "He is a judge. His picture should be on line."

Daniel found an official looking picture of Judge Fredrick Hurst standing in his courtroom in full robe. He turned the computer screen to show Noland.

Noland did not react outwardly at first, but his heart rate jumped. Involuntarily both his hands balled into fists and all his muscles tensed. He knew this man from long ago. The face had aged and he had changed his name. But Noland remembered him. He was no more an American Judge than Vladimir Putin was President of the United States. How long had he been lurking in the shadows. Then the realization hit Noland. This was all about what happened in Poland so long ago, he was taking his revenge through Benjamin. Noland couldn't hide his anger from the others in the room. His face was red now, it was obvious that Noland Savage had history with this man.

Mrs. O'Reilly spoke, "What's wrong Noland, do you know him?"

"I'm sorry everyone, but I have to go," was all Noland said.

Mrs. O'Reilly could read him like a book. "You need help this time Noland. You have friends here. Go to Commander Troy. This man is rich, powerful and dangerous."

Noland did not hear her as he walked out of the room and down the hall. He had a set resolute glare in his eye. He would need weapons. Lots of weapons!

Steve Mills and two of his college buds were excited about landing Jobs at the Renaissance Festival. It paid well and you got free meals. It was also just a lot of fun. People really got into it and would come decked out in full suits of armor riding awesome horses, others would dress as archers, soldiers, kings and queens, beautiful princesses, court jesters, all the staff had to wear clothing from the period. The festival hosted daily contests, huge outdoor feasts, blacksmith shops, fur traders, woodworkers, and other shops appropriate to the period. Everything modern was kept to the far south pasture outside the realm of the kingdom. This gave visitors an authentic medieval experience but still provided for that craving of a hamburger and a coke if desired.

New this year were the catapults, huge wooden structures that used counter weights to launch bags of sand hundreds of feet into the air. For five dollars a pop you could test your aim and skill by hurling sandbags at houses built out of hay bales. It reminded Steve of a glorified game of angry birds, the once popular game app. He did not want the job of putting the hay houses back together every few hours. That would be a pain. But he did want to run the catapults, that would be fun and he could look cool while doing it.

The highlight of the week was the last day "winner takes all" knight of the realm competition. The prize was twenty thousand dollars cash and it included an amazing archery competition, jousting in a full suit of armor on horseback and last and most lethal, a dual with swords. The waivers you had to sign off on were blunt about the risks involved. It was all supposed to be decided by a point system but when the competition got heated, sometimes mistakes happened. It attracted some real swordsmen from around the world and some real beginners who had no business holding an authentic steel rapier. There was a process of elimination that started on the first day, weeding out the less skilled and leading the contest to a final clash of highly competent and motivated individuals.

For those looking for a less physically challenging competition there were the daily chess matches also ending on the last day with an overall champion. For the kids there were races, tug of war games with mud pits in the middle, kid level archery, a corn maze and the gauntlet, which was a elaborate obstacle course suspended off the ground a few feet designed to knock little Johnny off his feet and safely into the soft feather filled burlap sacks below. At the finishing end of the gauntlet was the sword in the stone based off the old legend of King Author, if a kid made it to that point he could try his hand at pulling the sword out of the stone. The operator had a button he pushed that would release the sword.

Steve and his friends were loading all their things into the back of his pickup truck. They would just camp out on sight for the next three weeks. The first week would be spent just setting things up and then a week of festival activities and then the real hard work of clean up and tear down. They didn't pay you till it was all over to avoid dropouts.

"What's up with all the engraved stones in the back of your truck?" One of his friends asked.

Steve had forgotten they were there, "I'm holding them for a friend."

"Well, we'd have more room if you'd take them out," he commented holding up one of the larger ones with the words 'Never give up' engraved deep into the stone.

"The extra weight gives me better traction in the mud," Steve said grinning.

That answer satisfied his friends. "Cool, we'll just pack around them then, because we are going to do some serious mudding this week." End of discussion.

Benjamin and Timber found the well marked hiking trail

but decided to follow it from a distance, still weary of people. He would rather not have to answer a million questions about who he was and why he was alone. Even after leaving the National Forest and heading west toward the coast he was grateful to find plenty of cover between the farms and small towns. But the nights were getting colder and sleeping outside was not as fun as it had been in the summer, so he found shelter wherever he could. Timber was a good scout for empty barns. Benjamin had learned to trust him. If Timber didn't want to go near a house or barn it was because there was another dog or the smell of the people warned him of some unseen danger. Some outbuildings had hay inside that he could use to make a soft bed, others had chicken coups where he could take a few eggs, but as he got closer and closer to the city the wide open spaces started to get cut up into smaller and smaller lots, with more fences to cross, more and more people to avoid.

Finally Benjamin found himself at a country gas station. Folks were pumping gas and buying coffee and staring at the boy dressed up like a mountain man complete with buck skins, moccasins, a raccoon hat and bow with arrows. Nobody asked him any questions; they just looked and smiled like he was just a kid dressed up for a play at school. Maybe that's what they thought. There was a cork board just inside the door of the gas station. It had fliers about cars for sale by owner, a guy who would drop off a cord of cut wood at your door, two lost dogs, and other odds and ends pinned up, one on top of the other. But there was one full color poster that stood out from the rest. The first word was too big for him to make out but there were plenty of pictures. Benjamin froze when he saw the castle. It was the castle he remembered being taken to. It was the home of the dragon. Benjamin suddenly grabbed the color poster off the wall sending pins and ads flying to the floor and ran out the door with it. The owner of the station called after him but was not motivated enough to make a chase out of it. Timber was waiting for him behind the station and ran beside him into some nearby woods.

Once alone, he opened the crumpled poster and looked closely at the pictures and tried to read the words.

Noland approached the home of Judge Fredrick Hurst in full operational gear. He was prepared and intent on starting the hostilities himself. It was a starless cloud covered night. The wind was blowing just enough to cover his movements with the sound of rustling leaves and branches. Tents were already being set up in the eastern fields in front of the estate. It was some sort of festival that did not concern him. He would come at the estate from the west were the forest was dense. But before he could circle around to make his approach he spotted a guard or a lookout of some sort. He was in the way, cutting off his access to the back woods. Noland was not in a cordial mood, as a matter of fact, he was ticked. It would be a bad night for Hurst's men.

He silently edged closer and closer to the man, moving from tree to tree and was about to rush the final distance when unexpectedly the man was gone, vanished into thin air; instinctively Noland changed direction, dove sideways to the ground expecting gunfire, rolled back to his feet and circled back around farther out from the stone wall that surrounded the grounds. But as he did so, he spotted the figure again standing in his way. They stood there, each aware of the other, each weighing the possibilities. The mystery figure had not responded to him like he would expect an enemy to. Nevertheless, if he stood between Noland and his mission this night he would not be counted as a friend.

"You don't know what you're up against Noland." It was Commander Thomas Troy.

"You don't have the right to keep a father from rescuing his children." He was done talking and started walking right past Troy.

Troy put a hand on him to stop him. Noland hit him hard!

Troy stumbled to the side with the force of the blow as Noland walked on. Noland would regret it later but Troy was determined to make him regret it now! He came at Noland fast and swept his feet like a baseball player sliding into home. Both men went down but Troy elbowed Noland powerfully into the stomach, Noland felt his breath exit his lungs and Troy was up first. He took a few steps back, once again in the way.

"You are no good to your kids dead." Troy tried again.

Noland did not like being lectured to but needed a moment to catch his breath.

"So where are your boys?" Noland said looking around for Troy's men.

"I'm not here on official business. The mayor and the D.A. didn't want to hear it. The slave factory was bad enough for the city's image. A corrupt judge would blacken their other eye."

Noland expected as much. "Well then, we have nothing left to talk about. I suggest you get out of my way!"

Noland threw a punch so fast Troy couldn't move in time and took it in the face. Noland followed up with a rapid procession of sharp sudden moves that left Troy searching for an answer. Troy settled for an ungraceful head butt that stopped Noland cold but also left both men reaching for their balance.

"I'm trying to help you...you stubborn navy brat," Troy said as he was getting his eyes to focus.

"I never asked for a Marine's help in my life." Noland tried to stumble passed him.

"Even at the cost of your kids lives." Troy had to reach him. "You are walking into Ivan Zanderwin and his men."

That stopped Noland. It was like ice cold water waking his stubborn soul. Ivan worked for the dictators of whole countries and governments not common criminals. Hurst did not have the money... or did he? But Noland would not let himself be intimidated, not when his kids were being held hostage. He turned and faced Troy again with determination in his eyes.

"Then help me, right now, stop standing in my way and join me." The words sounded foreign to his own ears. How long had it been since he last asked another man for help?

"Just being here could cost me my career." Troy respected Noland and was trying to show it but Noland was still letting his anger cloud his judgment.

"I don't give a commies red flag about your career, this is about my kids, about your kids, this is about evil men taking over my country, taking over YOUR country and no one having the guts to face them."

"We need a plan Noland. We need to move with strategic purpose. Ivan is well practiced in fighting men like you and me. His men are as well equipped and as capable as my own and for him there are no rules of engagement. The word is, he took this job because of you. You have a reputation that attracted his attention. He is bored with killing less worthy opponents. He is waiting for you now. He has studied you and he knows your coming. You are walking into a trap. Don't fight this enemy on his ground and on his terms, come on man, you know better than that!"

Noland didn't like the fact that Troy was making sense. He wanted to hit the man again, fast and hard. Troy readied himself not knowing which way Noland was going.

Troy had one more ace up his sleeve. "I took some pictures tonight that you need to see." He pulled out a small scoped shaped camera and attached it to an iphone. The pictures were of four headstones with the names of the Savage family engraved. Noland felt a chill go up his spine. Benjamin's grave was covered over with fresh dirt. The others were still empty. Noland noticed the dates.

Troy saw the sanity returning to Noland's eyes and added. "Hurst wants a show, he plans on murdering Eric and Amy on the last day of the festival and if he can draw you out in the process all the better. But two can play at that game. We can use the Renaissance festival as cover just as well as him."

A faint sound came from the direction of the mansion. They both heard the movement at the same time and retreated fast and independently away from the estate disappearing into the night.

Ivan's men fanned out with night vision goggles and small drones probing ahead of them. As Noland and Troy ran, a high tech metal orb dropped from Troy's hand. The miniature E.M.P. blast disabled the pursuing drones and every other electronic device within one hundred yards, leaving Ivan's men in the dark. Moments later Ivan stepped out of the woods and picked up one of the downed drones. All around the area a green blue miniature aurora was flexing in and out of the visible light spectrum. He was pleased. This was something new. He was hoping for a challenge and maybe, just maybe, Noland would make this interesting.

Hours later Ivan Zanderwin stepped into Eric and Amy's elaborate room. If not for the guards you would think this couple was on their honeymoon. Ivan looked around at the extravagance shaking his head.

"The benefits of being held captive by one given to excess," he said gesturing around the room.

"Your father paid us a visit tonight." He let that sink in for a moment. Reading their faces he became aware of what was missing in their reaction, the obvious question of Noland's survival, over confidence perhaps? But he had another inquiry on his mind.

"He was not alone. Who do you think would have been with him?" Ivan looked at Eric.

"He always works alone," Eric replied.

"I know, that is why I'm asking you who was with him tonight." Ivan had a blade to Amy's throat before Eric could even react. "I'll ask you one more time, who do you think was with him?"

Eric tried to think of an answer, any answer. "It had to be someone new, his best friend was Gary Holland and Harvey killed Gary." Eric wanted to strike out at the man but he knew what would happen if he did.

Ivan trusted in his ability to read people and saw the honesty in Eric's eyes, he withdrew the blade. "Ok,… I believe you are telling me the truth. It seems I have lost the element of surprise with Noland and he is acting out of character. I admire that. But I will also change the game. You, Eric Savage, son of Noland Savage, will compete as a knight in the Renaissance Festival. Every day you survive the contest...," he pointed at Amy …, "she survives. If you are eliminated, she is eliminated. That should motivate you to do your best. If you reveal your identity to anyone, cry out for help or do any other foolish thing my men will kill your wife without delay. You seem to have recovered from your injures, good. You can start training immediately but always in your armor with your helmet on. It rains so much here no one will think it strange. But learning to fight with a helmet on, that will take some getting used to, I know. My men will take you to get fitted for your armor when you are ready. The three areas of competition are archery, jousting on horseback, and dueling with swords. The festival starts in five days. The eliminations start on day one."

Ivan walked away. He was certain Noland would use the festival as a means of cover. He would if he were in Noland's boots. His son, Eric, did not have the skills to win the competition but he might last a few days and unwittingly give away his father's location to the snipers.

Benjamin walked along the country roadside with Timber

beside him. Rolling green fields dotted with hay bales decorated the landscape. He hoped he was heading in the right direction. He held the crumpled poster advertizing the festival in his hand. His longbow was draped over his shoulder along with his quiver of arrows. There was a rumbling of thunder coming from somewhere behind him but when he turned to look there were no storm clouds in sight. Nevertheless the rumbling grew louder and louder. Then, suddenly rising over the horizon on the road, the first motorcycles came into view, followed by what seemed to be a never ending tide of Harley Davidson riders. They were all dressed like bikers from the same club from the neck down in their leather jackets, chaps and riding boots. But they all wore a medieval knight's helmet, the lead bike had a jousters lance attached to the side of the bike, its point cutting through the air, a medieval flag flapping in the wind as he rode.

They passed Benjamin in a roar of internal combustion engines. Benjamin stood still, watching them ride by with the full color poster in his hand. One bike broke off from the others and came to a stop next to Benjamin and Timber. This bike was different from the others in that it had a side car attached.

"That is a cool looking German Shepherd." The man said lifting up the front of his knight's helmet. He was smiling with a full face of hair and a mustache that sort of stood out. "I had a shepherd once, best dog I ever had; he used to ride with me everywhere." The man noticed the poster in the boys hand and asked. "Do you need a ride to the festival?"

Benjamin held up the poster and pointed at the picture of the castle. "I want to go here."

"Jump in the side car, you and your dog." He handed Benjamin a helmet that was too big for him, but for Timber, he pulled out a pair of goggles. "These were old Bruce's goggles but see if you can get your dog to wear them."

The gang of bikers rode on for about fifteen miles.

Benjamin loved it! He took the oversized helmet off and let the wind blow into his face. Timber seemed to be enjoying himself too with his tongue hanging out one side of his mouth and his nose sniffing at the breeze. The pack finally arrived at a property about a half mile down the road from the festival. They had been kicked off the festival grounds three years ago and had come up with their own camping site close enough to compete in the games but still live by their own rules off grounds. Benjamin and Timber were dropped off within view of the entry gate. Benjamin thanked the man and joined the crowds walking toward one of the entrances.

Chapter 12
Trapped in a suit of armor

On the first day of the festival everyone was in high spirits. It was a grand thing. The flags were flying high in the wind. The tents were laid out in winding rows creating an old European feel to the medieval city. The mansion of Judge Hurst was fitted with castle-like additions to enhance the illusion that this was indeed Camelot. All the new sights and sounds and smells satisfied the need of escape most had hoped for from the pressures of modern life. There were open areas in the middle of the city where people could gather and talk, various street entertainers attracted small crowds, one such juggler lit the ends of his torches on fire and dazzled those watching. The whole event was laid out in a half circle to the east of the house in the vast open fields with all roads coming from the outside leading back toward the castle and the larger events. There were three entrances to accommodate the masses, a north gate, an east gate and a south gate. The design gave the judge's home a commanding view of the kingdom, all entrances, and the camping areas beyond.

Ivan Zanderwin saw this world through the circler scope of a sniper rifle. He saw the two knights walk through the east gate jostling each other like good friends would or was it an act. He put his cross hires on the teenage boys sneaking in without paying behind the long line of port-a-potties which were kept just outside the perimeter. There was a husband and wife dressed up like king and queen in matching emerald and dark sapphire colors. A group of kids were at the gauntlet getting knocked off balance by the swinging arms of wood wrapped in feather pillows. He looked over the crowd of parents scrutinizing them with a careful eye. One old blind man with a stick was begging for money as he stumbled about. Ivan trained the scope on the old man's face. The state of the art computer in the riffle analyzed the structure of the man's features comparing it to dozens of images of Noland Savage. Ivan had his finger on the trigger ready to fire the kill shot. A red light came on indicating that it was not a match. Ivan searched on.

Benjamin Savage had received several complements on his costume by the time he reached the south entrance of the festival. One lady dressed as a huntress asked to see his bow and, in kind, handed him her bow.

"Wow, this looks authentic," she commented.

"My grandfather made it for me," Benjamin said with pride.

"Are those real animal skins?" she asked feeling his buckskins.

"Yes, my grandfather made those too."

"I would not let the people from P.E.T.A. know about that." She pointed to a group of protesters off to one side of the entrance.

Benjamin pulled out a piece of dried venison from his pocket and took a bite.

"Why not?" he questioned between chewing.

The lady just grinned and patted him on the head. "Never mind."

Benjamin was distraught when he was asked for money and a responsible adult to accompany him by the man admitting people.

"You have the best youth costume I've seen today and your dog is welcome as well, it makes the place seem realistic to have animals about. But I can't let you in without paying. Where is your family?"

You wouldn't believe me if I told you mister. Benjamin thought to himself.

He stood at the south entrance for some time trying to think of a way to get into the festival. Thankfully Timber was behaving himself with all the people crowding around. Benjamin told him to be good as kids came up to pet him. Two men in full polished silver armor walked up to him. Timber had never seen anything like these creatures and let out a low growl. But Benjamin hushed him.

The men stood there looking at Benjamin like he was some great specimen. They had their helmets on so Benjamin could not see their faces.

"You need to get in boy?" one man finally asked.

"Yes" Benjamin felt weary of them but at the same time really wanted into the festival.

"Come with us," they said and started walking toward the gate. They paid the man at the gate and lied about being his uncles.

Once inside Benjamin thanked them and took off. The two men looked after him as he ran with Timber beside him.

"I never expected to see him here!" one knight said to the other.

"Nobody could have, he is supposed to be dead," said the other knight.

They were wanted men, so they kept their helmets down. Chief Hobbs and Walker were there looking for revenge on one Daniel Lane. They had been to his house and after getting a lead that he went to the Renaissance Festival, followed his trail there. But they were disobeying Judge

Hurst's direct orders by just being back in the state of Washington, they could never let Hurst know. The rule was to always keep their distance from him so that no one could ever make a connection between them. But Hobbs and Walker just couldn't let it go! Daniel Lane the Boy Scout, Daniel Lane the baby faced novice, was now a hero in the press, giving interviews and having his face in the news, talk shows and magazines. They would make him pay and then just disappear before anyone was the wiser. Maybe that kid just looked like Tiny Tim. Hurst would never know.

The smell of freshly made bread was filling the air and drawing paying customers to the tent of Rose O'Reilly. She was dressed as a traditional fourteenth century Irish lady and Abigail was beside her in a beautiful cobalt embroidered dress, her red hair braided and her green eyes shining. This was a world away from life at the factory for Abigail. Mrs. O'Reilly was happy to see her smiling and talking more.

A wizard walked by the front of their tent holding a great staff in his hands. He smiled at Abigail and said, "What a lovely dress, young lady."

She smiled back but said nothing. The wizard walked on.

A knight in black armor rode into the festival on a fearsome looking stallion. His shield had a silver and black griffin surrounded by three crosses. He looked challenging and strong. He rode passed the lesser knights to the stables to care for his steed.

A humble priest with his head covered in a deep hood walked through the north gate. He had a large cross draped around his chest and carried a musical instrument after a type of violin. He walked to one of the center gathering areas and began to play the most beautiful music. It was soft and drawing, calling to the deep parts of the soul. Something about it resonated with the mood of the day and people began to congregate.

Eric Savage was seeing this world through the five slits cut into his helmet for vision. If he saw his dad in the crowds he would be careful to give no clue to those he knew were watching him. Anyone who approached him would be putting their lives at risk without knowing it. Yet it was impossible to not interact entirely. He had spent the last five days practicing for the upcoming challenges determined to keep Amy alive or die trying. He would have no problem with the archery competition but the jousting and heavy medieval sword fighting were new to him. He found many willing sparing partners and was not afraid to ask for tips. He watched the more experienced swordsmen with focused attention.

Due to the magnitude of participants, you had to choose one event on the first day of the competition. Large numbers needed to be eliminated in a short amount of time, reducing the field to only a few by day seven. Eric was walking toward the archery fields when it started to rain. It had been clouding up all day. The rain was not heavy like back east, it was more of a constant drizzle mixed with a dense mist. As he looked around at the crowd it was obvious to him who was a native Washingtonian and who was visiting from elsewhere. Washingtonians joked about having webbed feet and walked in the rain like it was liquid sunshine. Others put up their hoods or reached for umbrellas. Knights who had been carrying their helmets on their hips now put them on to shield from the rain. Eric realized the advantage this gave him. It would make him stand out less for having his helmet on and the sword fighting would be more about balance in the mud, as well as skill. He prayed it would rain all week and being the Pacific northwest that was more than a possibility.

It was simple, each archer had three shots and only the top twenty percent would advance to the next day. The targets were set up numbered one to thirty. On that first day the lines were long. Eric would take no chances. He would do his best. He got in line fourteen and waited his turn. As he watched those in front of him compete he weighed his chances as better than good. Many did not even hit the target. Yet several knights did stand out as serious competition for the days ahead, and that is what worried him.

Noland Savage was unaware of his son's presence in the line of archers. Noland was also waiting in line but far to the right, in line Twenty one. Daniel was in line five with helmet off, talking to those around him. The rest of their little band of operatives were spread out incognito in the land of Camelot. The plan was bold. They had hashed out the possibilities and settled on a strategy that carried great risks but would put Zanderwin in checkmate if successful. The plan depended in part on Noland getting to the final rounds of competition and he was determined to do so. That first day passed without incident, Noland, Troy, Daniel, and Eric all advanced to the next day. Unknown to them all, so had Ivan Zanderwin and several of his men.

Benjamin had no place to sleep that night and made his way back to the camp of the bikers. He did not come empty handed having bagged a rabbit in a small patch of woods between the festival and the Harley camp just before the sun went down. He walked into the loud rowdy camp and went directly to the huge bonfire and started skinning out his game. The conversations stopped around the fire and all eyes were on the boy with the rabbit.

"You gonna eat that rabbit?" one tattoo covered man asked.

"Yah, I'm gonna eat him." Benjamin grinned.

"Is someone selling rabbits at the festival?" a big man with arms like tree trucks questioned.

"No, I shot him with my bow," Benjamin said pulling the hide from the flesh with one last tug.

The eyebrows went up and the big man smiled. "You pulling my leg?"

Benjamin showed him the bloody arrow and the group let out a course of expletives.

He cooked his rabbit meat over the open fire and ate it. A few of the men ask for a taste and Benjamin shared his kill. "Not bad kid."

"Where's your dog?" someone asked.

"He takes care of himself, he's probably hunting rabbits too but he just eats them raw."

Benjamin made his bed of tree branches next to the fire and fell asleep. No one knew who, but in the night someone put a blanket over the boy.

Timber smelled him somewhere in the crowd. The quiet man from the mountains was here, but where? His scent was mixed with so many others that it was difficult for the dog to follow. Timber walked behind one of the tents where the man had been sometime that day. Abigail stepped out of the back entrance of the primitive bakery. Timber saw the little girl and came to her smelling the scent of the man close by. Abigail loved animals and was delighted with Timber. She rubbed under his chin and let Timber kiss her face. Timber could tell she was a kind soul but there was also a fire in this one, burning as red as her hair. He looked into her green eyes and saw a deep hurt.

"Are you hungry?" the little girl asked. "I know what it's like to be hungry and kept in a dog crate all day."

It was the same hurt he had seen in the eyes of Benjamin. He would search for the man later. There were things that men knew that timber may never grasp, but there was a depth of healing in the unconditional love a dog could bring, that man could learn from.

On the second day of the competition everyone had to compete in all three areas. This would test the knights in their overall skill set. The great black knight demolished his opponent at jousting, shattering his lance with a solid hit on the lesser knight. The defeated knight was lifted off his horse and into the air. His body crashed into the ground landing in a heap of vanquished armor. Eric was relieved that chance had not matched him up with that one. Never-the- less he was next in line to compete. Eric spoke to his horse in a kind gentle voice. Much depended on the speed and willingness of this animal. Eric did not recognize the green shielded knight he faced across the field but he was determined to stay on his horse no matter what. Inside of his helmet the sound of his own breathing and heart beat were amplified. He remembered Amy. He remembered the life they dreamed to have together. He remembered that Benjamin was still alive and needed him. He clenched his teeth and put all fear out of his mind, tightening his hold on the lance.

The trumpet sounded and the two knights raced toward one another, the point of their lances on deadly courses of unavoidable collision. The impact was simultaneous, Eric felt his lance hit and deflect, but his own shield was fractured and ripped from his arm leaving him fighting for his balance. He had to recover quickly, turn and charge again with no shield. He did so, beating the green knight in the second attack.

This time Eric had no defense but did have the advantage of speed, catching his opponent flat footed, he pointed his lance at the lower corner of his rivals green shield. The point of his lance struck pushing the green shield up and sliding into the belly of the man sending him to the ground. At the same moment Eric was hit in the shoulder and knocked sideways on his horse but he held on with one hand.

Ivan Zanderwin whispered into the microphone installed in his helmet. "The pup has survived, narrowly."

The men who held Amy withdraw the blade from her neck. "Your man pulled it off, but he's just hanging on by a thread from what I hear and this is only day two."

Amy knew her husband and would be proud of him no matter what these in-human excuses for men said. Eric had been weakened by his concussion and time in bed. He was not one hundred percent but he would grow stronger every day. The fight would bring out the inner strength in him. They didn't know the Savage men the way she did, he would learn from every near defeat and not make the same mistakes twice.

At the request of several bikers Benjamin competed with them in a homegrown archery competition of their own making. He had gotten very good with his long bow over the last months, having to depend on it for food and protection. They laughed and poked fun at each other for losing to a child and started calling him the jungle boy. He was welcomed to stay at their camp for the week if he liked. Benjamin enjoyed watching the sword play and the general roughness of the men, fighting each other in mock battles. Some of the men boasted about having advanced to the third day of competition.

Later that day, Benjamin walked through the crowds of people and came to the gauntlet. He watched as kids his age and older were laughing and having a great time trying and failing to run the course of obstacles. It looked like fun and Benjamin got in line but was turned away and told to go buy a ticket. The tickets were three dollars each and he had no money. Noland Savage just happened to be walking by the ticket booth in full armor and helmet at that moment. The sight of Benjamin froze him in his tracks.

Noland could not believe his eyes. What was Benjamin doing here? He could not risk approaching him now. But if someone recognized him he would be in just as much danger as them all. At that moment Abigail and Timber came walking around the corner. Timber went right up to Noland waging his tail and barking. Noland could take no chances; he turned and left without a word.

"Timber, leave that man alone." Benjamin called after him. A few heads turned but Noland was long gone.

"Is that your dog?" Abigail asked Benjamin.

"Sure is, he is the best dog in the whole world," Benjamin boasted.

Benjamin looked up and for the first time really saw Abigail. She was the most beautiful girl he had ever seen after his mother Amy. She had her red hair all braided and her big green eyes made his heart beat a little faster. Benjamin didn't know what to say to her.

Abigail broke the awkward silence, "He has been hanging around our bakery and I've been feeding him homemade bread." Abigail was a little disappointed that he belonged to someone.

"That's ok, I let him go where he likes. He's a very smart dog." Benjamin got on his knees and started petting and scratching Timber. Abigail joined in and the two of them gave Timber their attention.

"You sure are dirty, even for a boy." Abigail was not trying to be cruel. He really was dirty.

Benjamin had not noticed. "I guess you're right," he said looking at himself. "I really am dirty." They both laughed.

"It's OK, I'm only this clean because of Mrs. O'Reilly. She makes me take baths all the time and does my hair and makes me wear these dresses."

Benjamin wanted to tell her that she looked pretty in the dress but the words refused to come out. So instead he asked "Do you play hide and seek? Timber plays really well. He can find you no matter where you hide."

Abigail was not really allowed to be away this far from the bakery tent as it was, but she wanted to play with Timber and this boy seemed different in a nice way.

"I'm Abigail, what's your name?"

"Benjamin."

"Can you walk with me back so I can ask Mrs. O'Reilly first?"

"Who is Mrs. O'Reilly?"

"She's a really nice lady who takes care of me."

"Is she your mom?"

"No, silly, if she were my mom I'd call her mom. She is trying to adopt me."

Benjamin didn't know what to say after that and two walked on with Timber between them.

Eric Savage forced himself to walk right past the two without stopping or looking their way.

Once again Timber was following a stranger wagging his tail and barking. Benjamin called him back again, "What has got into you boy, I've never seen you this friendly."

Eric disappeared into the crowd praying no one had seen or understood what had just happened. Why was Benjamin here? Who was that little girl with him? Would Timber give him away and put their lives in danger? It was too much for Eric; he stopped and rested against the wood bench of a carpenter's shop. Eric could feel the fatigue coming over him, he was tired deep in his bones and he could not see himself lasting through tomorrows third day of competition. He prayed for strength.

The craftsman in the carpenter's shop was working on a piece of wood. The shavings came off the wood in long curled ribbons. The pressure was even with each stroke of the old fashioned tool moving in steady rhythms. The smell of fresh carved wood and the sound of work began to calm Eric. The man stopped and looked up.

"Can I help you?" he asked with an honest smile.

Eric looked around at the man's shop. Quality wooden lances lined the walls along with a few other hand crafted items. This man did good work and he did it the old fashioned way.

"I wish you could but nothing for now thank you."

"What about your busted shield?" the man questioned. "You can't win the competition with a shield like that."

Eric had forgotten about his shield. He had done well in the archery competition, but had barely survived the joust and sword events of day two, leaving his shield fractured and scarcely functional. His shield was a perfect reflection of his soul. It could not stand another blow. And he had overheard the talk. The real competition begins on day three.

"That's the day that separates the men from the boys!" one knight who claimed to be a three year veteran warned Eric earlier that day.

The carpenter had stopped his work and was gazing at Eric's shield.

"Can I see that please?" The man reached out his hands. Eric handed it over.

The man put his fingers into the gashes and deep cuts made by lance and sword with a concerned look on his face. It was like he was seeing what had happened, every vicious attack, every near defeat. He walked the shield into his woodworking shop with care, the way a surgeon would carry someone's wounded heart.

Unlike most of the medieval shops his place was actually a wood built structure and not just a tent. Eric followed him in and sat on a log stool. He had a fire going in a stone fireplace constructed in the middle of his store. Eric could feel the warmth of the fire through his armor. The man was checking over the shield but he was also studying Eric. There was something about the way the war torn knight held his head that spoke to the craftsman.

"So are you in it for the twenty thousand dollars?" the carpenter asked.

"No," came Eric's weak reply.

"For the glory?"

Eric just shook his head.

The man was silent then and Eric was content to just sit for a moment staring into the fire.

"Is it for a woman?" he had pulled up a seat by the fire next to Eric.

Amy's face flashed before his eyes and Eric woke up.

"Yes, my wife."

The man looked through the slits of Eric's helmet and into the eyes of a desperate man.

"I have not asked you why you always have that helmet on."

Eric stood to his feet about to leave. He was putting this man in danger.

"Hold it right there son. I don't know what kind of trouble you're in but you have nothing to fear from me."

"You're putting yourself in danger just by talking with me and I cannot tell you why," Eric said in a low voice.

The man considered that as if putting the weights on a scale.

"OK, fair enough. It wouldn't be the first time a carpenter gave his life for others. I think you stumbled into my shop for a reason. I think you need my help and whether you believe in God and his son Jesus or not, I do, and I feel him talking to me right now. Now sit down and let me help you."

Eric sat down.

"Your shield is all wrong. The way it's flat on the outside absorbs the full impact of a blow. It needs to have a curve to it so it sheds the force of each strike to the side. This will cause your opponent to shift his weight to that side and give you a chance to counter attack."

"Have you ever competed in the games?" Eric thought it a fair question.

The man simply glanced up to a wood shelf with a line of dusty trophies. Eric had been too exhausted to left his head up that far.

Eric walked over to get a closer look. They were all from three and four years ago but there were no second places among them, First Place Renaissance Festival Dallas, TX,... First Place Renaissance Festival Kansas City, KS,... First Place Renaissance Festival Seattle, WA. *This guy was doing something right.*

"I'm all ears, sir; anything you can help me with would be greatly appreciated."

"Come with me." He led Eric to the back of his shop to a simple but sturdy looking trunk.

The man opened the heavy top lid to reveal a beautiful shield and sword.

"They aren't magic but they were designed and redesigned in the hot furnace of competition." He first handed the shield to Eric. "You've been wasting most of your strength on bad equipment. This shield is half the weight and will do twice the work for you."

Eric was amazed by the way it felt on his arm. His shield had been big, heavy and clumsy. This shield felt like an extension of himself, it moved with him.

Then he pulled out the sword. Eric could see the quality

of workmanship before he even touched it.

"This was made by a man I greatly respect as the best sword smith in the world. It would cut straight through some of the lesser quality blades I've seen in action this year."

Eric felt the balance of the sword in his hand. He knew there was no possible way for it to be true, but his arm felt stronger just holding it. Next, from the wall above his new friend hoisted down a regulation length wooden lance and carefully walked it outside.

"Nothing really special about this lance but I'd bet twenty dollars it's better than the one you've been using," he commented looking back at Eric's busted shield and gashed up sword now in his junk pile outside. "Whoever supplied you with that rubbish should be shot?"

Eric didn't answer but it was ironic to think about. *I'd shoot them if I could*, he thought to himself.

For the next four hours they talked and the man walked Eric through moves he had tested and perfected with lance, shield and sword.

Ivan's men paid them a visit pretending to shop for wooden lances. After a while they must have gotten the all clear because they left.

Eric thanked the man and walked away with his new better weapons. He had a set time to report back to his handlers and dare not be late. When he was half way there he realized he had never asked the craftsman for his name. He had been so tired and so intent on learning all he could. It was too late now. He would have to find him again tomorrow.

Chapter 13
Heart of a warrior

"Did you know that Noland Lee Savage ran track in high school and never really did that well?" Ivan walked Amy Savage by the arm out of the back door of the house toward the mock family cemetery. She knew she lived on the edge of a knife and prayed for strength. It was the early morning of day three.

"He wrote poems for a magazine his senior year, did you know that about him?"

She made no reply.

"ANSWER ME WOMAN!" Ivan shook her hard.

"No,.." Amy replied starting to cry, "I never knew that."

Ivan pulled himself together. It was just the two of them, his men were not around, that outburst would have surprised those who knew him best. Ivan was usually cold and calculating and not given to emotional winds. He talked on as if nothing happened.

"I really liked one of his poems. It spoke to me, so I did something special for him."

They walked within view of the headstones and Noland's was now engraved with a poem.

Amy remembered the poem but would not share family memories with this man.

She slowly read it to herself, letting the strength of it speak to her.

"Heart of a warrior, Soul of a Lion, I will not fear the battle, I will return to the fight, again and again and again, not counting the times defeated, till the sweet taste of victory becomes my happy home."

It was simple, to the point, yet there was something deep about it, something from the heart.

Ivan talked on and on about how much he knew about Noland and about how he could now anticipate his every move. But Amy did not hear him. She was lost in the last three words of Noland's poem, *my happy home*. That was all she wanted. To be with Eric and Benjamin and maybe another child in time. Why was that such a threat to these men, such a danger to the armies of evil that attacked on every side? Strong families protected one another and grew like stout solid oak trees. Maybe that was it? These men preyed on the weak and unprotected. Family stood in the way of that, if it really was a family.

"...and what do you think I should do about that Amy?" Ivan asked her

She had no idea what he had been saying but suddenly she knew what she wanted to say. "I think you need to write a poem."

"I don't follow?" Ivan questioned.

"You need to write a poem." But this time she gestured toward the tombs.

"I think that is wishful thinking on your part."

"At least tell me your date of birth."

He almost lost his temper again but this time he caught himself. She had made him think. What would be on his gravestone? He quickly dismissed the idea like he had practiced doing his whole life and instead wrapped himself in the comfort of his deceit.

Another man approached them at that moment. He was

an average sized man dressed in a grey suit of armor.

"There you are!" Ivan was pleased with his arrival. "Amy Savage meet Jason Rio."

The knight saluted his captain.

"He is one of my best men and has been competing in the games next to your husband Eric. Jason shares my enthusiasm for swords. It has been arranged that today Jason and Eric will face each other in combat. Day three has been known as the most deadly day of competition. Amateurs who made it this far by luck get desperate and make mistakes and people get hurt. And although Hurst has that ridiculous rule about anything modern being at the games, we have installed some hidden cameras with you in mind. You will watch. So if I were you, I'd start writing a poem for your husband."

He ordered that she be taken back to her room. Soon this would be over and the Savage family would all rest in the wet muddy earth.

Noland was relieved when Mrs. O'Reilly told him that Benjamin was now with her and that she had informed him of the whole situation. He had made the right decision to leave if the mountain lion had come into his camp but Noland never dreamed he would find his way here. There was no time to take him to a safe place now. He was a part of this.

The next day would be day four of the games; the King would finally show himself. Judge Hurst would begin overseeing the competition sitting on his grand throne. He would be surrounded by body guards at all times but would have a lavish private tent set up close by as a retreat from his throne. Noland had to survive day three and advance on for the plan to work. If he could do that, anything was possible.

The retired Navy Seal was a warrior no doubt but not an expert with these weapons. He had been watching his competition and saw some men who would challenge him. He was at the sword arena when Eric and Jason walked in full armor to the center of the showground. It started to rain again as the two faced off. All he saw was the grey knight against another knight who carried a new fancy looking shield and sword. Noland had been watching the grey knight, he was good. The other knight had not impressed him and his new costume jewelry wouldn't help him against a better skill set. Noland turned to leave uninterested in this clash as he was almost certain of the outcome.

The ring of metal striking metal is what drew his attention back to the fight, the pitch was distinctive. At first he thought that perhaps the fancy sword made from cheap steel was the source of the usual tone and he was half right. It was the origin of the sound but it took Noland five seconds of serious observation to realize he had been mistaken about the weapons and had dismissed the underdog knight too quickly. He was making a fight of it. The grey knight was fast and advanced first with an onslaught of rapid strikes bent on a prompt victory, but his blows were being misdirected by the shape and design of the newer shield without causing much damage and from the looks of it, without much effort from his challenger. The grey knight was wearing himself out. Unexpectedly the grey knight stopped his advance and backed away, realizing what Noland had realized and taking a second look at his opponent. But Eric Savage would give him no time to gather himself and attacked with a fresh ferocity that surprised everyone, handling his new sword like a pro. The grey knight fended off the attack but not without effort and Noland judged them an even match now.

Ivan was not entertained in the least.

Amy Savage prayed for her Husband.

This time the grey knight did not charge straight ahead but strategically attacked to the left side of the underdog knight, swinging his blade in short quick bursts, forcing him to defend to his left. Noland could see what was coming. The grey night was setting him up for a reversal attach to his right. But suddenly, the underdog slammed his shoulder into his foe, in his heavy armor the gray knight lost balance and stumble back giving the challenger an opening. Eric lunged forward with the tip of his blade and received the first point in the match. The grey knight was stunned. The point of the blade had penetrated through his armor like butter. If Eric had not pulled that thrust he would have been badly injured.

Noland also noticed the cut in his Armor and viewed the new sword with suspicion. Who gets a new sword and shield in the middle of competition? And where had the new moves come from. Unless this Knight had been hiding his skills on purpose? One of Ivan's men perhaps?

The grey knight knew he was in trouble. If he lost this match he would have to face Ivan for his failure. He took his time now not letting Eric get an advantage. Thrust, parry, thrust, parry, Jason Rio waited for his moment. When he finally made his move, it was a very technical action, one he was probably saving for the last days of competition. Eric fell for the trick move and suddenly found himself disarmed, his sword landing seven feet to his right. The grey knight quickly landed a point and pressed his attack before Eric could retreat, getting between Eric and his Sword. The underdog was in trouble, completely on the defensive. It was only a matter of time now. The grey knight battered Eric's shield with strike after strike, than rammed him shield to shield, knocking him off balance the same way Eric had done to him. Before Eric could right himself the grey knight landed his second point. One more point and he could claim victory. Eric was being backed into a corner, his sword farther and farther away. The sword-less defender made a desperate play, rushing to the inside of the grey knight's next swing, Eric smacked him in the helmet with the edge of his shield with all his strength, Jason's head collided with the inside wall of his metal helmet, the soft grey matter of his brain slammed into his skull. The grey knight collapsed like an empty suit of armor. Knocked out cold!

Noland scrutinize the victorious knight as he walked back to retrieve his sword and then away from the fight without the least bit concern for his opponent's condition. There was something familiar about the way the man moved but Noland could not pin the thought down. His lack of interest in his fallen foe was unnatural unless this knight was truly one of Ivan's men or perhaps Ivan himself, concealing his abilities until the final days of competition so no one could learn and anticipate his techniques. Noland also noted how he never took off his helmet and had an escort back to the mansion every evening.

Benjamin wanted a real sword. Everywhere he looked men and women were walking around with swords in hand. Like other kids his age he played with whatever he could find. One bully challenged him to a dual with a wooden sword made with a blunted tip. Benjamin had an oak branch he had been carving into the shape of a sword. He looped a rope around one end for a handle. He defeated the bigger boy in a fair match but the bully wouldn't let it rest and got a group of kids to tease him for the way he smelled. That's when Abigail stepped up and punched the bully square in the nose. Mrs. O'Reilly had them both by the ears in no time.

"What am I going to do with the two of you? That poor boy's mother was beside herself."

"He was calling Benjamin names Mrs. O'Reilly," Abigail pleaded.

"That is no reason to punch him in the face Abigail," Mrs. O'Reilly said sternly.

"But you fought with those men at the factory?" Abigail felt justified.

"Abigail, that was different, those were grown men trying to seriously hurt us."

Benjamin remained silent. He felt bad for getting Abigail into trouble but was secretly proud of her for standing up for him the way she did. She was his first real friend and she was turning out to be an extremely loyal one.

Mrs. O'Reilly looked at the two of them. They appeared so different from each other. One wild looking and dirty, the other spotless and dressed like a princess, but inside they were very similar. Benjamin; kidnapped at the age of five and kept as a slave around hard cruel men. Abigail; passed from foster home to foster home enduring who knows what and finally sold as human cargo. Would they ever be able to adjust again to normal childhood? They would be different from other children, more protective and in some ways more appreciative of what they had. But Abigail struggled with nightmares. Benjamin had the advantage of still having a family that loved him but Abigail had no family, no one to belong to. Mrs. O'Reilly loved her like she was her own but at her age could she really be what Abigail needed? She hoped so.

"You two behave yourselves; we do not need to do anything that would attract attention."

Mrs. O'Reilly was worried that their little shenanigans would put them all in danger and yet had a hard time staying angry at these two. Knowing what they had been through, it seemed to her, they deserved a little grace.

"Is there a constructive activity you could find to occupy your time without getting into fights?"

"You could let me and Abigail go visit my biker gang friends. We could just watch them fight each other, they seem to think it's fun," Benjamin said with a smile.

"Not a chance young man! Your mom and dad would not approve of you hanging out with those hoodlums."

Benjamin dropped his head at the recollection of his parents. He missed them terribly.

Mrs. O'Reilly saw the distressed look in Benjamin's eye and tried to change the subject.

"Benjamin, it's time for you to have a nice hot bath. I've set up a tub in the tent. It took me forever to heat up enough water on this fire. I can beat the dirt off your.....deer skins….Just hand over your shirt, and..."

She reached out to help him get his shirt off. Benjamin looked horrified and backed away. He did not want Abigail to see his many scars.

"Don't be afraid boy, it's just a bath..."

But Benjamin turned and ran.

"Benjamin!" she called after him concerned more about the boy then the bath.

Abigail ran after him without asking.

"Abigail, you get back here this minute!" But it was too late. Mrs. O'Reilly was beside herself.

Timber looked up at her the only obedient one among them.

"Follow them Timber, keep them safe."

Timber gave Mrs. O'Reilly a confirming bark and darted out of the tent after Benjamin and Abigail. Abigail found Benjamin with the help of Timber. He was sitting on the ground behind the blacksmith's shop throwing pebbles at the canvas roof top and watching them roll back down the slope of the roof with the rain drops.

Abigail said nothing at first. She didn't want him to run off again. So she just picked up a pebble and joined in. Abigail liked having Benjamin around and she had to think of a way to get Mrs. O'Reilly and him to get along.

"Did you see that sword stuck in the stone?" she asked him.

"Of course, the one at the end of the gauntlet," he replied.

"I bet you could pull that sword out." Abigail was thinking of a plan.

"No one can pull it out unless the guy running the game presses the release button, I'm not stupid." Benjamin had already tried his hand at the sword in the stone and figured it out.

"But if you got through the whole gauntlet without falling or getting knocked down he would have to let you have the sword," Abigail shot back at him.

"It costs three dollars a ticket to run the gauntlet," Benjamin said in a discouraged voice.

"Hmmm,...." Abigail said dramatically, "Where could we get some money? Mrs. O'Reilly has been making money selling fresh bread. Maybe she would give us some?"

"Mrs. O'Reilly just wants me to take a bath."

"She really, really wants you to, doesn't she? Too bad we couldn't get on her good side and ask her for twelve dollars. With twelve dollars you could run the gauntlet four times. You could get that sword if you ran the gauntlet four times."

Benjamin stopped throwing pebbles. *I could get that sword if I ran the gauntlet four times*, he realized as if the thought was his own.

He turned and asked Abigail, "Do you really think she would give me twelve dollars?"

Abigail had him now, "If you took a bath I bet she would."

Ten minutes later Benjamin was chest deep in hot water scrubbing himself with a soapy wash cloth.

Daniel Lane was the only one of their team who came to the festival publicly and showed his face around on purpose. After the news coverage of him in action at the factory and the story of his involvement in exposing the criminal ring, he became a local celebrity with people recognizing him at the festival and asking for his autograph. Noland told him not to let it go to his head. On day three Daniel was eliminated from the competition but continued to socialize around the festival, his role still important to the plan.

On the start of the fourth day the king of the kingdom walked toward his throne with much celebration, surrounded by his best knights and the nobles of the realm. Judge Hurst had invited the winner of the Miss Washington Beauty Pageant to play his queen for the day. The procession marched from the elaborate tent set up behind the stands of the main show grounds to the high throne. They came flanked by knights on horseback, flags and trumpets. The king was dressed in an ordinate royal robe made especially for this year. His crown looked dazzling. His queen for the day was adorned with matching robe and crown. Being a surviving contender, Noland Savage was able to get in close enough to secretly photograph the king from several different angles. He would continue to collect photos throughout the day. The photographs were sent directly to their team of designers who were making an exact duplicate of the crown and costume. Leonid Volkov had been practicing his lines for weeks now, with his beard grown out and a little makeup he looked exactly like Judge Hurst. They were both Russian and had about the same build. If Ivan happened to speak to the king in Russian Leonid could reply without hesitation.

Eric Savage could feel his strength returning to him. He may not be able to save Amy from their ultimate death on day seven but he could buy her more time. He owed an enormous debt to the carpenter who had equipped him with his own sword and shield. He was returning now to thank him but when he entered the shop the craftsman was not there, instead none other than Jason Rio, the defeated and shamed grey knight looked up at Eric with an insidious smile.

"You should know better than to make friends." he said tauntingly.

Eric pulled out his sword ready to finish what he started yesterday.

Jason Rio sat calmly amused by Eric's reaction. "You and I both know what would happen if you did that."

Eric did not sheath his sword but asked through clenched teeth, "Where is he?"

"If you survive the games today you will be sharing a cell with him tonight. Sit down Eric, let us talk warrior to warrior."

Eric did not move and would not sit with this man.

"You have nothing to fear from me today, I have loyal friends among Ivan's ranks and some jealous enemies."

Eric did not care about the man's personal life and turned to leave.

"What if I helped you win, just for today?"

That stopped Eric.

"I'm your biggest fan now you know. You made me look bad yesterday in front of the others. Today you will fight Anatoly. If he defeats you when I could not, well... I would look even worse. But if you defeat him, what could he say and Ivan would not kill us both. Today is the coin toss. The man tossing the coin is loyal to me. The winner gets to choose the event."

Eric had no choice. For the moment, the enemy of his enemy was his friend.

Jason Rio saw the willingness to be reasonable come over Eric.

"Good! You are a practical man. I like that."

"Before this is all over you may change your mind and

wish you had let Anatoly kill me." Eric wanted Jason Reo to know how he felt about him.

Jason shrugged his shoulders, "We all make our choices, don't we." And then he got to the point.

"Do not fight him with swords, you are good but he has seen your moves and you will not surprise him the way you did me. I have seen you joust; we both know that is out. So listen to me now, the archery maze is your best option against him. He is strong and powerful and deadly accurate with a bow but would be slower than you I think. The arrow tips are supposed to be blunted and in your armor you are safe. But I would not put it past Anatoly to have a few armor piercing tipped arrows in his quiver by accident, so keep your shield handy. If he thinks he is losing he would use them for sure."

Eric walked away wondering if he could trust the information. But did it really matter, if he won the toss the archery maze would be his best option anyway. He prayed for God to make him fast and accurate.

The gauntlet was a long wooden structure that snaked with turns to the right and left, it lifted up to various levels of raised platforms and ended with an impossible leap to catch a hanging rope and then swing like Tarzan to the elusive sword in the stone. It was divided into four parts. The first being a web rope climbing challenge. The whole rope net would tip upside down at the slightest imbalance sending most kids plummeting and others hanging on by fingers and feet.

Next was a series of padded swinging arms, the kids that made it this far were met by an attendant, they had to continue one at a time to avoid heads bumping into heads. The swinging arms came at them from all angles knocking them off the platforms.

The third was a long balance beam just two inches thick. Streams of shooting water would come on automatically from the side and caused most to lose their concentration without even touching them.

After that was the wall climbing challenge. Once an attendant fitted a harness on the child attached by a rope that would catch them when they fell, the kiddies could climb up the wall by the attached hand holds. Very few made it to the climbing wall and those who did found less and less handholds as they struggled higher and higher. Those who failed here would be lowered safely to the ground.

At the top of the climbing wall was a flat square platform. In the distance, hanging from a crane like arm was a rope suspended above a deep pole of water for safety. The victor would jump from the platform, catch the rope and swing to a lower platform and the path leading to the sword in the stone. No child had ever made it.

Benjamin handed his ticket to the attendant and stepped passed him for the first time and toward the net made of rope. The net was jammed with kids stuck halfway up hanging on. Benjamin waited, not wanting to start until he saw a clear path. Suddenly, two boys rushed onto the right side of the net, the weight spun the whole thing upside down and more than half the occupants fell off.

Benjamin saw a clear path in the center of the net open up. He had been watching this obstacle for days and knew the center was best. He quickly climbed up and over the net challenge before it flipped again. He was headed to the swinging, spinning, dropping arms.

When his turn came, Benjamin moved forward, the first arm came at him from the left, the second from the right, then front high, front low, and then slam! There was an arm hidden from view that hit Benjamin from behind. He stumbled forward and into the spinning arms pushing him off the platform and onto the cushions below.

Benjamin heard the voice of Harvey in his head. "*You're nothing but a stupid idiot. That's why your parents didn't want you. Tiny Tim!*" Benjamin felt the fear come over him. He crawled off the cushions and looked up at the gauntlet. It looked bigger and more intimidating than he remembered. Just then the bully who had teased him the other day appeared.

"I saw you fall like a girl!" He shouted and pointed at Benjamin.

Abigail stepped between them facing the bully with fists up. "How's your nose feeling?" She asked.

The bigger boy got a look of terror on his face and rushed away into the crowd.

Abigail turned back to smile at Benjamin, but he was gone and this time Timber had went with him.

Eric stepped up in front of the crowd and was now standing across from his opponent for the coin toss. The man officiating looked normal enough. He gave no indication that he was nervous or doing anything underhanded. Eric felt uneasy, was he being set up, if so, how? The official said that Eric's opponent had the higher ranking between the two of them, more points scored so far overall, so he got to call it, heads or tails. Eric did not like leaving his fate to chance but there was nothing he could do.

"Call it in the air." the official shouted as he tossed the coin up with a flip of his wrist.

"Heads" the man across from Eric said in a deep voice.

The coin spun end over end, Eric watched closely, heads, tails, heads, tails, up it went and down it came. It hit the ground with a ping and jumped a little back into the air flipped over a couple more times and landed squarely on heads. But suddenly, it flipped over to tails. The official called it before anyone could grip. Was he that fast with his hands? Was there a magnet under the platform?

"Just one minute!" the losing party growled. "I want to see that coin."

The official handed him the coin. He looked it over suspiciously and then pulled a magnet out of his pocket to the surprise of everyone. But the official looked calm. He touched the magnet to the coin and there was no pull. Nevertheless, he warned in a low threatening tone, "If I find out that Jason Rio has had his hand in this fight in any way, you are a dead man." He was speaking to the official. The official continued like nothing happened. Looking at Eric he asked, "What's your pleasure, sword, jousting or the archery maze?"

Chapter 14
Courage has its day

Benjamin escaped into the quiet woods behind the mansion of Judge Hurst. Timber sensed something was wrong and stayed close. Harvey's voice was in his head, *stupid, loser, dumb kid, nobody's missing you anyway.* Pain like fire flared up on the old scars that crisscrossed his back. What was happening to him? He thought he was going crazy! He sat down on the soft thick layer of pine needles covering the forest floor. He put his head between his knees and cried. Timber laid his head next to him feeling his dismay. Benjamin struggled to dam up the tide of emotions that had suddenly washed over him like a flash flood. He could only handle so much at one time.

The distraction he needed came in the sound of footsteps and voices coming his way. The warning of danger eclipsed the emotional overload in his mind. The crying stopped and his thoughts cleared. Timber dropped low without a sound and Benjamin held perfectly still knowing that it was movement that gave most people away. The two guards were talking about the upcoming match between Eric Savage and Anatoly. They said it didn't matter how good Eric was because of the hidden archers in place to kill both men. The large round hay bales were hollowed out with the men inside so everyone would think that the arrows had come from inside the match and that each one had killed the other. Benjamin waited until he was sure they were long gone.

Then he raced back to the fairgrounds. He had to retrieve his long bow! He had to save his father! Whatever hold the past had on him was broken for now.

Eric was handed a dozen blunted arrows and a bow. He examined the arrows and tested out the bow for strength. They seemed un-tampered with. Looking through the crowd he saw Jason Rio giving him the thumbs up but the smile on his face was mocking. Eric couldn't worry about him now. He had to focus on the contest before him. The maze was formed by tall walls of hay bales with confusing twists and turns interrupted by long shooting lanes open left to right and back to front. It would not be hard to get pinned down attempting to cross an open lane or ambushed coming around a blind corner. The key here would be fast action and unexpected changes in direction. Eric was not confident he could fire accurately on the run but he would have to try. The match started the moment the two holding gates opened from both sides of the maze. Eric's opponent fired immediately down the open lane. Eric lunged for cover, the arrow whizzed by only inches from his head. Anatoly had already tossed the rules out the window by notching an arrow before the gate was even opened.

Eric hurried out of the open lane and into the safety of the maze. He ran one way and then the other. The other knight had disappeared into the maze along with Eric. Both men were now trying to find their way through numerous dead ends and endless loops.

Benjamin barged into the bakery pushing passed Mrs. O'Reilly and Abigail grabbing his long bow and arrows. Without stopping to explain he rushed out of the tent and ran toward the archery maze with Timber at his side. Abigail darted after them. Mrs. O'Reilly decided that this time she would not be left behind and pursued them both as fast as she could.

The raised wooden stands around the maze were jam-packed with onlookers. Benjamin hurried to the top seats where he could see the two knights in the maze trying to find each other. One was his father but he had no clue which was which. He looked at the larger rounded hay bales that lined the perimeter of the maze, the archers had to be hidden in some of those. The stands were built right to the upper edge of the larger hay bales, suspended by a wooden support structure.

Abigail caught up to him just then.

"Benjamin what's going on?" she asked.

Benjamin had no time to explain, "This is dangerous, go back to the bakery." he ordered and took off under the stands toward the bales. Abigail bristle; she would do no such thing.

Anatoly correctly anticipated Eric's direction and released his arrow just as Eric came around the corner. Eric got his defenses up just in time. The arrowhead struck his shield with a hard thud and penetrated about three inches passed the hardened wood. It was an armor piercing tip that sprang open on impact. Eric snapped the arrow off of his shield and fired back in the direction of the shoot as he moved to better cover.

Benjamin turned to Timber for help. "There's too many hay bales for me to check them all. I need you to find the bad men for me." Timber set his nose to the ground and started toward the first hay bale. But Benjamin had no idea what he was going to do. He notched an arrow and followed Timber but could he really shoot a man, maybe even kill him, he was terrified but if it came down to his dad and his fear, he would overcome the fear. Timber cleared the first hay bale and moved to the next. At the fourth hay bale Timber signaled to Benjamin that something was up.

Jason Rio's man inside the hay bale was intent on spotting Eric and Anatoly; he was whispering to the archer on the other side of the shooting lane through a mic piece. They were ordered to shoot when the two knights were in line with each other so that it would look like the shots were fired simultaneously from within the maze. The man's attention was on searching for the two men, he had no idea what a large beast of a dog was about to attack him from behind.

The crowd above them gasped at some close call in the contest and then let out a loud cheer. Before the cheer reached its zenith Benjamin pulled back the concealing flap exposing the archer inside and ordered Timber to attack. The large shepherd took the man by complete surprise. He was not dressed in armor. Using his four long canine teeth as weapons, Timber latched on to the man's thigh, his bite penetrating the skin and deep into the muscle. The man was paralyzed with pain and dropped his weapon. Timber dragged him out of the bale. Benjamin was about to shoot him at point blank range when suddenly a wizard appeared. He was a tall African American man with a large staff in hand. He struck the man on the head knocking him senseless. Benjamin felt the tension in his heart relax even as the tension on his bow relaxed. He would not have to kill.

The man was unknown to Benjamin but was obviously a friend. The wizard smiled at the boy and motioned him to the next hidden archer.

Abigail had seen the whole thing and ran to report it to Mrs. O'Reilly. "We need to help him Mrs. O'Reilly!" She pleaded.

"Go and get my cast iron pan, fill it with the fresh rolls and bring it to me under the stands." Mrs. O'Reilly ordered.

"But how will that help Benjamin?"

"Trust me child, have I ever failed you yet?"

Abigail took off running back to the bakery tent.

Mrs. O'Reilly slipped under the stands unnoticed and crept to the opposite side of Pastor Marcus Johnson and Benjamin. She stopped short of disappearing around the corner and waited for Abigail to being her cast iron pan.

Abigail came under the stands fast as lightning; the rolls were falling all over. She handed the pan to Mrs. O'Reilly and they both disappeared around the corner.

The second archer that Benjamin encountered tried to fight back by hitting Timber with his bow. The dog leapt for the man's throat and brought him down like a cut tree. This reminded Benjamin of why they called him Timber back at the factory.

Mrs. O'Reilly held the cast iron pan at the ready and crept behind the hay bales on her side of the maze until she found what she was looking for. Abigail pulled back the camouflaged blind for Mrs. O'Reilly, the man turn his head just in time to see a blackened cast iron pan fill his line of sight, then, WHACK, the lights went out.

Eric was losing the contest, two hits to his one, and needed a game changer. He removed the armor from his right leg and arm, including the hand piece and set them protruding out of a corner hay bale. He then slipped away to be in position to spring his trap.

The second Archer on Mrs. O'Reilly's side heard something strange going on through his microphone piece but didn't want to leave his position. When he could get no response from his partner across the maze he decided to go investigate. He opened the back flap on his hay bale and stuck his head out.

"THUD!" He was out cold.

The last standing hidden archer was on Mrs. O'Reilly's side and he finally had Eric in his sights; Eric's choice of positioning had backfired, he was in the firing lane. Anatoly was about to step into the same lane. The corresponding archer on the other side was being shaken like a rag doll and dragged out of his hollow. Benjamin overheard a voice come over the man's mic, "Savage in position, Anatoly in position, I'm going to take the shot, prepare to fire!"

Benjamin was already moving! The boy quickly took up

the position of the vanquished archer, drawing back his own long bow and looking beyond the two knights to the large rolled hay bale on the other side of the lane. He imagined where the man would be.

"Fire on three," came over the mic. "one…" Benjamin fired.

Eric turned, spotted his opponent and fired, at the same time Benjamin's arrow passed him, high and to the right. He heard a gargling sound behind him as the arrow disappeared into a hay bale. Eric's own arrow struck Anatoly in the shoulder. It was a tied match now. Both men vanished back into the maze.

Pastor Marcus and Benjamin rushed around the perimeter of the maze under the stands to Mrs. O'Reilly's side. When they rounded the corner there were two men down with Mrs. O'Reilly and Abigail still standing over the second with an iron skillet. Pastor Johnson opened the flap of the last Archer that Benjamin had shot from across the maze. He simply closed it after looking and said. "All accounted for. We need to disperse in different directions. Walk away, do not run." He advised.

They all did just that, exiting from under the stands from diverse and discrete points. All but Benjamin, who was about to leave but hearing a gasp from the crowd above, feared his father needed him again. He peered through each hiding place until he located both men; he took a guess that his father was the knight with the blunted arrows, while the other knight carried the armor piercing points. Benjamin watched as the other knight was getting in position behind his dad. Benjamin spotted a microphone piece protruding out of a hollow hay bale directly behind Anatoly. He picked up the connected mic on his side and attached it to his bow, then pulled back hard. Anatoly heard the faint sound of a bow tensing behind him and instinctively turned and fired.

Eric, drawn by the sound of Anatoly's movement, caught

sight of his foe and fired.

Later that night Daniel walked out of the festival grounds in his knight's costume through the parking lot area toward his car. He planned on changing back into his blue jeans and getting some sleep and a hot shower. His helmet was off and he was unaware of the two silver knights waiting for him in ambush. The parking lot was deserted at that time of night. They rushed at him from opposite sides, one swinging a sword low and the other high. Daniel's feet came out from under him and he fell with a crash. Both swords raised high over him about to spear him through. Daniel rolled into the legs of the closest knight knocking him down on top of him to avoid the swords. Daniel then rolled out from under his attacker and just kept rolling. He knew that getting to his feet while in the armor would take forever, so his best bet was to keep rolling.

The one attacking knight still on his feet came after him but now the parking lot slopped downhill and Daniel was picking up speed. His pursuing enemy discovered quickly that running down hill in a metal suit of armor just doesn't work and slowed to a walk. The fast moving rolling metal knight collided into a line of Harley-Davison Motorcycles, causing them to smash together and fall like dominos. Daniel toiled to get upright while the world was still spinning. He pulled his sword out like a drunken pirate and faced the four silver knights, which reduced to two after his double vision settled. The silver knights took off their helmets. Daniel was stunned to see the faces of Chief Hobbs and Walker grinning back at him with a glare of revenge.

Daniel looked around at his options. He had a sword and knew more about how to use it than he did three days ago.....maybe he could fight his way.... but then Hobbs dropped his armor gloves and pulled out a gun from up his sleeve....or maybe not.

"You are a lot like your father." Hobbs commented, pointing the gun at Daniel. "But in the end, just like him, the good guys always finish last."

"Did you kill him?" Daniel asked.

"I gave him a choice. He could have been smart and lived like a king instead of struggling along on what they pay police officers. I wasn't going to let him stand in the way of my future."

Daniel was stricken with emotions. Now he knew the truth. His dad was the real deal, not part of the corruption. He had always known that deep in his heart. Another emotion was there too, one that demanded justice. Hobbs was not just a corrupt officer. He had just admitted to playing a part in his father's murder.

A low rumble from the other side of the parking lot shook the ground. Fifty riders sped forward at the sight of the fallen Harley-Davison motorcycles. They circled around the three knights closing them in, cutting off all exits. The headlights from all the bikes turned night into day. One guy jumped off the back of a bike where he was a passenger and ran to his tipped Harley like a parent would run to their hurt child after seeing them fall off the monkey bars at a playground. He was erupting with expletives as he looked over the dents and scratches.

Someone gave the order and the loud growling engines were turned off. There was a moment of silence like this was a funeral for the collapsed bikes. The circle of metal, leather, and men, looked like a school of piranha surrounding three gold fish. Hobbs didn't even lift the small .22 caliber handgun, he just moved it a little; the sound of leather holsters being emptied filled the night air along with the unmistakable sound of a shotgun being loaded. He slowly placed the pea shooter on the ground and backed away with his hands up.

Someone recognized Hobbs from TV. "Hey, you're the Chief of Police aren't you? You're the one that everyone's been looking for," he said.

"Isn't there some kind of reward out for you?" another man asked.

Daniel decided it would be a good time to speak up, "One hundred thousand dollars to be exact, and another fifty thousand for his brainless sidekick."

Walker fumed!

Chief Hobbs thought he had an ace up his sleeve, "I'll double it, just let us deal with Mr. goodie two-shoes here first and then we'll ride to go get your money."

The leader of the gang of bikers looked at Daniel Lane. "You were at the factory of slaves the night it was raided; weren't you with that old Navy Seal guy, Savage?"

"Ya, I was there helping Savage." Daniel replied.

"Is Savage around?" he asked. "I saw the footage from the airport, that man can move and shoot like nobody I've ever seen."

Hobbs did not like his offer being ignored and made a critical mistake. "You afraid of Savage?" He was looking at the leader. "We already have Savage on the ropes... if you take my offer..."

The leader stepped off his bike and slammed Hobbs in the jaw with a right cross. "I was just having a conversation with baby face over here!" he shouted at Hobbs, feeling disrespected.

That's it! I'm growing a beard, Daniel thought to himself.

"Why are you so set on offing a fellow officer anyway? I understand the bad cop good cop drama here, but you went out of your way to get this man, why?" He looked at Hobbs and Walker demanding an answer.

Hobbs didn't know how to put it into words. "He offends me."

"Why?" The biker had turned philosopher.

"Because he's weak." Hobbs wasn't a deep thinker.

The leader of the gang was smiling and shaking his head at the whole situation, he took another look at Daniel and then at Hobbs. Daniel was smaller and had that respectable look to him. Hobbs was big and tough looking, but there was something in his eyes that said 'pretender.'

"I don't like police officers in general," he said looking at Daniel. "But I hate traitors to their kind even more!" he seethed looking over Hobbs and Walker. He had made his decision.

"Is the reward for dead or alive?" he questioned.

Someone found it on their smart phone, "Yes sir, dead or alive!"

They stripped them of their armor, cuffed all three, put them in side cars and rode away.

Eric Savage was man handled by the guards and drug down some stone stairs to a dungeon like lower level of the Hurst mansion. The veneer of good treatment had worn off and the sting of his victory in the archery maze that day probably didn't help any. He was thrown into a cell with a man that looked like he had been beaten to within an inch of his life. His face was swollen, bloody and bruised beyond recognition. At first Eric thought he was dead as he lay there lifeless but then he moved and let out some muffled words.

Eric got down beside him and tried to make out what he was saying.

"How did they handle for you?" the man asked.

Eric thought the man must be delusional. But then he spoke again.

"My shield and sword, how did they handle for you?" he asked louder and then coughed up some blood.

Suddenly Eric realized he was the carpenter. He did not look at all like the strong man he had met two days ago. They had broken him. From the amount of blood he was coughing up Eric suspected that he was bleeding internally.

"My God, help him!" Eric pleaded calling down the echoing empty stone halls.

"How did they handle?" The man knew he was dying

Eric could see he was really bad off and saw no way to help him. So he answered his question.

"They were magical." Eric finally said. And then remembering the man's words about God and Jesus, rephrased adding, "They were blessed weapons, blessed by great workmanship and blessed by God."

"Did you win?" His voice was weak, but there was still some determination in his soul.

"Yes, with your help, I did win." Eric didn't feel like celebrating.

"I've been praying for you Eric. While they beat me I prayed for you." But then he had a bad coughing attack and couldn't speak for awhile.

Eric didn't have the words to respond. This man risked his life to help him and would probably pay with his own.

The Carpenter had something to say before he died and struggled to hold on till it was said. The man didn't want to die. He still had dreams left unfinished. He had a wife and kids he wanted to say goodbye to and a grandchild he would never see. He talked to Eric about life in general and he asked Eric about his faith in God. His words grew weaker, like a dying flickering candle, he was at the end of his journey.

"Do not treat time as if you have an endless supply. Do something with the life God gave you Eric, do something that matters." Those were his last words.

Eric stayed next to him and wept and realized too late, he still didn't know his name.

Ivan looked at the handmade arrow with the flint tip. It was the best clue they had as to who attacked his men. It was unique. The fletching was made from real feathers. If he saw another like it he would have his killer. The explanations as to why his men were stationed there in the first place did not please him. Jason Rio was executed on the spot. Ivan stared down the rest of his men. No one dared to look him in the eye.

"Find me the maker of this arrow and no more fighting among ourselves." His men left into the night searching for more clues and the owner of distinctive weapon.

The lights from one hundred and twenty motorcycles lit up the huge old rock quarry. It was like a natural amphitheater with a fighting arena in the middle. The walls sloped up all around it like it was the Grand Canyon of skater parks. But instead of boards, men and women on Harleys raced up and down the walls. There were natural jumps here and there and some rock formations left standing in the middle of the great floor, like pillars in a coliseum.

"Welcome to our games, gents," the leader said with a grin. "It seems to me you two have it out for each other," he said looking at Hobbs and Daniel. "It's time to go man to man and see who can handle the way we play."

He lifted his hand and the great rock bowl cleared of bikes, save two. On opposite sides of the bowl, dueling Harleys revved their engines waiting for his hand to drop.

The men on the bikes were in suits of armor and under their right arm, a long medieval lance pointed the way. His hand dropped and the two Harleys roared toward each other. Without flinching the riders pointed their lances in the direction of their rival and collided in a heap of splintering wood, flying bodies, and run away bikes. The crowd went crazy.

Hobbs shrugged his shoulders like this was no big deal.

"You two will not be wearing any armor," the leader informed them.

Hobbs hesitated. "Without armor that's a death sentence. You are throwing away money here. I'll triple my reward money, how about it? That's three hundred thousand dollars."

The man in charge just shook his head. "I can't trust what a man says, when I know he's about to wet himself. Besides, we'll collect that reward money and your three hundred thousand," he said as he looked back at Walker.

Hobbs looked like he would cry. He started to get angry and then started to plead and beg.

Daniel turned away and started walking on his own over to his starting position. A pieced together motorcycle was waiting for him there. On the way, he turned to a guy playing music out of the back of his truck. "Do you have that old song, Bad to the Bone, it was my dad's favorite."

"Sure do!" the man answered. "You want it to start when you get the bike started?" he asked willing to accommodate last requests.

"That would be great!" Daniel answered.

The leader of the gang heard the exchange and grinned.

As Daniel walked to his side of the bowl he had that John Wayne swagger in his step, like a man who knew who he was, and didn't give a damn what you thought of him.

Hobbs, after being forced half way to his bike, finally found his pride and walked on his own.

The two Harleys started up, bellowing a rumbling thunder that echoed around the rocks mixing with the loud music. Daniel took hold of the lance. It did not feel that unfamiliar in his hands after jousting at the festival. He had ridden a bike before but promised himself that if he survived the night he would buy himself a Harley-Davison. The leader held his hand high. Daniel pointed the heavy lance up, if the tip got caught on the ground he would be poll vaulted to his death.

The leader's hand dropped and so did the two bikes into the rock bowl. Daniel struggled to control the steering with one hand and hold the lance with the other. The speed picked up fast on the way down and the front suspension absorbed the impacted as the bike leveled out. Now he could see Hobbs screaming like a madman, his fat belly bouncing with every jolt. He had murder in his eyes and not a rational thought in his head. Daniel knew it was suicide to play by these rules and at the last minute dropped the tip of his lance into the front tire of Hobbs' bike. It flipped up and as it did the tip of Hobbs' lance caught onto an edge of stone, Hobbs was holding so tightly to the lance that it propelled him through the air. He landed on his side rolling over and over. Daniel lost his seat when his lance hit the wheel and was sent off and to the right, safely away from the Hobbs' flipping bike.

Both men suffered deep cuts and bruising, if not a broken bone or two covered by adrenalin. Daniel found his fallen bike and next to it a circle of good rope. After a few tries he got the bike running again and shot straight for Hobbs. The bigger man was running up the side of the wall holding a limp and bleeding arm. Daniel thundered after him and jumped from the bike unto Hobbs back, using the momentum to push Hobbs down, slamming his head into the hard stone ground. All the fight, all the tough talk, all the facade was gone and the true nature of evil showed through in his weakness. Daniel used the rope and hog tied Hobbs like a cowboy taking down a steer on the run.

Daniel stood over the man and took a moment to speak his mind.

"The good guys do not always finish last. It took courage and strength to live the life my father lived." Daniel said. "You took the easy way and it's the quick and easy way that always makes men weak." He tightened the rope a little more until Hobbs cried uncle.

Chapter 15
It's all on the line

On the morning of the fifth day Benjamin found the courage to stand in line once again at the entrance of the gauntlet. On his second try he made it passed the swinging arms and onto the balance beam. He was almost to the end when a powerful stream of water hit him from the side knocking him off balance and onto the wet soft mat only two feet below. Other kids tried to cheat and get back up before the workers would see them but Benjamin wanted to win this fairly. On his third try he made it passed the balance beam and after getting fitted with a safety harness started up the climbing wall.

On the other side of the climbing wall decisions were being made that Benjamin was unaware of. The two teenage workers had been poorly trained. They were supposed to circulate the water in the deep pool at the end of the gauntlet. Instead they accidently pulled the wrong valves and drained the pool entirely. They flipped the valve that was marked, "water in" and nothing happened. They were oblivious to the fact that there was another shut off valve up the line. The guy who normally worked in this area had a family emergency and was gone for the day. They did the responsible thing and told someone. That person passed it on to someone else and someone made the decision that it really didn't matter since no kid had ever made it to the swing of death. But just in case, the workers at the climbing wall were told that the gauntlet ended with them today and no kid was allowed to reach the high platform above. The helper who usually stood on the platform came down to help in other areas. He decided to raise the exit ladder out of reach for safety.

A group of about a dozen rough looking bikers were walking passed the gauntlet when one spotted Benjamin on the climbing wall. He stood out even among the other costumes, wearing his authentic buck skins and moccasins. The one outlaw biker pointed out Benjamin to the others, "Hey, isn't that the jungle boy?" They all stopped and looked at Benjamin making his way higher and higher up the wall.

"He's gonna make it!" one of the men said.

But Benjamin was stuck. The next hand hold was just too far for him to reach.

The voice in his head ridiculed him, *too small for your age, Tiny Tim?*

Benjamin leaped from the foothold and went air born, reaching for the hand hold above, stretching with all his might. His fingers grabbed hold of them, but suddenly he felt a pull on the harness. He was pulled away from the wall, away from his victory and lowered safely to the ground. He was fit to be tied angry.

The voice in his head laughed, *See, no matter how hard you try, you will always be Tiny Tim.*

"I was almost there!" he said to the attendant.

"You did great!" the attendant tried to be positive. " But today we cannot…"

Benjamin didn't wait around to hear the explanation. He was back in line with his fourth and last ticket. The watching dirty dozen gave him the thumbs up as he ran past them.

"I want to see this," one man commented. They all agreed.

While waiting in line, other boys and girls played games

on their smart phones. People were discouraged from having them at the festival but it was impossible to police. One boy kept bragging to Benjamin about his great exploits in a particular game. Benjamin was trying to concentrate on the gauntlet but the boy wouldn't stop talking. Benjamin finally told him, "You are risking nothing by playing that game, if you lose it doesn't hurt you, if you win there's no reward."

Benjamin handed the attendant his last ticket. He waited for the net to flip and raced up the middle. He had the swinging arms memorized and took them like a pro. The group of rugged bikers started chanting, "Jungle Boy, Jungle Boy!" And the crowd grew in size wondering who they were watching. He was on the balance beam when he had his first close call. The stream of water hit him and he almost lost balance but righted himself at the last split second. It was there, at the end of the balance beam that he saw what was happening. The helpers at the climbing wall were pulling kids off the wall by their harnesses when they felt they were stuck and not giving them a chance to work it out. This was his last ticket and his last chance at the sword in the stone.

Benjamin waited until all the workers were distracted and jumped on the climbing wall without a harness. The crowd saw it and tried to get the attention of the help but by the time the attendants noticed him he was half way up and well out of reach.

"Hey, you! Get down here now! You need a harness on!"

Benjamin climbed higher and higher, passing all the others.

The crowd below saw the danger and ordered the workers to go up after him but they were harnessed to other kids and first had to pull them off and lower them down. One father jumped over the small fence and up the steps to the wall and started climbing after Benjamin himself. When the boy stopped, nearly at the top, it looked as if he was stuck and the father would catch him.

The crowd gasped in fear as Benjamin made the leap to the hand holds that were just out of reach. Mothers held their hands over their mouths wide eyed with fear, feeling sick to their stomachs. Even the leather clad posse held their breath. For a moment, Benjamin's hands fumbled to get a grip, his feet dangling on nothing, then his hands clamped down and he held on and up and over the top he went.

The father, thinking the danger had passed, made his way back down. The frantic festival workers, after clearing the wall of other children, scrambled up the climbing wall after Benjamin.

Benjamin stood on the high platform and took in the view of the Kingdom. He could see the city of tents, the show grounds, the four catapults lobbing sandbags at houses of hay; he could see the mansion of Judge Fredrick Hurst. To him it was the layer of the dragon who had renamed him Tiny Tim, the man who ordered him beaten and ridiculed.

People below thought it was over until Benjamin made a practice run to the edge of the platform to test the distance. The long rope hung above the empty pool below. People shouted at the top of their lungs, "The pool is empty, do not jump!!"

Benjamin saw the empty pool. But this was his moment. He felt that if he turned back now he would be Tiny Tim forever. It was time to silence the voice in his head. It was time to become who he really was. Tiny Tim would never make this jump but Benjamin Noland Savage would.

Benjamin backed up to the edge of the high platform and got ready to run, tying his moccasins tight. The workers were almost to the top and set to grab him by the leg to stop him.

People were calling 911 in advance seeing what was about to happen. The crowd below had grown to fill the entire available space around the gauntlet. From every vantage point throughout the festival people could see the lone boy on the high platform.

Noland bullied his way through the crowd trying to get within earshot of Benjamin to stop him.

One festival worker was finally within reach of the boy. He grabbed at his moccasins, grasping over the edge, but the smooth leather slipped away as the boy burst forward.

Benjamin ran for all he was worth. The rubber pad on the platform gripped well with the leather on his feet and he felt the strength of his stride propel him. He had no thought of fear or pride as his feet left the edge and he leaped out into empty space.

The crowd below watched him fly. Kids lifted their heads from their hypnotizing little glowing worlds and wondered if he'd make it or would need to buy another life with an on-line code. Parents prayed he would catch the rope. Other looked away unable to bear what their imaginations had already envisioned.

Benjamin reached for the rope; it was coming at him fast but he was dropping faster. It would be close. Noland watched and hoped the boy's training would pay off now when he needed it most. The length of the rope seemed to pass him but he reach up and caught the knotted end at the last possible second and held on for dear life. His body jerked with the change in direction. His momentum carried him in a wide circle passed the lower landing platform, back the way he came and over the awe struck crowd.

Someone started to clap their hands in relief, not knowing what else to do. Soon the applause grew and spread throughout the area. Other people sat down, emotionally exhausted from the whole ordeal.

Benjamin landed on the lower platform his second time around and was greeted by some very angry staff.

"You disobeyed direct instructions from our workers and are forever banned from this festival. You will have to leave the festival grounds with your parents NOW!!" the white faced man barked.

"I want my sword first." Benjamin pleaded.

"No prizes for people who break the rules!"

"But I finished the gauntlet?"

The man grabbed Benjamin by the arm and lifted him off his feet, dragging him along, passed the Sword in the Stone.

Three imposing men in motorcycle jackets stopped him. "Let the boy go, now!" the lead man demanded.

"Get out of my way, I'll call security on you."

But security was already there and fearful to move as more gang members crowded the area, their wide shoulders forming a wall around the group.

"We're not afraid of your security." The leader put his finger in the man's chest. "You have a choice to make sir, we start a riot right here, right now, or the boy gets his sword. Your choice Mr., but I'm not bluffing."

The man saw the seriousness in the rebel's eyes and backed off, letting Benjamin go. The crowd cleared a path to the sword in the stone and Benjamin walked through the on-lookers to his prize. He stood in the place of destiny, put both hands on the sword's handle and pulled with all his strength. The man in charge nodded to the attendant to push the button. But Benjamin still struggled to get the sword out of the stone. One tattoo covered guerrilla of a man put on a pair of brass knuckles and stared at the head staffer man impatiently.

"It's just a little stiff," he explained. "It's never been removed before this."

Benjamin kicked it with his foot to loosen it and then tried again.

He pulled once more with all his might; the magical stone seeing the courage of the young man and the future destiny that was before him began to release the sword to his care. It slid out of its place with a ring and Benjamin held it proudly over his head.

Somewhere, hidden in the crowd, Noland Savage's heart swelled with pride at the sight of his grandson holding the sword of victory. It was a moment worth waiting a lifetime for.

Later that same day, one of Ivan's men spotted the unique looking long bow and handmade arrows resting in the corner of Mrs. O'Reilly bakery tent. Mrs. O'Reilly and Abigail where there alone, Timber had been placed in the care of the Harley-Davison camp after his involvement at the archery maze.

"Whose bow and arrows are those?" he asked as casually as possible. "Are they for sale?"

Mrs. O'Reilly realized how foolish they had been to leave them in sight. "Oh those, we don't know where the owner is, we found them behind the tent this morning. We were hoping someone would come back for them today."

He looked at Mrs. O'Reilly and Abigail and was convinced that neither of them could be the archer he was after and decided to just stake the place out to see who was coming and going.

The man paid for a morning roll covered with cinnamon and walked away, but not far. He was impressed with the fresh baked roll. *That old lady can bake.* He hoped he wouldn't have to kill her.

Mrs. O'Reilly sent Abigail to see if her suspicions were right and Abigail confirmed it. The man sat just a little ways down the street of tents watching them.

This presented a problem for Mrs. O'Reilly. Today was day five. It was time to spring their trap but if she left the tent and the man followed her, all would be lost.

After watching Benjamin ride off in a parade of roaring Harley-Davison motorcycles, Noland returned to the competition with the feeling that his cover had been compromised. The knight that he was scheduled to face did not show up for the match. He was being reassigned. Also, posted on the gate of the showground was a new notice to competitors. The victor from each match going forward was required to remove his helmet before the king. The reasoning was that they needed conformation that a team was not filling the same armor with fresh rested men going forward into the final rounds. It was too late to change the plan now. Noland waited nervously in the arena for his new rival to appear. He had a bad feeling about this.

Ivan had narrowed the pool of men that could be Noland Savage down to just a handful. He was eliminating the possibilities one at a time. He had a suspicion that the match he was setting up for that day would be the final act in this drama. He ordered that Eric be removed from the dungeon and suited up to face the knight who could be Noland. This was a win, win situation in Ivan's mind. The sniper was at the ready for Noland. Amy's life was over if Eric lost.

To Eric's surprise he was given back his sword and shield and escorted to the main show grounds. The stands were packed and waiting. The king was sitting on his throne enjoying some imported wine and laughing with whoever had agreed to be his queen that day. Ivan was waiting for Eric at the gate. He had something in his hand. As Eric approached he noticed that it was the stone of Courage that Benjamin had given to Amy.

"You are facing one of my best men today." Ivan said turning the stone over in his hand.

"That's what you said yesterday and the day before." Eric was determined to survive as long as possible. But he was hoping Noland would make his move soon.

"For good luck than," Ivan handed him the stone and walked away.

Eric stepped through the challenger gate and faced his foe. The two knights walked to the center of the show grounds staying about twelve feet apart from each other with helmets on. It was a rare sunny morning and Eric noted where the sun was, so as not to blind himself in the fight. Noland was thinking the same thing. They both faced the King for a moment but neither man bowed. The king excused the offence and waved his permission to proceed. Eric still had the stone in his hand and suddenly realized he had no pockets. Noland drew his sword and Eric had to drop the stone in front of him to pull his.

Noland recognized the "Courage" stone and understood that Amy was the last one who held it. What message was this man sending by lobbing it into the mud at his feet just before their match? Had this man killed his daughter-in-law? Anger boiled over in Noland's heart. Eric was determined to keep his wife alive at all costs.

Father and son clashed in a volley of sparks and swinging swords.

The sniper watched the fight through his scope. They suspected that this was indeed Noland Savage but would wait until he won the match and removed his helmet before taking the shoot. It would be blamed on a lone crazy gunman. At the same time, when Eric lost to his father, Amy would be eliminated. The king watched the drama with enthusiasm.

Pastor Marcus Johnson was now dressed just like he had been on the day he visited Judge Hurst. He convinced one of the king's guards that the note to the king was very important. Indeed, when Hurst read the note he dismissed himself from the match to meet with Pastor Johnson right behind the stands. Ivan was so engrossed in the deadly match between father and son that he did not notice the judge's speedy departure.

"Please tell me that you brought it with you, I want to see it! Whatever you've been offered I'll double it, it would be the crown jewel of my collection." Hurst had been drinking and while Johnson knew he had baited him with the Ark of the Covenant of Slavery artifacts he was still surprised at this reaction.

Johnson had a locked case with him which was labeled with the name of the item. The judge's eyes grew with excitement. But Johnson cautioned, "It is very old and to expose it to direct sunlight could be harmful." Johnson thanked God for the break in the clouds.

"Of course, of course!" said the king and gestured for Johnson to follow him to his tent nearby.

Four guards followed them over to the king's tent. Two went inside with them and two kept watch just outside the entrance.

Mrs. O'Reilly and Abigail readied the bread cart. The rectangle shaped box was big enough to hide a king inside. But she could do nothing with this man following them. But neither could she be a second late outside the king's tent. The cart was designed to be light weight but with a full grown man hiding inside it was quite heavy for just her and Abigail. Where was Daniel Lane? He was supposed to be here to help? The man following them got closer and Mrs. O'Reilly had an idea. An old saying came to her mind; *keep your friends close and your enemies closer.*

"Would you be a saint and help me get this cart over to the king's tent?" Mrs. O'Reilly asked with a smile. "The king loves my cinnamon rolls and has ordered me to deliver enough for his whole court."

The man felt discovered but if he refused to help he would feel awkward following them there anyway, so he grunted his agreement and pushed the cart all the way to the king's tent arriving just as Daniel Lane came stumbling up. Daniel smelled strong of alcohol and he looked falling down drunk. Mrs. O'Reilly was shocked. He seemed like such a responsible young man to be drunk at a time like this.

Eric Savage knew that the time for fun and games were over. This man was obviously determined to kill him. The points had added up and passed the necessary number to win, yet no one would call the match. The superior shield and sword that Eric wielded helped to hold Noland at bay up until now but suddenly Noland spun low hitting Eric first with sword, then with shield and finally sweeping his legs out from over him. It was a one, two, three, strike that happened so fast Eric didn't know what hit him. The crowd let out a cheer thinking it was all part of the show. First, Noland kicked Eric's shield away and then stepped down on his sword hand pinning it down and leaving Eric defenseless. Eric tried to roll but Noland had him trapped.

Daniel was making a scene outside of the king's tent. "I… want..to see …..the…king!" He slurred his words like a real drunk man. "I….want…him to…" He let out a belch! "To…knight …..me ….SIR…..Officer….Daniel…..Lane."

The guards inside the tent with the King and Johnson stepped outside to help handle Daniel who had pulled out his sword and was swinging it in wild circles. Ivan's spy was also distracted as he parked the cart exactly where Mrs. O'Reilly instructed. Mrs. O'Reilly stood and watched Daniel be subdued. The regular festival security was called in to haul Daniel away. The guards turned to return to their duties as the king stepped out of the tent with Johnson, they shook hands like they had come to some agreement. He turned to Mrs. O'Reilly and thanked her for the cinnamon rolls, best he ever had, and walked back to the sword match. Ivan's spy wasn't about to help unload the rolls or haul the Cart one foot farther and decided to return to the bakery tent and get a closer look at those arrows while the old lady was away.

Noland held his sword high over his challenger.

Eric just wanted to see his family one last time and said aloud. "Tell my wife I love her!" He doubted the words would be passed on to her but had to try.

Noland recognized his own son's voice but had already sent the orders to his arms and the sword was coming down fast, somehow he willed it off course to the right and it penetrated Eric's Armor only, missing his flesh by inches.

"Kick me now!" he ordered.

Eric hesitated for only a moment and then kicked up his right foot hitting Noland in the back and sending him forward and off of him. Noland rolled back to his feet and faced his son. Eric now had both swords, pulling his father's from his punctured armor and Noland had both shields, picking up Eric's as he rolled. The two men were grateful that their helmets hid their tears as they both realized what could have happened if one had not spoken.

Eric attacked with both swords and spoke to his father between the sound of each strike.

"If" … "I"…"Loose"… "Amy"… "Dies"

Noland defended himself and then using the edges of the shields went on the attack to keep the show going.

"Trust me" he said as he dropped both shields and opened himself up for Eric to strike.

"Do it now!" Noland commanded his son.

Eric had no choice but to trust his dad and thrust the duel swords into his father's armor. Noland fell to his knees, both swords penetrating through his armor and seemingly into his chest; the pain on his face was real. Eric stood there in shock. What had he done?

The mass of on-lookers went crazy! The king ordered a medical crew to carry out Noland's body, Eric was surrounded once again by Ivan's men and escorted back to the estate. The crowd was confused and some worried about what they saw. Others said it was all part of the show and that they could tell the man was acting. They were even more confused when they walked back to their tents and saw nailed up notices posted everywhere. It was a ransom notice for the return of the king in exchange for the release of Eric and Amy Savage and Leonid and Yalina Volkov!

Ivan was accompanying the king back to the estate when one of his own men caught up to them and showed Ivan the ransom notice. Ivan read the notice thinking it must be a joke, but then a disturbing thought came to his mind and he turned to observe the king. Leonid took off his wig and said in Russian, "Noland says this would be the first time in your career someone under your protection has been abducted. He fears for your international reputation. Perhaps the judge should get a refund? "

Ivan tore the ransom note in anger. Punched one of the king's guards and ordered his men to turn the festival upside down in their search for Judge Hurst. Savage had played his cards well. Ivan's flawless reputation was his Achilles' heel. He made hundreds of Millions because he never failed. If this embarrassment got out he would just be another hired gun. His enemies would say he had lost his touch. Ivan was already doing the math. He had to get Hurst back at whatever the cost.

He ordered his men to get out the high tech weaponry, night vision, thermo imaging, he wanted armed drones in the air. The new smart ammo never missed. He wanted to dominate the field of battle, he ordered his specially equipped helicopter to be at the ready on the landing pad atop Hurst's mansion. Enough with the show, Camelot had fallen, it was time to fight this his way.

The exchange would take place that evening just after sunset between the mansion and the festival grounds. Leonid had the message from Noland Savage memorized. None of Ivan's men were to be on festival grounds after five pm, they were to be ordered back to the mansion. Ivan needed to understand that he would be matched man for man, sniper for sniper, drone for drone. It was the old time proven strategy of mutual assured destruction. Many festival guests were upset about the invasion of privacy as Ivan's men searched the festival armed with newer versions of the AK-47, not exactly a medieval weapon. People were leaving early, demanding a refund and making threats to sue.

Commander Thomas Troy received Chief Hobbs and Walker into his custody and had them singing like Canaries, their confessions were all Troy needed to acquire the green light for his unit. If a firefight broke out at the festival his men would be ready. The Commander held the small metal orb's in his hands. The new tech was risky. He wondered if Ivan had noticed that the effects of the miniature E.M.P. blast were temporary. The magnetic pulse released disrupted electronic circuits but did not destroy them completely. It was designed to neutralize an enemies weapon systems, overrun their defenses and turn those same systems against them when the effects wore off. But the distance between the Hurst mansion and the festival grounds was too slight. Any use of the tech would neutralize both camps' weapons and the effects would fluctuate unexpectedly. It was a last resort.

Steve Mills would not leave the festival, in part because he needed to get paid and in part because of the names on the ransom notices, Eric and Amy Savage. He needed to know what was really going on here. He had witnessed the demolition of their beautiful little house and watched the news reports about Noland Savage. He felt somehow a part of all this. Benjamin was kidnapped while Amy was aiding him. No one had ever blamed him, the Savage Family never mentioned it, but he felt guilty that it was his foolishness that gave some creep the opportunity.

They were out of sand bags at the catapults and someone had to drive out in the field where the hay houses sat demolished and load them up. That is where Steve was when Troy's men started infiltrating the festival grounds. Ivan's mercenaries spread out in the woods on both sides of the Hurst Manson and at every window and rooftop vantage point. Steve was out in the field alone. He did not receive the warning to evacuate that was being circulated throughout the festival. The sand bags were heavy and Steve had no help. He loaded them one at a time into the back of his truck, over the engraved stones from the Savage house.

Troy ordered his men to dig foxholes in the ground and pile the dirt high. The tents of the festival only gave the illusion of shelter. Even the wood structures would not last long if things got nasty. His snipers were ordered to locate all enemy snipers and eliminate them first. Ivan's men had the woods around the mansion and the estate itself as good cover. The exchange would happen in less than an hour.

Chapter 16
The Savage stones

Noland Savage was face to face with Fredrick Hurst, the man who had enslaved his grandson, killed his best friend, and forced him to fight his own son to near death. Troy had been worried about placing Hurst in Noland's care.

"Just remember friend, we need him alive." Troy understood the struggle Noland might feel.

But Noland was the best man to make the exchange. He could ID three of the four hostages and Leonid could surely ID his own wife. More importantly, if things went south Noland could think on his feet and adapt to the situation.

Hurst was shaken by his abduction but had confidence that Ivan would never let it stand. Yet sitting across from Noland Savage in the back of the armored vehicle alone was like being caged with a cobra. Savage would not take his eyes off the man. Hurst had always feared him, ever since Poland. That fear had in part motivated his abduction of Benjamin. Maybe having power over his grandson would diminish the envy and phobia he felt for the Savage name.

Hurst opened his mouth like he was about to speak. The cobra struck so fast, Hurst never got the first word out. He could be carried to the exchange. Noland wasn't in a talking mood.

Ivan himself walked the two couples from the mansion steps across the open field toward the festival grounds. Eric and Amy were blind folded and had been told nothing. Ivan walked behind them alone just as instructed. Leonid and his wife walked in front of the group without a blindfold and unguarded. The group stopped half way across the field and waited.

Noland helped Hurst stay on his feet as they walked from the opposite festival side of the open field. Troy had a hundred eyes on the situation and enough fire power to start a small war. Hopefully, that would not be needed and the exchange would go off without a hitch.

The two groups met halfway. Ivan and Noland faced each other for the first time.

Ivan removed the blindfolds from Eric and Amy but kept them close, a gun in Amy's back. He first ordered Leonid and his wife to walk on. As they passed, Noland told them to keep moving all the way home. Next, Ivan ordered Eric to move forward. But Eric refused.

"Not without my wife," he stated.

"Noland, talk to your son. I am following your instructions." Ivan called over.

Noland didn't like it. Ivan was too calm, too smug. His eyes were looking passed them to Leonid and his wife. What leverage would Ivan still have with Leonid and Yalina Volkov....Noland suddenly remembered their missing daughter.

Eric could read his father's expression of horror and slammed into Ivan while pushing the gun away from Amy, the massive explosion that happen half a second later knocked them all back toward the mansion. It came from the festival just as Leonid and Yalina Volkov reached the front line of Troy's men. The couple was told that the explosive vests were just bargaining chips. That their daughter would be exchanged for Chief Hobbs and Walker if they obeyed, it was just another lie, like all the lies they have been told since leaving their home in Russia. The fireball of their betrayal consumed Troy's front line of operators and blinded his command center. His armed drones were damaged by the shock wave and fell, crashing from their hovering positions. They no longer had eyes on the Savage family. But Troy's snipers had already locked on to their targets and even through the ball of fire performed with excellence. Then all hell broke loose.

From the far away fields to the north Steve Mills was caught off guard by the sound of the explosion. He would have guessed that perhaps a large propane tank had just ignited but he didn't remember seeing one at the festival. The following firefight had Steve completely stunned as the thin long lines of tracers from the sudden exchange of gunfire crowded the space between the festal and the mansion. The two forces had taken up positions just after dark, Ivan had swelled his team with terrorist cells from up and down the west coast promising them a match up against Americas best.

"Armor forward, now!" Troy ordered.

Through the burning tents charged a fast moving juggernaut of an armored Hummer. Several shoulder fired missiles came streaming toward it from Ivan's men in the woods but were intercepted by Troy's advanced defense systems. There was no time for the rescue vehicle to stop or even slow down much. Noland and Eric were pinned down by enemy fire behind a large stone water fountain. Noland tossed an extra gun to his son and they were both returning fire with everything they had. As the armored vehicle came within range, Amy was the only one able to jump through its' open door on the run while receiving cover from all directions. Several of Ivan's armed drones fired at the wheels of the vehicle and one blast found its mark. The upsurge of the detonation propelled the Hummer up on two wheels and shredded the armor covering its' front passenger side tire. The weighty armored juggernaut righted itself, landed hard with a resounding racket of metal and moved on with Amy safely inside, taking heavy fire.

Ivan Zanderwin and Fredrick Hurst had both disappeared into a tunnel of some sort. One minute they were both downed by the blast and the next Ivan had Hurst up and running. They had both vanished into the ground though some trap door. Ivan re-emerged moments later fully armed and followed by dozens of his men.

Outnumbered and outgunned, Noland and Eric ran toward the festival for all they were worth. Troy sent in what was left of his drones to cover their retreat.

"Code Merlin!" Noland screamed into his microphone as he ran. "I need Merlin now!"

Troy agreed and launched the orbs. His men were pinned down by the higher vantage point of the mansion, the better cover of the trees and the unexpected advantage of the initial explosion. It was time to change the game.

The five small orbs fell from the sky unnoticed along the lines of battle. The green blue aurora glowed in the night. Troy had prepared for what was about to happen. Out of the blue, the lights went out, the systems shut down, every high tech gun stopped firing, every drone dropped from the sky. For a moment all was dark and silent. Troy left the useless command post and dawned his black knight armor and mounted his horse. The line of archers was assembling behind the festal grounds. A long line of ready men and women he had recruited over the past weeks in preparation for this moment, some from the festival itself.

Ivan's Men checked and rechecked their weapons. Ivan Zanderwin shouted for shield and sword as soon as he could. Noland and Eric made their way back to friendly ground, their swords and shields waiting. Once dressed and ready they waited for Troy's signal.

It had been a long time since father and son had a

moment of time together. Over twelve long months had passed since they parted on bad terms. Noland wanted to say something to his son before heading back into battle. Eric missed his dad and felt terrible for words they had both spoken in anger.

Sometimes you just start somewhere.

"Sorry for trying to kill you earlier today." Noland turned to face his son.

"What are you talking about? You got us both out of an impossible situation and saved Amy's life at the risk of your own," Eric said putting his hand on his dad's shoulder. "I never knew you were such a good actor, you really looked like you were in pain."

"The pain was real! When I fell to my knees the metal joint in my armor pinched my skin." He got serious then. "I could never have lived with myself if..." Noland started to say but Eric interrupted. "Please forgive me for not calling you for the last twelve months. I should have never let it go that long."

Noland remembered their argument. "You were right to stop the search for Benjamin to take care of Amy and save your marriage, things were getting out of hand," he just said it.

"Benjamin is alive, dad, because of you." Eric was proud of his father.

"And he has a family to come home to, because of you." Noland was no less proud of his son.

A lone torch appeared behind the smoldering tents of the festival. The long line of archers waited with arrows at the ready. The torch started moving, right to left, igniting the tip of each archer's arrow as it went. Ivan had studied warfare, from the Romans to the American Apache, he saw what was coming. His men were foolishly advancing out of the tree line. Communications were down. Ivan shouted orders at the top of his lungs, some heard and understood, other did not.

Commander Troy rode down the line with his torch, lighting every arrow. It was Ivan's turn to take some losses. Once every flaming tip was burning, Troy shouted the order.

"Take aim!" Drawing his sword and pointing in the direction of the mansion.

"Fire!!" he ordered and then charged toward the enemy followed by a small army of highly motivated special operation units hungry for payback.

The volley of burning arrows lit up the night sky for just a moment, and then fell forward raining down fire and pain on Ivan's men. The two armies collided in a heated exchange of close quarters combat.

In the middle of the chaos, Ivan and Noland squared off, Sword to Sword.

"Your Russian friend and his wife went out with a bang, didn't they?" Ivan taunted him

Noland liked Leonid, he was a simple trusting man. Whatever he did, he did because he thought it would free his daughter. He was not trained to fight this kind of evil.

Noland struck first, testing the waters. Ivan easily parried and attacked with expert skill. Noland had to give ground to avoid his opponent's blade. As the dual progressed Noland noticed he was being pushed back into the woods south of the mansion but could do little about it, Ivan was the better man with a sword.

Benjamin watched the battle from a distance carefully

hidden from sight. He knew both his father and grandfather were engaged in this fight. He would have to get dangerously close before he would know for sure where they were. It would require him to be just about invisible, camouflage alone would not do. The boy set his mind to the task at hand. Every cloaking skill he had learned would now be put to the ultimate test. Benjamin moved from tree to tree, painstakingly covering the ground, unseen by human eyes. Only Timber detected his movement.

Steve Mills had no plans of returning to the festival. He was hiding behind his truck out in the north fields afraid to attract any attention to himself. One of Troy's men scouting the area arrested him and brought him in. But when Amy Savage saw him she vouched for him. Steve was full of questions. Amy was worried about her family. One of Troy's men finally filled him in.

Steve Mills pulled out his cell phone. "So that's why it's not working."

"We call it the blue zone," the soldier said. "Right now the only weapons that matter are those without electronics, and now days their shooting smart bullets even out of the old guns."

A soldier arrived back from the front lines, "We need our archers targeting that roof top!"

Steve mills had an idea, "Why just our archers, when we have catapults?" They were not paying attention to the young man. So he said it again, louder!

"Why just archers, when we have catapults?!"

That turned a few heads.

The idea caught on quick. "Let's do it!" The soldier was on board. "What's their range?"

Steve had been operating them all week and was a good

judge of their range. "Help me get them to the main show grounds. From there they'll pulverize that roof top."

"Let's move them fast," the man said and ordered others to help.

Noland was fighting for his life in the woods, cut off from help. Ivan started nicking him up with flesh wounds. Nothing fatal, just a tenth of a second faster here and there. But Noland was bleeding and beginning to weaken. Ivan saw that his victory was coming.

"You have made my time here worth it all Noland!" Ivan taunted

Noland backed away willing to let the man talk, hoping for a second to breathe. "Two more days of competition, I thought."

"I'm afraid not!" Ivan said and lunged forward so fast that Noland could only deflect the tip of his blade into his shoulder away from his heart. Noland ignored the pain and tried to thrust his own blade into the man but Ivan evaded him. Noland backed away again, trying to buy time.

"We have a grave all ready for you Noland. I even put that poem of yours on the marker." He was mocking him now. "Heart of a Warrior, Soul of a Lion, I will not fear the battle, etc, etc." Ivan was ready to bring an end to the legend of Noland Savage and would enjoy the prestige and fear it would bring to his own name.

Noland stopped retreating and stared at his nemeses. The poem was dear to his heart and it angered him that this man would have it on his lips. Noland picked up the fallen words. "I will return to the fight…" Noland sidestepped Ivan's next thrust and kicked him back. "Again and again and again.." Noland gathered his strength and attacked with all he had. He got close, he moved fast. "Not counting the times defeated!" Noland shouted in anguish not wanting his dreams to die there. But it was not enough. Ivan was able to answer his every action.

Ivan was impressed but not wounded. "But the sweet taste of victory will be mine Noland. And you can keep your happy home crap for Tiny Tim and his mother."

Suddenly, the bark on the tree just eight feet from Ivan came to life. Benjamin let fly an arrow that hit Ivan in the side.

"My name is not Tiny Tim, its Benjamin Noland Savage!!"

Ivan was distracted, completely caught off guard, he lifted his sword toward Benjamin.

Noland lunged forward with all his remaining strength and plunged his sword into the chest of Ivan Zanderwin. Ivan was a dead man but stumbled toward Benjamin with sword held high and one last act of vengeance in his heart. Timber had been speeding to the scene the moment Benjamin moved. He leaped from the ground on the run eight feet away from his target. His long white canine teeth reached Ivan's neck and clamped down hard puncturing the main artery and taking him down for good. Ivan's lungs filled with blood. He was drowning in it. His eyes still looked at Noland with hatred, un-repented and un-willing to consider anything but clinging to his evil in death.

"…Till the sweet taste of victory becomes my happy home!" Noland needed to say it even if a man like Ivan Zanderwin would never understand the love of home and family.

Noland collapsed to the ground exhausted. Benjamin came to his side.

"Are you ok? Do you need me to run and get help?" Benjamin saw his many wounds and wondered what to do.

Noland spoke into his microphone hoping the power was on again, "medic needed in the south woods, Noland and

Benjamin Savage here, alive for now."

After a minute, when no one answered Noland struggled to his feet and with Benjamin's help started making his way back to the festival grounds. Once out of the woods they were spotted and picked up by a team of medics. Noland was placed on a stretcher and carried back to the field hospital.

The catapults were in position. But the effects of the orbs began to flex. Some lights came on in the mansion and then went back off again. Eric and Amy were helping to load sand bags into the catapults. All four catapults fired at the roof top but came up short, with sand bags crashing through windows and colliding with the outer wall. Steve was upset with himself because he forgot to consider the slope of the land, the mansion sat on higher ground.

"Again!" someone yelled.

They moved all four catapults closer to the mansion and spread them out farther from each other and loaded up the slings. Noland and Benjamin were taken to a medical tent and treated but Noland refused to leave the area and seeing Eric and Amy joined in next to them. Amy grabbed Benjamin and gave him a bear hug. But there was no time. The power came back on in the festival area, to Troy's men, and those helping arm the catapults reached for their guns and surged forward with the others. Ivan's men were pushed back into the far woods with some holding up in the mansion. Noland watched the action unfold through the scope of a rifle as Amy tended to his wounds.

Then Noland saw him, Fredrick Hurst getting into a helicopter under a camouflaged blind on the roof of the mansion. The lights of the chopper kicked on and off, the blades started to turn and then stopped.

"NO!" Noland looked around for a shoulder launched missile but saw nothing that would reach the roof. The power flexed again and the lights on the festival side went dark and the mansion came to life. The helicopter blades started to turn.

"The catapults are ready to go," Steve reminded him.

Noland pulled the lever on each catapult followed by the sound of wooden gears straining against the weight of the sling. The sand bags reached the roof top taking out several men and one nearly hitting the chopper's blade, but no real damage.

"We need to reload!" Noland was desperate.

Steve and the others went back to the truck for more ammo but they were out of sand bags. Eric and Amy were immediately fascinated at the sight of all their memories sitting in the back of Steve's pickup. Everything their family stood for cut deep in stone.

"The engraved stones," Amy touched them like they were her hopes and dreams. She had collected them, large and small, from fifty pound boulders to five ounce smooth stones that would fit in the palm of your hand and everything in-between.

The chopper was hovering over the mansion now, facing the four catapults, weapons hot.

A missile launched from one side of the chopper sending everyone diving for cover. It struck the wooden catapult to the far left blowing it to burning pieces.

Amy grabbed the "Faith" stone and a pile of "Love, laugh and live" and started loading the middle catapult. Eric handled his big, "Nothing is written in stone", bolder. Benjamin picked up the, "Never give up!" and "Make it happen" stones. Steve retrieved the "Phoenix" stone from his cab and dropped it in the huge sling. Other stones followed, "Wonder," "Strength," "Dreamer," "Be the Change," "Unforgettable," and "Find a way."

Noland followed their lead keeping a wary eye on the helicopter. The blue aurora remained above the mansion. Hurst's pilot was trying to fly away but was contained in a sweet spot of power. Every time the pilot steered the chopper higher its' power would start to drain. Hurst was trapped for the moment.

Noland was as surprised as everyone to see the family heirlooms, many of them gifts from his late wife, in the back of the pickup. He retrieved "The 23rd Psalm." And "God, Guts and Guns" and loaded up the other remaining middle catapult.

Unable to fly away, the helicopter fired again taking out the catapult to the far right and raining down shards of wood on the Savage family.

Benjamin and Amy placed the "Family" and "Courage" stones in one sling together, and then Amy got Benjamin to back away from the catapults to a safer place. She was not going to lose him now after all they had been through.

When Noland pulled back the lever to the first catapult the sound and energy of a powerful force unleashed! Eric pulled the lever on the second remaining catapult just a second later with an even greater release of meaningful words engraved in stone. It was as if the whole of the stones were more than the sum of their parts. They shot out of the two slings with a vengeance. The mass of engraved stones launched up and forward, over the heads of Ivan's defeated men being rounded up below, sailing through the heavens. They each had a name, a memory, a story to tell. In flight they seemed to spread out, maybe she was just imagining it but when the lights from the helicopter caught them in motion Amy swore she saw a perfect circle of stones form in the middle of the troop. They arched high and came down fast, rotating as individuals but as a group stayed dead on target, flying like two waves of fighter jets in formation.

"Faith", "Hope," and "love" struck first, cracking the front windshield, followed up by "Nothing is written in stone" which shattered it. "God", "Guts" and "Glory" took out the back rudder sending the helicopter into a spin. Then there was a rapid procession of impacts, puncturing the metal skin of the craft with holes, shredding its outer protective layer and exposing those inside.

Judge Hurst was seeing his worthless life flash before his eyes, his power disintegrating around him. But it was the whispers that horrified him most. From the inside of the helicopter he could hear them. As each stone struck there was a whisper, every engraved word spoke its name! Simple truths like "Forgiveness", "Trust", and "Togetherness"; ideas that the man had never understand the strength of before, suddenly cut the darkness like double edged swords. The "Phoenix" stone hit the frame of the helicopter turning it belly up. The circle of stones came in last, among them the "Family" stone and the "Courage" stone, together they struck the fuel tanks and blew the entire rooftop and helicopter to smithereens.

Amy Savage watched as the fireball turned night into day. From behind the mansion she saw the long shadows of their tombstones rise like demons from the deep and then fade to nothing. For a long moment she just stood there letting her mind and emotions get the beginnings of closure. The immediate threat of death was over; the long nightmare had finally ended, but how long would it take to truly heal. She purposely looked away from the burning rooftop, unwilling to give Hurst another moment of her life. She walked back to her family with Benjamin beside her. They gathered in a circle which included some friends, soldiers and one Germen Shepherd dog. They all thanked God for being alive. Then the Savage family walked away together. No one said anything at first, they were just happy to be breathing the same fresh air. The fight was over and the lights came on everywhere. Commander Troy sounded the all clear on both the mansion and the surrounding woods.

They wandered across the front lawn of the mansion, passed the heavily damaged water fountains and ended up at their mock family cemetery. It was an odd feeling to stand there looking at their own graves, intentionally dug with them in mind. Eric and Amy hugged and held each other close. Benjamin looked at the grave of Tiny Tim satisfied that he was truly dead. Noland surprised everyone by his reaction to seeing his own tombstone up close.

"I actually like my grave marker! Damn good poem if I do say so myself. I think I'll keep it!" Everyone laughed.

But there were things still left unfinished that would not be easy for them. Gary Holland lay dead out in the woods and his wife had been lied to by Hobbs' man as to why he disappeared. She needed to know the truth. He was a hero and he died while protecting his own with a courage she could be proud of. There needed to be an appropriate memorial service. Noland would take it hard. Gary was his best friend and as far as anyone knew, Noland's only friend.

It was difficult for them to think about Leonid and Yalina Volkov. But who knew what they had been through in the hands of a desperate Ivan Zanderwin. What if their daughter had been hauled out in front of them and threatened and then the idea presented that a trade could be made if they cooperated. The bottom line was Leonid was a part of the team and had helped make the plan a success even if in the end he was deceived and used. His daughter was still missing and Noland decided right then that he would make an effort to find her.

That night Mrs. O'Reilly tucked Abigail into bed after her prayers. She would do everything in her power to adopt the child. Just before she turned off Abigail's light she caught her own reflection in the mirror and was reminded of her age. But love was a conqueror, an over comer, a way maker and she loved Abigail.

Pastor Johnson continued to feed the poor and homeless in the forgotten parts of Seattle but also used his platform to raise awareness of the growing problem of slavery in

America, the term "Human Trafficking" just seemed too politically correct for him.

The Savage family purchased a new home with three large wide leaf maple trees in the backyard. Together they built a tree house for Benjamin to play in. Benjamin had a good start down the road to healing. He had discovered his true name, found his family and vanquished the negative voices that haunted him. He would still have to face the challenges ahead with courage. There were always going to be those who would do anything for a profit, even prey on the lives of innocent children. **The Savage Family was determined to protect their own from a world sinking deeper and deeper into darkness.**

The End.

A note to the reader

I am a first time, novice writer who needs your help. If you enjoyed this story, please go now and write a good review for me on Amazon. It would be greatly appreciated. Thank you!

Watch for book two in the Savage Saga!

In a humble home on an unassuming street Mrs. O'Reilly sat at her desk gazing with determination at a pile of unpaid bills from the light of a single lamp. She kept the rest of the lights off in the house and the heat on low to save money. A lot of good it was doing. She could barely put food on the table to feed Abigail and herself. She loved the little redheaded girl sleeping soundly in the other room like she was her own daughter. Mrs. O'Reilly rescued Abigail from the clutches of modern day slavery. When the little girl looked her in the eye with desperation and bagged Mrs. O'Reilly to keep her it touched something deep in the soul of the old Irish woman. Abigail needed her and being needed gave Mrs. O'Reilly something to live for. She would walk through fire for Abigail. Indeed, Mrs. O'Reilly had already pawned her good silver and many of her late husband's guns. If Robert was alive he would have approved. He would have adored Abigail.

The State of Washington was still the legal guardian of the girl. The adoption was still pending. They had been straightforward with Mrs. O'Reilly from the beginning about their concerns. She was above the age limit and it would take an order from the governor to make a special exception on her adoption of Abigail. She wrote a letter to the governor and so had many of her close friends. Yet she had heard nothing. In five days the DHS workers would be paying her a visit. If the power was turned off and there was no food in the kitchen she was sure of what would happen. They would take Abigail from her. And she could never let that happen. Not as long as she had breath.

Noland was on the move again, even though the blizzard had intensified. His plan to hold up in a snow cave had been interrupted by the sound of wolves' howling in the night. Something had disturbed them or they wouldn't be out in this weather. Noland checked his six and spotted the lights in the distance and the sounds of pursuit. There were three military grade light assault vehicles called Hägglunds on his trail. They were articulated tracked vehicles made to move fast through any winter conditions, even a blizzard in the mountains of British Columbia. The beams from their headlights penetrated through the thick falling snow and their tracks broke through the tallest drifts, they were making good time. Noland did not know how they found him, only that they were not far behind.

Through his snow shoes, he felt the ground level out beneath his feet and realized he had stepped onto a frozen lake buried in blanket of snow. The temperature being what it was, it was defiantly safe for a man to walk on. It was probably even safe for the Hägglunds vehicles that pursued him. But Savage was looking for trap, some way to throw off, slow down, or thin out his pursuers. He knew that many lakes in this part of British Columbia were fed by hot springs. That knowledge may give him the edge he was looking for. The ice would be thinner closer to the spring. Noland pulled out a small laser pointer and tested the depth of the ice and continued to take measurements at even intervals. As he got closer to the middle of the lake the ice defiantly thinned out, but would it be enough?

The lead vehicle came crashing through a snow drift at the edge of the lake and continued straight at him, its' headlights spotlighting Savage. He stood there with his hands up for just a moment but then saw his opportunity. In the bright lights of the Hägglund he could see the outlined oval shape of a drop in the snow blanket caused by warmer water below, a circle of thin ice about twenty feet in diameter lie hidden beneath it. He kept his hands up but continued backing up, baiting the driver to come after him. He suddenly turned and ran. The tracked vehicle surged forward intent on running the man over. Savage could hear the ice cracking behind him as he dashed forward. He did not look back; the abrupt disappearance of the headlights told him all he needed to know. The glassed in cab of the Hägglund shattered as it hit the thick edge of the ice sheet, freezing water poured into the vehicle. It sank like a rock to the bottom of the lake. One down, two to go.

The following vehicles came over the snow drift and stopped, surprised to not see the lights of the lead Hägglund. The place where it fell through the ice was already freezing over and the snow would soon have it camouflaged completely. The crews were dumbfounded, where had it gone? They checked their instruments, nothing on thermo, and nothing on radar, and no radio contact. It was blasted hard to see anything in this blizzard visually. Noland hid his heat signature behind a large edge of ice pushed up like a continental fault line.

"Command, this is snow fox two. We have lost visual on snow fox one. Can you confirm their location?"

"Snow fox two be advised, they went off radar three minutes ago seventy-five yards to your west, directly in front of you."

But they saw nothing.

Noland half undressed himself in the bitter cold while laying on his back. He would need something dry to change back into if he lived through the next four minutes. Without a heat signature he would almost be a ghost in this blizzard. First, he clipped the high powered explosives to himself knowing his hands would be useless later. He went into the freezing waters aware of what to expect. The bitter cold sucked the life from him like a vampire. As a Navy Seal he knew how far he could push the limits. He was on the edge now and one slip would send him into the abyss. He struggle back out of the icy grave, half dead and dying, but invisible to his enemies.

The invisible half naked frozen man painfully walked behind the two vehicles and detached the explosive devises from his body and kicked one under each fuel tank. He then struggled back to where he had positioned the detonator and fell on it.

KAABOOOM!!!

Both vehicles exploded up and forward, flipping over and smashing into the thick unyielding ice at the lakes edge. The dual fireballs and black smoke from the Hägglunds went billowing up into the falling snow. Noland had no time to be picky about where he warmed himself. Standing between the infernos of his pursuers was just practical at the moment. The heat that was death to them could bring him back from the edge of hypothermia.

"Sir, now all three signals are down. Do you think it's the cold weather?" the operator looked to his commander for answers.

"No, I don't think it's the weather. I think it's a Savage!"

Made in the USA
Columbia, SC
17 June 2019